Mark of Ascension

# MARK OF
# ASCENSION

JOSEPH Y. KIM

CHRISTOPHER BOOM

ISBN: 9780578595832 (E-Book)
ISBN: 978-0-578-59585-6 (Print Book)

This is a work of fiction. Names, characters, business, events and incidents are the products of the author's imagination. Any resemblance to actual persons, living or dead, or actual events is purely coincidental.

Cover design: cheriefox.com
Interior formatting: Sarco Press

*To those who guided us along the way.*

# Prologue

· · · · · ● ● ● · · · ·

A THICK HAZE CLOUDED my mind like a veil of fog as silent tears rolled down my cheeks. Ms. Lambi, someone who usually embodied joy, no longer had her lips curled in her trademark smile.

"Ms. Lambi?" I called weakly, grasping at the hem of her flower-patterned blouse. A bed of crimson splayed out beneath her, the thin red coating covering the smooth concrete floor. My heart started pounding against my chest, shaking my entire body in irregular shudders.

"Mr. Jackson! Help!"

The heavy metal door crashed against the wall violently with a reverberating thud as a furious man—someone who was *not* Mr. Jackson—marched in with his gun trained on me. My heart jumped, and I scuttled back toward the opposite wall as the barrel of the gun chased me down until it paused just inches away from my forehead. The small Beretta I was gripping clattered out of my hands.

"Chase! Stand down!"

"Give me one goddamned reason! You saw what he just did! You look at that Bastard's brand. Look at his neck! Give me one good reason why I shouldn't shoot him on the spot!"

Mr. Jackson murderously glared at Chase, who was still

1

holding the gun against my temple. "You'll be making a big mistake. He's only seven for Christ's sake. Now *stand down.*"

Chase appeared to be at war with himself, but soon, the barrel slowly lowered, and the grip dropped out of his hands. The weapon clattered onto the ground with a short, metallic clang. With a heavy sigh, he leveled a venomous glare at me, and I wondered if he was going to kick me like he did the last time. He didn't. Instead, he turned and walked away with heavy steps, knocking into Mr. Jackson's shoulders as he stormed out of the room.

"Mr. Jackson?" I asked, looking up toward him. His usually gentle expression was replaced by something foul: his eyebrows were scrunched together, lips pressed into a thin line.

"Ethan, I think it's time for you to leave."

# PART 1:
# Bearing the Mark

· · · · · ● · · · · ·

# Chapter 1

*October 21, 2102*

·  ·  ·  ·  **●**  ·  ·  ·  ·

I WAS RUNNING FROM *something*. As the pitter-patter of rain filled the cityscape with ambient noise, a hulking figure hidden by shadows chased after me, its powerful legs bounding forward one step at a time. I didn't dare look back, knowing that just a moment of hesitation could spell the end for me.

It was the same dream. I *knew* that it was a dream. But knowing that fact didn't slow down my pounding heart which kept on shaking my body in rhythmic trembles. It didn't stop my legs from continuously running despite my efforts to stop and stand my ground.

"...Ethan!"

The pounding of the beast's feet against the ground echoed off the building walls, the sound surrounding me from every direction. Was there one of them? Two of them? Ten? I couldn't tell. All I could hear was the increasing pace of the beast's running. The beat of its feet pounding against the pavement accelerated by the second like a building drumroll.

"Ethan!"

The beast let out a terrifying roar and finally, curiosity got the better of me, and I whipped my head around to look back. But before I could get a full view of my predator, a tall, wide-open maw of jagged, glinting teeth soared through the air toward my face. It came closer, closer, closer, and-

"Ethan, wake up!"

I spluttered and shot up in bed as a wave of ice-cold water splashed over my body, shocking me back into consciousness. The gray pajamas that I had worn to sleep were now clinging tightly to my body, the chilling dampness freezing my skin.

"Hannah! How many times did I tell you not to wake me up like that!" I shouted angrily.

She let out a soft snort. "What are you going to do about it?"

"I will *literally* make the fact that you exist agonizing, and I'll do the same to you."

"Only if you ever wake up before me, and who knows in what century that'll happen," she scoffed. She was still dressed in her panda-themed onesie with a white kitchen apron draped over her neck. Setting the small water bucket down by the foot of the door, Hannah jauntily skipped out of the room, adding, "Breakfast will be ready in ten minutes."

"Alright."

The door closed with a soft click, and I mocked in a high-pitched voice, "Oh yeah, breakfast will be ready in ten minutes."

I rolled my eyes with a heavy sigh and kicked off the soaked blanket. The small analog clock sitting on my night-stand read 6:15. Reluctantly leaping out of bed, I walked over to the closet and fished out my Academy uniform. I tossed on the white button-up, layered on the outside with a forest green suit jacket. The cold droplets of water on my skin clung to the shirt like a sticky coat of glue.

"Ethan!" Hannah hollered from the kitchen.

"Coming!"

Snatching a towel off the laundry bin, I scrubbed the remaining bits of water out of my hair and dashed out with my school bag loosely held over my shoulders. A sweet aroma wafted out from the dining room, and I saw Hannah already sitting at the table, waiting patiently. She had laid out three neatly plated servings of scrambled eggs and Canadian bacon slices.

"Where's Tony?" I asked, sitting down at the table.

"He was working on one of his projects until late in the evening, so he's probably not going to be up until early afternoon. The plate's there just in case."

"Is he still trying to crack the AI code rejection paradox?"

Hannah shook her head. "I think he gave up for now. He's been working on one of those auto-programming bots. School project."

"It took him, the 'Great Engineer Tony,' that long to finish a school project?" I asked sarcastically, emphasizing Tony's self-proclaimed title.

"You know him. He probably spent most of that time playing games."

I chortled, seeing Hannah's annoyed countenance. Her ongoing crusade to burn all of Tony's games was more or less a failure. She never got anywhere close since Tony always managed to find some obscure place to hide them.

I speared a slab of bacon on my fork and started feasting. Breakfast today was a quiet affair, the only sound coming from the methodically ticking clock backdropping our meal.

"Being here feels kind of nice," Hannah started, breaking the silence. "It kind of reminds me of things way back to primary school. Remember when we were in Sector 54 and you tried roping Tony into rewiring all of the teaching devices?"

"I thought we agreed to not talk about that. It was really

embarrassing when they caught us trying to do that," I begged. That particular experience was something that I could do without remembering. It had gotten us in far more trouble than we had bargained for.

"Hey Hannah, sorry that we had to move again."

Hannah laughed off my apology like it was nothing. "Stop being so melodramatic. I'm used to it by now. Don't worry about it. Remember, you're the 'dumb' one, and I'm the smart and responsible one, right?"

"Yeah…" I muttered. That was the phrase we'd been using to describe our dynamic ever since we were seven, when we met at the orphanage in Sector 47. My parents, who had illegally given birth to me without government consent under the PDHS Act, were still rotting in prison while Aunt Teresa died in a railroad accident while on a business trip near what was formerly Washington state. Hannah, on the other hand, came to the orphanage under undisclosed circumstances. Although we didn't get along very well during our first couple of months, we eventually got close through an odd agreement of companionship.

Hannah was an outcast because she was too smart. The words that came out of her mouth—such as asphyxiation and obdormition—were far beyond the reach of the other seven and eight-year-olds. On the other hand, I was a reject of the system since I was a Bastard, an illegal child that didn't even exist in legal databases. The other kids shied away from me when they saw the tattooed brand above my collarbone—a wolf-like figure that looked like it was biting into my neck. So, when Hannah was forced to leave the orphanage when she turned ten, I followed her, the orphanage being more than eager to let us go.

Our first stop was in Sector 48. During our three years there, Hannah discovered that her "word problem" was not a boon, but a talent. Within the year, she was being hailed as the

"Genius of Medicine," although Hannah would joke that she was only the "Genius of Knowing Big Words." Her newfound status meant that upstanding Academies and research facilities constantly sought for Hannah to attend their institution with the hopes of increasing their name value. They always offered a hefty stipend that covered far more than just our living expenses.

From there, we lived a very redundant lifestyle. Every few months or so, the Academy that ran in our sector would kick me out, and we'd be forced to relocate to somewhere else. Not once did they ever tell me a formal reason, but their nasty glares directed toward my neck told me enough. "Bastard," some would even have the guts to say.

As this continuously happened over the years, I started considering ourselves to be nomads, people on a journey who bounced around from place to place every few months or so.

"Hey, I'm done with my food, so I'm going to go get ready for Academy, okay?"

"Yeah, I'll finish up and get ready too," I replied, biting at another spoonful of eggs.

Hannah shot me an awkward smile before taking her plate back to the kitchen. Meanwhile, I sat there, mulling over my negative thoughts. My gaze shifted over toward the last plate of food on the table whose owner was still dozing off in his room.

Tony had been an interesting addition to our "family." We picked him up around three years ago while we were living in Sector 78, the second sector that we visited during our travels. We found him wandering around on the streets feeding off food from trash cans after he had been released from the local orphanage, and Hannah offered him a place with us.

It turned out that her decision was both beneficial and a bit of a persisting curse. On the positive side, Tony was very adept in the computer science department, and his skills were far beyond those of his peers. Also, it helped that he had a penchant for pranking other people, one of the few qualities that we had in common.

"Ethan! Why haven't you finished your food? You're going to be late!" Hannah frantically chided, running out into the living room with her white school uniform on.

*What is she talking about?* The last time I'd checked, I had plenty of time to spare. But just to make sure, I took another look. It showed 6:43 A.M. Academy started at seven. It took about fifteen minutes to get there.

"Whoops."

# Chapter 2

*June 19, 2103*

· · · • • · · · ·

T HE PRINCIPAL WALKED onto the stage with a rolled-up sheet of paper grasped in his hands, and each step he took left a reverberating clack that echoed in the large auditorium. When he reached the podium set on the center of the stage, he unfolded the paper, then took a moment to look out into the crowd.

Sitting in the way back, I could barely make out the features of the principal. Even worse, I was sitting in the column right next to the Military Academy kids who were shooting me piercing glares of anger for no apparent reason. My hands felt clammy as a thin sheen of sweat covered my palms.

The graduation ceremony was set up as it was every year, with every single department "coming together" to celebrate. Ironically, the seating was set up in separate columns where students from each career track had about ten seats in between themselves and students from other fields. What a great "coming together" it was.

To the far left, the engineering students were sitting up prim and proper in their sleek gray uniforms. Next to them were computer science students in their navy blue. So on and so forth, each career track was represented by a unique color.

The principal began speaking in a throaty voice, half-shouting. "Finally, to end this graduation ceremony, I would like everyone to welcome the valedictorian for the Medical Sciences Class of 2103. Even at such a young age, she has crafted herself a stellar reputation in the upper echelon of the medical world. Through her revolutionary applications of newly discovered techniques to medical procedures, she has redefined the process by which we mend and research the human body. While working with renowned medical professors and practitioners such as Dr. Francis Collers and Dr. Jeric Eng, she refined and expanded the literature on human processes that are written in her works such as *Applications on Surgery Processes* and *Revolutionary Technology.* Please welcome to the stage, Hannah Kamiya."

She was wearing a silky white graduation gown that shimmered like a pearl and rippled like water with every step she took. Her neck was adorned with various honor cords and accessories accumulated through her accomplishments and accolades. A pure white student cap sat on top of her head and hanging from it was the ever so desired golden tassel, the mark of the valedictorian.

As she stood at the center of the stage, I saw her hands trembling as she brought out a bundle of loose-leaf papers from inside her gown. She searchingly gazed around the auditorium before her eyes came across mine. I shot her a cheeky smile and a thumbs up. Her nervous visage transformed into a relaxed smile as she took another gaze around the auditorium. As she stood underneath the single shining ray of light coming from a spotlight fixture, I had the fleeting thought that she looked ethereal, like an angel.

Her soft but powerful voice reverberated throughout the large auditorium.

*"We are all gears inside of one gigantic machine. Without one part, we cannot function. Our talents are*

*not given to us but are cultivated through the time and effort that we give to the cause of bettering ourselves. Although we may have been uncertain where life would take us before, now we have clarity and a purpose for how we can serve our country.*

*"As we were going through Academy and started discovering more about ourselves, we found that what we were good at was not always the thing we were most interested in. Instead, there were often times where we would find both pleasant, and unpleasant surprises.*

*"We all started like little seeds: misguided and unfruitful. Perhaps some of you thought that you would never see above the ground. But now, the flood-gates have opened. Our path has been drawn for us, and people support us in various ways. Now, we are not merely waiting for our time to bloom but are stretching toward the expansive sky. We have no limits.*

*"I can't speak on everyone's behalf of what the Academy must have been like since I personally have moved around multiple times during my years of childhood. However, I'm sure that there have been acquaintances and colleagues that you have met throughout your time here who will help you along your journey in the future.*

*"I only wish the best of luck to everyone and send you off with the hopes that we may all live to better serve this Republic with our dedication and skill. Thank you."*

The noise level in the auditorium climbed in a gradual crescendo as thunderous applause filled the hall. As Hannah stepped off the stage, people stormed around her, barraging her with compliments and questions while thrusting cameras in her face. I could barely see over the wall of human flesh that suddenly formed in front of me. Hopping on top of the chair I was sitting on, I took a sweeping gaze around the auditorium. The principal was panicking, trying to wave off the reporters and students while Hannah glanced toward me with a beaming smile. She seemed so calm in contrast to the raging cacophony that surrounded her.

But soon, she disappeared behind the crowd, and the principal hurried her toward the back room behind the stage. Again, I was left alone under the shadow of the balcony. Sighing in exasperation, I sat down and started sifting through the graduation pamphlet, figuring that it would be a good way to tune out the noise and pass some time.

The first page on the inside featured the classic anti-Blighted propaganda poster, with the pages following it showing images and information regarding those genetically modified creatures' exploits. Along with that was the one-page political propaganda about the Bastards. It was a "cute" little infographic showing the "enormous" amounts of tax dollars they cost the Republic coupled with near-fanatical hate messages that called Bastards "children of the devil." I always scoffed when I saw them but apparently, the people bought into it.

More uninteresting information about the staff and the administration followed shortly after that. Then, I got to the student biographies for the valedictorians and I was transfixed, stupefied by the extensive resume of every single one of them. Just like how the principal described Hannah, each and every one of them had national connections and field experiences with their given subject.

A pang of guilt stung at my heart as I wondered if Hannah would've had the same extensive opportunities given to the others had we not moved around so often. As I turned toward the back pages, I reached the last page, which was Hannah's blurb.

*"Hannah Kamiya is a hardworking, dedicated student that defines a new peak for her generation. Within the walls of the Academy, despite only being in Sector 36 for a short while, her grades have been top of the class, and she always goes beyond the parameters for projects, assignments, and practical trials. Overshadowing many of her peers, her work is already elite class and on par with many of the professionals in the upper echelon of the medical field. Despite her less than ideal childhood circumstances, she has managed to find time to balance her academic work with moving in and out of different sectors. When she was thirteen, she worked closely with Dr. Francis Collers of Sector 48 to develop the theory of artificial cell replication, which has since become a national curiosity in the medical world, although practical experimentation has not begun. Just a year later, in Sector 125, she worked with Dr. Jeric Eng in developing artificial human body parts that could have military and commercial implications. Unfortunately, her work was abruptly halted by another move, and the project has been put on stasis with the hope that it will be completed in the near future. Her most recent accomplishment, co-facilitated by the Sector 36 Academy Medical Sciences School Supervisor Dr. Sarah Choe was the creation of an experimental serum for physical enhancement. This serum is currently in the experimental testing phase, and the project is estimated to be completed soon. Unfortunately, she-*

"Hey!"

I jumped and tore my gaze away from the pamphlet to meet Hannah's hazel brown eyes. Surprised, I glanced behind me and saw the clock reading 7:49 P.M. It had already been thirty minutes since graduation ended.

"Are you ready to go?" she asked. "What have you been doing?"

"N-Nothing," I stammered as I rolled the graduation pamphlet into my pocket. When I looked around, I finally noticed the silence of the auditorium. Everyone else had left, leaving the large hall empty.

"Okay then."

Together, we walked from the large auditorium out to the atrium. When we passed through the Academy's front gates, the marble architecture gave way to nature's constructs. The surrounding greenery shifted with the breeze like a fluttering blanket, and the sky was alit with orange and yellow hues as if an artist had splashed buckets of paint on the horizon.

"This is going to be the last time that we're here," Hannah noted. "I'm really going to miss this place."

"Yeah…" I mumbled mutedly.

With that parting thought, we began our trek home as our surroundings quickly shifted into the gray cityscape. The honking, yelling, and urban sounds filled my ears, and dim lights lit up the city as people walked to their destinations at a leisurely pace.

"What do you think you're going to do now?" Hannah asked, kicking at a loose pebble mindlessly. "I mean, Career Day is also coming up soon after all."

"I don't really have a choice, do I?"

She hummed while kicking at the same pebble, skipping across the sidewalk. "Well, you were kind of admitted as a general studies student since they couldn't figure out where to place you. Maybe you'll get to choose."

"Fat chance."

Before Hannah could kick at the pebble again, I snatched it up with my feet, sending it away far out of her reach. She glared at me playfully, and we started a little game, kicking the little pebble around the block like little kids. I had just knocked it toward a railway station when suddenly, a shrill feminine screech of panic tore through the loud urban sounds. Pedestrians stopped their walking and stared into one of the dark alleyways. Heads bowed, they ran away as quickly as they could.

Turning my heels, I prepared to run, preferring not to become involved with what some might call the "Late Night Alleyway Shenanigans." But before I took a single step, Hannah roughly latched onto my sleeves and leveled a harsh glare at me.

It was *that* look. "Come on, really?" I asked helplessly.

Her eyebrows were scrunched together in anger and concern while her lips pressed into a thin line. "Ethan," she threatened in a low voice.

My eyes flitted back and forth between the large railway station just several paces away and the dark alley, which disappeared behind a bend like an empty void. Droplets of sweat started running down the side of my face. I couldn't decide which was more frightening, the prospect of going into a dark alley in the city at night like an idiot, or risking Hannah's ire.

"Alright, I'm going, I'm going! Make sure you call the police first and get them here. If something happens to me, I'm holding you liable."

She grinned triumphantly. "Sure thing. Go on. I'll make the call, you start investigating."

Hannah hurriedly typed in a number and ran over to the intersection to look at the street signs while I continued to peer into the dark alley with trepidation. Loud banging was reverberating from deep within the alley, and eerily, it reminded me of the methodical footsteps from the beast in my dreams.

Suddenly, a pale white arm shot out and roughly grasped my arm, dragging me away from the safety of the streets. Even though their fingers were long and bony, their grip was firm, much firmer than any of the kids I had brawled with at the Academy. As he dragged me further and further away from the city lights, I kept clawing at the hand, making my captor grunt.

"You little brat! Stay still!" the owner of the pale hand shouted.

He jerked me around to the left and right, which provided me a window of opportunity to tear my arm away from the man's grasp. Under the single flickering wall light of the alley, I peered at my arm to see it sporting an angry red imprint of the man's bony fingers.

"What do you want from me?" I questioned, glaring at my captor.

A group of men from the shadows started cackling with raspy, worn-out voices. The one who dragged me into the alley, presumably the leader, stood in front of me, staring me down with the top half of his face hidden by the hood of a jet-black sweater. He mocked in a high-pitched squeal, "'What do you want from me.' He says, 'What do you want from me.' Get a load of this crap."

The guys in the back started cackling like banshees again.

"Look, kid, we weren't trying to 'want something from you.' Me and my boys were just having a little bit of fun, but then you and your little girlfriend walked by talking about how you was gonna report us to the police, so call it self-defense. It wasn't because we had a 'what do you want from me' moment."

The others laughed with him mockingly, and my teeth gnashed in anger. Without thinking, I shot back, "She's not my girlfriend. And what do a bunch of low-life gangsters like you have to do in an alleyway during dusk anyways? Did your mothers kick you out of the house because you were unemployed?"

The guys in the back stopped laughing, and the person with the hoodie shot me a strained smile. "Ouch, let's not get all 'insulty' now. Even 'gangsters,' as you put it, have stuff going on. Leave us be and call off your girlfriend, or there might be some...unintended consequences."

I saw his eyes flitter to the base of my neck before his eyes widened in glee. The brand started itching, and the guy erupted into a chorus of cackling. "It's my lucky day! No one will care if I decide to off a little Bastard!"

I grit my teeth, body shaking furiously. A tense silence settled down in the alleyway as an unnerving breeze blew several loose strands of hair out of my eyes.

As if they were given a silent cue, the five "minion thugs," who had been sitting around in the background, all charged at me, the leader staying back with a smirk on his face. I silently prayed, hoping to come out of this encounter unscathed and as some kind of hero. But it wasn't even close. As the five guys charged at me with their fists reared back, I only landed one feeble punch on the guy at the front before the rest kicked and pummeled my head into the ground.

My skull bashed into the concrete repeatedly, the assault rattling my brain. I tasted a metallic liquid on the edge of my lips. Relentlessly, they kept on hitting me with all they had and before long, my vision became hazy and the edges of my vision started fading to black. Soon enough, my grip on reality faded away.

# Chapter 3

*June 22, 2103*

· · · · · ● · · · ·

A SHARP PAIN JABBED at my eyes as the soft rays of morning light filtered in through the windows. My head throbbed with the force of dynamite and moving my arms and legs even the slightest took a lot more effort and pain than usual.

"Oh, you're finally awake."

Squinting my eyes, which were slowly adjusting to the lighting, I took a quick scan of the room that I was in. The walls were pale white, decorated minimally with some pictures of random plants here and there. A small 32-inch TV was mounted on the wall directly in front of me. To my left, monitors and machines were beeping away, many of them having tubes that were connected to my arms and legs.

"Who brought me here?" I asked. "Where's Hannah?"

The nurse's face lit up. "Dr. Kamiya left for Career Day at the Academy just around half an hour ago. She was hoping that you would be awake in time so that you two could go together, but unfortunately, you were still unconscious. She'll be so delighted to see that you're awake!"

"*Doctor?*"

Her face twisted into a puzzled expression. "Yes, Dr. Hannah Kamiya. She was certified around two years ago?"

"Oh…" I responded dumbly.

"Anyways, please rest up just a little longer. Dr. Kamiya will be doing a checkup when she returns and should be releasing you fairly soon. In the meantime, if you need anything, make sure you call for one of us and we'll be there to help!"

"Thank you."

With a bright smile on her face, she backed out of the room, leaving me alone. I looked down at my hands and legs which were all tightly bound with a hard cast. I groaned. Hannah definitely went overboard with the treatment again. Experimentally, I tried wiggling my arms and legs around, but a searing pain ran up my body as if someone had dug a thousand daggers deep into my skin. Maybe her treatment wasn't so overboard.

That fact also meant that I was stuck in this uncomfortable position for God knows how long. I looked around the room once more. The only form of entertainment available in the room was the TV, but the remote was out of reach, sitting on a coffee table next to the bed. Ignoring the large spikes of pain that erupted across my body, I wiggled toward the edge of my bed and stretched my casted arms across my body toward the remote. I was almost there. Just a little bit more.

But as luck would have it, just as I made to grab at the remote, the sliding room door slammed open, and the nurse from before walked in holding an E-Board against her chest with a furious look on her face.

"Just what do you think you're doing?" she questioned.

"Um…exercise?"

Her stormy look merged with one of absolute disbelief. "Exercise?"

"Yes."

The room became silent. Without another word, she grabbed a small stylus off the top of her E-Board—the "modern clipboard" as some called it—and wrote down a couple of sentences, whispering, "Patient appears delirious, a mental check is recomm-"

"Hey!"

She stifled a laugh. "It's my responsibility to make sure that all patients are given the correct treatment and recommend them to the doctor. But in all seriousness, from now on, if you have anything you need to do, please call for me through the button on the right side of the bed."

She bent down, picked up the remote, then handed it to me.

Nodding to her gratefully, I fumbled around with the remote a little bit before finding the buttons I wanted. The screen flipped to the local news channel.

"-come back to the important topic here! You're telling me that not a single person has any idea of why the Blighted have instigated these assaults?" a reporter shouted on television.

"Yes, that's exactly what I'm telling you. Remember James, we've tried to figure out what the objective of these people is for years and all the government led searches have failed and gone rogue. As of now, we don't have a single clue as to why the Blighted attacks on our southern border are taking place," another reporter responded. "All I can tell people along the border is to watch out. This genetically modified race, created by Professor Wallens in the 2030s, is dangerous and-"

"It does seem like the media has gotten more and more curious recently, doesn't it?" the nurse noted. "I've been hearing lately that their activity on the southern border has gotten more and more frequent. I'm just hoping that they don't try to move inland further than that."

"Yeah…" I despondently replied. "Why haven't we asked for help from other countries?"

The nurse guffawed. "No other country is going to help the Republic. Not after what the United States pulled during the thirties when they bombed India to oblivion."

"But that was the United States, right? Also, wasn't it India's fault in the first place for bombing our southern coast?"

"Tell that to the small-minded idiots out in the world. The rest of the world doesn't care who did what first. United States, United Republic. The rest of the world could care less what comes after United, they still consider us one and the same."

After seeing some grueling images of people lying in the rubble of buildings, I didn't feel like watching the TV anymore. Pressing the red power button, I shut the TV off. "Hey, uh…"

"Kathy."

"Hey, Kathy. I'm going to try and go to sleep. Could you tell Hannah to wake me up when she comes back?"

Kathy wrote down a couple of notes on her E-Board. "Sure thing. I'll let her know."

"Thank you."

She shut off the lights to the room and closed the window blinds before leaving. The room was now dark, and I could barely see the outlines of my arms and legs. The beeps and whirs of the medical equipment lulled me to sleep.

---

I WAS BACK within my mind listening to the pitter-patter of rain as torrents of water poured down on the deserted city. A thick wave of water washed down the metallic building walls like a waterfall. *Drip, drip.* Only this time, I wasn't running half out of breath as a monster trampled after me. Instead, I was held still by something invisible, watching my own reflection through a disfigured building window that made me look like a piece of abstract art.

Staring at myself, I couldn't help but notice the differences between the reflection and myself. The small boy in the reflection did not have the added height that I had gained during puberty, nor did it have the sharper, defined features that came with my slimming down.

In fact, the reflection looked half the age that I was currently.

"You're pathetic."

I continued to blankly stare at the reflection, still enraptured by the novelty of the experience.

"Hannah wouldn't have kept you if she knew how untalented you were."

A trickle of irritation started bubbling under my skin, and I opened my mouth, shouts of fury building in the depths of my larynx. But the only sounds that made it past my lips were strangled cries as if I was choking on my own breath.

"You know it's true," another voice whispered.

My eyes drift over toward the right. Fading into view next to the younger reflection of myself was the spitting image of Tony, complete with everything that pissed me off including his arrogant smirk, bad taste in clothing, and condescending body language.

He taunted, "If you weren't here, Hannah could've been famous. People would be lining up at our doorstep just to get a glimpse of her face."

I stared back into the building windows, and my face overlapped with my younger counterpart's. All I could see was a scrawny little kid, still stuck in the past with a negative attitude and no motivation to improve.

*Maybe they're right.*

"Of course we're right," mini-me and Tony chorused.

"We know everything about you. We *are* you."

Tony and mini-me started growing larger and larger in the windowpanes until their reflections extended to the height of the buildings themselves.

"You're pathetic."

"You're useless."

"Worst of all…"

WITH A STARTLED jolt, my eyes fluttered open, and I felt a trail of tears streaking down my cheeks. To my left, Hannah's hazel eyes were hovering over me, a concerned look on her face. Instead of the sweatshirt that she normally wore at home, she was garbed in a navy-blue scrub with a white coat over it. An M-Reader—a multi-purpose medical analyzer—loosely hung around her neck.

"Ethan, how are you feeling? You were sweating a lot and talking in your sleep. I tried calling your name a couple of times, but you wouldn't wake up."

I barely even heard her. My mind was spinning, thoughts still fixated on the vivid dream that had overtaken me during my sleep. Sweat was pouring down my face and body, drenching the hospital gown with dark stains.

"Ethan?"

My head snapped toward her voice. Seeing her nervous

expression, I chuckled and waved off her concerns with a flick of my hand. "Yeah, I'm doing fine. What those thugs did to me probably left me a little rattled."

"Are you sure?"

"Yeah. I'm doing fine."

Hannah picked up an E-Board that was sitting on my bed before scribbling some notes down. "If you say so, Ethan. But I'm going to have to keep you here maybe for another day or two just to make sure that you're completely fine. Sorry, it's more of a procedural thing."

I groaned. That meant more days in these restrictive casts. Hannah went through some routine checks, and after she prodded my arms and legs with some kind of rod, she nodded in satisfaction. "Alright, you look good for now. I'm going to go back home for the evening. If you need anything, ring up Kathy. She can help. Hope you get better soon!"

"Yeah, thanks."

With Hannah gone, the sinking feeling in my stomach returned. The hospital room felt even lonelier than it had been before. I sat there, staring at the blank white walls for a good half an hour, thinking about life. What else could I do?

Remembering the scathing comments that Tony and mini-me had made in my dream, my thoughts turned slightly negative. *In Sector 125, maybe she would've finished that project that the graduation pamphlet had mentioned*, I thought. *Maybe she would've had more chances. Maybe-*

A loud click tore my strands of thoughts into ribbons.

I glanced at the door and standing there was the one person that I could've done without seeing during my stay in the hospital. "What are you doing here Tony? Aren't visiting hours over?"

He strutted over to my bedside as if he was walking on a red carpet. Each step screamed, saying "Look at me!" His hands were stuffed in the pocket of his baggy brown hoodie while a black cap adorned his head.

"Special permission from Hannah. I couldn't bear thinking of the idea that you were all here alone without company, so I absolutely had to come," he cajoled. Thick sarcasm bled off every syllable he spoke, and all I wanted to do at that moment was introduce his ugly, freckled Mexican face to my fists.

"So, how'd you manage to do this?" he inquired, rapping his knuckles against my casts.

"None of your business."

"Ouch, you're so cold. Are you just mad that Hannah had to save your loser self again?"

The hairs on my arms bristled. "Shut up."

Tony tilted his head up in a mocking gesture and glared at me down the bridge of his nose. "Make me, Bastard."

I clenched the railings of the bed until the knuckles on my hands were white as I fought the urge to lash out at Tony. My jaw vibrated as my top and bottom teeth gnashed against each other.

"Piss off."

He smirked down at me as he stood right beside my bed. "Why are you even getting angry? You know it's true. It's always the same story. You get hurt because you're stupid, and Hannah comes to save you. It should feel routine at this point."

Embarrassed, I closed my eyes.

"This is why Hannah has to save you all the time. Because you run from your fears rather than facing them. You're an embarrassment."

I heard the rustling of Tony's clothes and his hot breath

hovered over my right ear. Opening my eyes, I angrily stared back at Tony, who was staring down at me condescendingly.

"Remember your place, Bastard."

# Chapter 4

*June 29, 2103*

· · · • ● • · · ·

"YOU'RE ALL SET to go Ethan. We're lucky that this hospital had accelerator tech, or you might've been stuck here for several more weeks," Hannah noted dully.

"Gee, thanks for the thought."

It had been a whole week since the little fiasco with Tony, and to be honest, it all went in one ear and out the other. Of course, Hannah would never find out about it, and I shoved the memory down deep inside to bundle up my conflicted emotions. Just as usual.

"Alright, I'm going to remove the casts now. Hold still," Hannah warned. She pulled out a small cast saw and started working on my legs. The high-pitched buzzing of the little blade vibrating filled my ears as I silently watched Hannah do her work. It took around ten minutes for Hannah to remove all the casts.

"Just one more final check and then you should be ready to go."

She tapped my arms and legs with the long rod wired to the wall before nodding in satisfaction. "Looks good!" she remarked cheerfully.

Hannah wrapped her arm around my back to gently help me get off the bed. Moving my body was still a painful endeavor, but it was much better than what it had been about a week ago. There was still a noticeable limp in my step. "I'll wait outside while you change."

She stepped outside, and I changed into some normal clothes that Hannah had brought from home: a plain white t-shirt with athletic shorts. I guided my feet into a pair of red sneakers and limped out of the room. Hannah was sitting on a bench in the hallway, and her face lit up when she saw me.

"Let's go," I told her in a hoarse voice.

The hospital hallways were very plain and candidly similar to the hospital room. White walls lined the corridor and the only specks of color came in the form of the little pictures that hung off the walls.

Right when we were about to leave, a gruff voice called, "Ms. Kamiya, are you done with your business in the hospital?"

Hannah and I turned to face a man of large stature. He must've been around thirty or forty years old. He was wearing a similar garb to what Hannah was wearing, and a small goatee was growing on his chin; he looked tired, as indicated by the sinking dark bags under his eyes.

"Yes, he's all healed now. I apologize for the slight inconvenience."

"Yes, *slight* inconvenience."

A heavy tension settled in between the two who appeared as if they were just a few ticks away from full out brawling. The man snorted. "I would recommend that you check your professionalism from here on out Ms. Kamiya. Not all people are so accommodating of the behavior that you've displayed. Your status and accomplishments do not give you the right to shortcut the traditional procedures. Keep that in mind."

"I will, Dr. Kay," Hannah responded smoothly. I heard an unusually irritated undertone in her voice. With a scowl, Dr. Kay clicked his teeth and shot me a dark glare before leaving us at the entrance of the hospital.

"Who was that?" I asked.

"He's the head of this hospital. Don't worry about him. I think he's just a little mad at me for doing his job. Probably did it better than he could."

"Won't you get in trouble for that?"

"Nope! After all, I did have a justified reason for doing what I did."

"Alright, whatever you say, I guess…"

The walk back home was near-silent, and although Hannah's face portrayed happiness and joy, her body language said otherwise. Her legs were dragging behind her as she walked, and her shoulders were hunched over. Occasionally, she would look down at the ground with a downtrodden expression on her face.

By the time we reached home, the sun was low above the horizon, letting a soft orange glow enter through the windows. When Hannah saw me heading to my room, she suggested, "Why don't you get some sleep? I know it's still a little early, but it will let your newly mended bones to have more time to recover. Trust me."

"Alright," I responded. Truthfully, I didn't feel too tired. After all, it was only seven o'clock in the evening. But at the same time, I'd gladly accept any excuse to get away from the awkward air.

"I'll see you tomorrow Hannah."

I walked into my room but froze, reminded of something. Poking my head back out of the doorway, I asked, "By the way, do you know what I'm supposed to do for career shadowing?

I never went to Career Day last week, so I'm not really sure what I'm supposed to do."

"I-I'll figure it out and let you know tomorrow, okay?" Hannah stuttered. She crossed her arms against her chest and refused to meet my gaze. Her feet kept on shifting nervously, and she glanced kept flittering back and forth between me and her room.

"Alright, I guess."

Ducking back into my room, I flopped down on the bed, wincing as my body protested in pain at the sudden movement. Closing my eyes, I willed myself to sleep but to no avail. Random thoughts kept running through my head, plaguing me with random questions that went unanswered. I must have been in that state for at least an hour, a weird limbo between sleeping and staying awake. Through the wall, I could hear rapid typing sounds coming from Hannah's room.

As random thoughts ran through my head, my mind inevitably wandered back to the "exciting" week that had just passed. After years of Academy, I graduated, only to be beaten up by a bunch of gangsters. Now, out of the hospital, I felt nothing but a dull numbness in my body and mind. This wasn't what I had imagined when people described the "post-Academy" high.

"I can't sleep," I muttered.

Pushing my sore body up, I sat down on the edge of the bed, legs dangling off the side. My back was arched over forward, my eyes never leaving the ground. I glanced at the clock. It read 8:23 p.m. With a heavy sigh, I pushed myself off the bed and walked out to the living room despite my body protesting. There was a lingering aroma of food that remained in the kitchen, and oddly, a dirty plate was still sitting on the dinner table with some leftover lasagna on it. It was warm to the touch. A letter, stained with wet tear droplets, was sitting next to the plate. Gently, I picked it up and started skimming it, becoming increasingly furious as I read on.

> *Dear Ms. Kamiya,*
>
> *Due to your recent infraction at St. Arc's Hospital (284928), your doctor's certification and right to perform procedures during times of emergency will be put on freeze until your appointed job shadowing overseer deems that you are fit to return to the line of work. This infraction will be marked in your academic and professional records. Additionally, to smoothen the process of reentering you back into the field, it is recommended that you enroll in the remittance course offered by Dr. Joseph Collins at Comen's Hospital titled "Proper Procedures in the Hospital" (008283).*
>
> *Any attempt to violate this decision will have additional consequences.*
>
> *Sincerely,*
>
> *Dr. Kay*

I clenched my teeth, fists balled up tightly until my knuckles turned white. *Is this what has Hannah dejected? But why would they do something like this?* I thought. At the same time, a heavy pang of guilt settled into my heart like a ten-ton weight. *She's suffering because of me,* I realized. My mind wandered back to what Tony had suggested to me back in the hospital room.

Gently, making sure that I wouldn't rip up the wet parts of the paper, I grasped the letter in my hands and walked toward Hannah's room. But before I passed through the small archway leading out of the living room, an oddity caught my attention. On the living room couch, which was normally filled with little pillows, Hannah's bag was lying ajar with papers spilling out of the main compartment. The pillows, which normally belonged on the ends of the couch near the armrest, were tossed to random positions with one sitting on the TV stand while the other was outside on the apartment balcony.

I picked up the pillows and placed them back where they belonged. Grabbing Hannah's bag, I started organizing the papers into one neat pile, but a lone envelope caught my eye. It wasn't anything special, just a blue-tinted envelope that anyone would use while mailing letters. But it was addressed to "Ethan Holfstras."

Surprised, I dropped the other letters on the couch and held the single blue envelope reverently in my hands, as if it would turn to dust at any second. My heart started pounding with anxiety, temporarily replacing my previous confusion. The letter had the official mark of the Academy in the left corner and was addressed by the principal.

I considered asking Hannah about the letter first but decided against it. Gently opening the flap of the envelope, I saw a cream-colored letter inside along with another white slip. My hands were trembling as I held the short letter in my hands, the butterflies in my stomach flying around as if they were angry bees as I started to read.

> *Mr. Holfstras,*
> *The Board of Education for Sector 36 has evaluated the results of your time spent at the Academy. We have concluded that your results, while far better than initially expected from someone of your status, are incompatible with the requirements that are necessary to join the workforce. As a result, we are assigning you an alternative path and career opportunity.*
> *You are required to attend Camp Daedalus, which will be directed by a member of the Republic Military Executive Board, General Kyle Bergen. The program will last approximately two weeks (subject to change) and will focus on improving the current skill sets that*

*you have and potentially, discover possible new talents that may have laid dormant in the past.*

*This program will not only develop your skills but offers an opportunity for you to work with a Military Executive Board, and potentially a way into becoming a member of the U.R. Military, one of the most coveted career tracks in our educational program.*

*Further details regarding the program will be detailed to you when you arrive at the destination. As a reminder, this camp is mandatory, and there is no other option should you want to continue forward after Academy education. A vehicle will arrive at your location of residence on July 16th at approximately 0600 hours to transport you to the camp. A packing list is enclosed along with the letter.*

*Sincerely,*
*The B.O.E. of Sector 36*
*June 19, 2103*

The letter evoked mixed emotions. First and foremost, disappointment. I had hoped that proving myself somewhat would dissuade criticism of my "status," but it didn't appear to have worked out that way. Second was excitement with slight uncertainty. I for sure hadn't signed up for such a program, yet it seemed like I had struck gold. This was pure luck, a kind of dumb luck that I usually was never associated with. Third was anger, directed toward Hannah. Disbelief that she would keep me in the dark about such an opportunity. Anger fueled by a sense of betrayal. By the looks of it, the letter had been written a week and a half ago, yet she hadn't said a thing.

Setting both Hannah and my letter on the living room table, I cleaned up the rest of the papers and put them into Hannah's backpack. After, I gathered the two letters in my hands again and trekked toward Hannah's room, rapping my knuckles against the wooden door. "Hannah? Can I talk to you for a second?"

The clacking of Hannah's keyboard abated, followed by several seconds of silence. Slowly, the door creaked open, and Hannah's head peeked out.

"Who is it? Tony?"

"Um, no."

She didn't look too pleased to see me. With a scowl on her face, she admonished, "Didn't I tell you to go to sleep? If you keep wandering around, the muscles and ligaments around the bone will continue to get agitated which could delay your healing."

"Sorry," I apologized with a weak smile. "I was lying down in bed, but the little jolts of pain were aggravating, and I couldn't sleep. Can I talk to you for just a second?"

Hannah's brows scrunched up, a questioning look on her face. "Sure."

She opened the door, letting me pass through. As I sat down on her bed and twiddled my thumbs, she popped open the window and let the warm summer breeze through. Her room was sparsely decorated. The walls were painted in a light baby blue with several picture frames hanging on all four surfaces. Some of the pictures were from when we were younger and still in the orphanage while others were more recent.

The bed was plain, the covers and blankets all a pure white, and the last piece of furniture, discounting her closet, was the desk that was sitting right in front of the window which looked out into the city. Her computer was still lit up, the cursor blinking on the last word she had typed.

"What did you want to talk about?" she asked, tucking a long strand of hair behind her ear. "I don't have a lot of time, though. One of the doctors has been pushing me to finish one of the research papers we've been working on."

I glanced toward the computer screen. The screen showed an email, not a research paper.

"Listen, I wasn't really trying to look through your stuff," I started nervously. "I just wanted to ask you about these."

I held out the two letters for Hannah to see. "Why did you keep them from me? Maybe you didn't trus-"

My words died in my mouth as I watched Hannah's expression go from calm to furious. Her small hands balled into fists, and her brows scrunched up in fury. For the first time, she was glaring at me with genuine anger in her eyes. My heart sank in sorrow, and I felt completely exposed as she stared down at me.

When she spoke, each syllable was chipped, her voice cold as ice. "Where did you find those?"

"W-Well, one was on the table-"

"Give them to me," she growled, ripping them out of my hands. I remained rooted as she started shredding them in halves, sprinkling the remains onto the floor. The anger I initially felt at my discovery all but disappeared as I watched Hannah tear apart the letters viciously. It was replaced by fear and nervousness.

"Please leave."

"But-"

"Now!"

Hesitantly, I got off the bed and under her harsh glare, left the room. Outside, as I slid down the wall in disbelief and confusion, all I could hear was sobbing coming from Hannah's room. My heart clenched in guilt.

*I'm the worst.*

# Chapter 5

## *July 4, 2103*

· · · · **●** · · · ·

THE COLD MORNING air rushed past me as I continued my morning jog around the block. It was only five in the morning, meaning that people were still tucked in bed. The streets were silent save for the occasional car that drove by.

I pulled out my phone, clicking back through my messages. The text from a couple of days ago was still at the top of my messaging list. *"Come out on the 4th. The usual place. Jimmy."* It was the only thing I'd been looking forward to throughout the week. Ever since the spat with Hannah happened about a week ago, she hardly gave me the time of day, even during the rare occasions I would catch her outside of her room.

*"Hannah?"*

*It was the first time that I saw her outside of the room since our argument, and she was looking worse for wear. Her hair was disheveled in frazzled knots and her eyes were bloodshot, bags hanging low under her eyes.*

*"Are you okay?" I asked nervously.*

*"..."*

*"You look a little bit tired."*

"..."

*"Do you need anything?"*

"..."

*She brushed past me without so much as saying hi and stepped into the kitchen. Grabbing a large pan, she started up breakfast. Every time she swiveled toward me. her eyes glanced over me as if I was just another piece of furniture. Just under twenty minutes later, Hannah had breakfast laid out on the table and immediately started walking back toward her room.*

*I grabbed her shoulder gently. "Can we please just talk?"*

*"No, we can't."*

*Roughly brushing my hands off, she pushed past me, shutting herself back in her room.*

*That was so stupid,* I seethed as the memory resurfaced. My desire to "ask for forgiveness" had waned after that encounter, and all I felt now was simmering annoyance. Hannah annoyed me. The Academy annoyed me. My own self annoyed me. I glanced back at my phone. It was 5:35, just about time for Jimmy to open shop.

As I ran along the outer edges of Sector 36, I passed by a long line of stores and stalls. This was the "Lower Strip," a long path filled with small stalls, stands, and companies that couldn't keep up with the competition in the business district downtown along with the rare Bastard shop-owner who was barred from selling in the city. Inevitably, they were forced to relocate here if they wanted their business to survive. My eye caught the hunched over figure that I'd been looking for.

"Jimmy! What's up?"

"'What's up' yourself," he responded tiredly, rubbing his eyes. "I'm still half asleep but dad still wanted me to come to this place. Story of-"

"-my life, yeah?" I finished amusedly. It was the same

corny line from him every single time. "So, what's going on now? Why'd you call me over?"

"Why else do I call you over? Same old, same old. Brand hid as per protocol?"

I rolled my eyes and pointed toward my neck. The wolf-mark was covered by the high collar of my long-sleeved undershirt. "Of course. Got it covered."

Jimmy was a little bit of an aberration in society himself. Born from a father who was a Bastard and a mother who was completely normal, he was an outcast while at the same time, not really. For anyone that didn't know him personally, he was just Jimmy, a normal, unbranded citizen who worked at the "Lower Strip" in the mornings.

"What do you need to be done today? More set-up work?"

"Nah, not today. I didn't call you for work-related things. Just thought that you might keep me entertained throughout the day. Maybe help out during the lunchtime rush as well..."

"Oh."

As Jimmy popped open the door of his small stall, I stepped in and sat down in a reclining chair that looked out toward the open store window. Soon, other owners also started walking by, some waving toward us heartily while others glared at us. Holton, an old man who had been working in the Lower Strip for decades, shot us an especially nasty glare.

"That guy's still on about getting you out of here?" I asked exasperatedly as I watched the old man pass by.

"Yeah, persistent geezer too. You think he'd give up after five years."

"Old habits never die, I guess."

As the morning hours passed, customers and owners alike appeared en masse, and by noon, the Lower Strip was in full swing. Jimmy's shop was starting to get overrun with orders.

"Can I have a hot dog?"

"I think this order is wrong!"

"Is it going to take much longer?"

"Why isn't my food out yet?"

Multiple voices clashed against each other, and my head felt like it was splitting in two. How Jimmy did this alone on a normal day I could not even begin to fathom. But in a sudden decline, the chatter died down to low murmurs, and I noticed that the packed mob of customers had thinned. In fact, they had nearly all disappeared. I poked my head out of the window and saw owners and customers alike gather toward the central plaza of the Strip.

"Do you know what's going on? Is there some kind of concert or something?" I asked Jimmy, who kept rubbing the back of his neck nervously.

"N-Not a clue."

"Man the stand. Let me go check it out."

"Stay here, man. It could just be that people aren't hungry," Jimmy suggested uncertainly.

"Fat chance."

"Wait, you-"

Before Jimmy could stop me, I took off my apron and set it on the counter, hurriedly rushing out of the shop. As I ran toward the central plaza, I noticed a big crowd packed together, forming a large circle around the area. I could barely see above the wall of bodies.

"What's going on?" I asked the person nearest to me. The guy was grinning with a can of beer in his hands despite it only being noon.

"I don't know for sure man, but I think it's a Hunt! Holton's gone wild!"

My blood froze in my veins, and my head snapped toward the central plaza where people were cheering wildly. Pushing in between people aside hastily, I squeezed my way through the crowd until I was at the front of the crowd. When I finally saw what was happening, my teeth gnashed against each other, a red haze filling my vision.

There were six people standing inside the large circle that the wall of people created. Holton notably stood out among the rest. Three middle-aged men also stood beside him while the last two, maybe in their early teens, stood opposite of them. One was a short girl with frazzled brunette hair while the other was a slightly taller guy with messy brown hair. They both looked like they were on their last legs, blood trickling down their arms and legs. But my eyes weren't focused on that. They were fixated on the distinct wolf-marks tattooed on their necks.

"Hunt! Hunt! Hunt! Hunt!" the crowd chanted, and searing lava flowed through my veins.

Of course, it was the Fourth of July. How could I forget?

"Hunt! Hunt! Hunt! Hunt!" the crowd continued to chant, and I felt my heart drop, fists shaking in rage when I saw Holton approaching the two teenagers with an SMP-9 pistol loosely held in his hand.

"Who wants to see some hunting!" Holton roared. His voice was hoarse as usual, bordering on wheezing. For a split second, as he swiveled back to stare at the two kids in front of him, I swore that he paused mid-turn to meet my eyes.

Holton started walking forward with his handgun held out in front of him, a glint of satisfaction in his eyes as he saw the two kids in front of him trembling. I started dashing forward toward Holton, but a firm hand on my shoulders stopped me. I whipped around and saw Jimmy standing behind me, shaking his head.

"Jimmy-"

"No."

"But-"

I turned around just as the crowd gasped in surprise. The teenage boy was starting to step forward, and Holton retreated slightly. I silently cheered as the kid dashed toward Holton, hand outstretched toward the pistol with his face contorted in anger. The kid nearly had his hands on the gun, and I grinned in glee.

A loud gunshot rang out in the plaza, followed by many loud screams. My heart stopped, and I watched as the teenage boy staggered and reeled back, falling to the ground in a pool of blood. Holton, who had been holding the gun confidently before, slowly dropped it, hands trembling while his eyes widened in fear.

"I-I didn't mean to k-kill him. H-He jumped at me! It was self-defense!" he shouted wildly as the crowd hastily dispersed. Children were quickly ushered out of the area by their frightened parents along with other adults who were grimacing. The sounds of loud chanting and excited whispers diminished as the crowd disappeared, replaced by the teary weeping of the teenage girl who was crying over the boy's body. I grimaced with a hollow feeling in my heart. Death was a somewhat common sight, but never a pretty one.

Jimmy tugged at my shirt once again. "Ethan, let's go."

"Jimmy-"

"You can't do anything for them."

I closed my mouth and was overtaken by overwhelming sadness because I knew he was right. I couldn't do anything. Not when I held the same burden that they did.

"Let's go back to the shop," Jimmy suggested pleadingly,

tugging at my shirt once more. I looked back at the crying girl with sympathy, then glared toward Holton, who was still standing rooted in place.

"Fine," I spat.

The rest of the day was very subdued. Customers weren't coming as readily ever since the "Hunt," and most of the owners had closed shop and left. While deaths during the Fourth of July weren't uncommon, they always left a bitter taste in peoples' mouths.

As the sun was starting to set over the horizon, I spotted Holton leaving his stand as well. His steps were weak, and his eyes seemed hollow as if he was merely a shell of himself. An unknown source fueled my anger as my head started pounding wildly.

"Jimmy, I'm leaving,"

"Alright. Don't do anything stupid."

I hesitated. "I won't."

I packed up everything that I had brought into the shop and opened the door, pausing to call back, "When's the next time you're going to call me back to do something like this?"

"I don't know, man. Don't you have your little camp thing?"

"Yeah, but that's not until like, two weeks later."

"I don't know," Jimmy muttered, staring down at his phone. "Maybe I'll figure out stuff you can do later if you're so eager to work."

"Alright, just let me know," I chortled, stepping out of the shop. "I'll see you later."

"See you later."

He never noticed one of his cooking knives disappearing from the counter.

To my surprise, Holton didn't go toward the suburbs of the sector, but instead went downtown. I followed him at a medium distance, staying as a part of the crowd. Occasionally, he turned around and stared in my general direction, but if he had noticed me, he didn't give any indication of it. I watched as he went around several different blocks before he hurriedly ducked into an alleyway as if he was being chased.

I cursed and trailed after him, barely registering how the bright city lights seemed to dissipate as soon as I entered the alleyway. After settling down to a slow walk, I saw Holton standing in front of a dead-end, staring at me with a tired expression on his face. It made me feel sympathetic. Almost.

"What do you want?" he asked.

A sense of deja vu overwhelmed me, catapulting me back to the day of graduation. Except this time, I was in the reverse role. "I don't want anything in particular, just a quick question. Why did you kill him? Back at the plaza."

"It was an accident."

"But you were smiling when you shot him, weren't you?"

Holton's breathing thinned as he started exhaling and inhaling at a quickened pace. He fumbled around with something near the hem of his jeans, and I watched him wearily. My heart stopped and I hesitantly stepped back when I heard a metallic click of something being disengaged. When his hands came back up, he had the same SMP-9 pistol from the afternoon held tightly in his hands.

"Get the hell away from me!" he shouted crazily, pointing the barrel of the gun toward me. His fingers were trembling, and his breathing was becoming even more irregular.

I held both hands up in surrender, my breath also quickening in response. As I stared down at the glinting metal, I took a large gulp. My life started flashing before my eyes as fear bombarded my mind.

"Come on, old man. Don't do anything you'd regret…"

He hesitated and I saw his grip falter for a moment, but it tightened again, his finger hovering just over the trigger. "What are you going to do? Tell other people about how I killed a stupid little Bastard? They won't care!"

"I know that they won't care," I growled angrily, slowly putting my hands down. "So put the damned gun down you senile old man."

I waited for the barrel to lower, but the gun was still held toward my head, standing at attention rigidly. Holton had a crazed look in his eyes, and he didn't seem to have any intention of lowering the pistol anytime soon.

Slowly, I reached into my back pocket, Holton tensing in response. I slid out the small cooking knife that I had stolen from Jimmy's shop, holding it out in front of me. It only gave me slight comfort while staring down the barrel of Holton's SMP-9 pistol.

"Do you really think that's going to do something?" Holton asked with a cackle, grating on my nerves. I stayed silent, watching him as he fingered the trigger. He looked a lot more confident than he was before.

"Why do you even care, anyway? It's the Fourth of July. They'll all get over it in a couple of days. I just have to wait that out and everything will be back to normal," he said curiously.

I grit my teeth at his nonchalant dismissal of killing a person, and the mark on my neck felt like it was twitching, as if it was alive.

"So, what if I kill one of them? It's not like it matters anyhow."

My vision clouded over with a red haze and I took a step towards him.

"Nobody cares, kid. Move past it. He was just a Bastard."

By breathing grew steadier, and it felt like my body was getting more powerful with every breath.

"So, what are you going to do? Take another step and I won't hesitate," Holton threatened.

"I won't hesitate either."

An unsettling breeze tunneled through the alleyway, and I felt something inside me shift. My mind went blank, and it felt as if something had taken over my body, urging it forward. Holton's certainty wavered, and fear began to rise in his face. The redness in my vision deepened. I took a couple of paces forward, and Holton hesitantly stepped back. For a split second, Holton lowered the barrel of his gun, and I leaped at him, tackling him to the ground. He fired off a few shots past my head and my ears rang from the deafening sound.

My body surged with energy, and I wrestled the gun out of his hands. The edge of my vision was blurry, and Holton's shouting and struggling became muffled as if they were coming from some distant world. To my surprise, he was stronger than I originally thought, and he kept grabbing at my neck, tightly holding my collar in a balled fist. A breeze blew against the crook of my neck and I saw Old Man Holden's eyes widen.

His grip slackened a little bit, and I could barely see beyond the red haze that overcame my vision. Surging forward, I lifted the knife to his throat as he choked on his breath. His eyes were wide in panic. "Stop! What are you doing, you parasitic demon?!"

Even my own mind was screaming, the brain firing off warning signals to the rest of my body. But there was no response, and my body kept moving without pause as my hands dipped down toward Holton's neck. I felt horror and a sick sense of satisfaction the thin metal face sunk into his neck, blood oozing out from the thin line of red that appeared in the wake of the blade's path.

He kept on struggling, but soon, his grip became weak, and his harms flopped back onto the ground, stilling. Numbly, I stood from his struggling body and leaned close to the cold concrete ground. The face of the boy from earlier flashed in my mind, and in a burst of inspiration, I carved the tip of the knife into the ground as Holton's choked gurgles started dying down. A roughly etched wolf in the ground stared back at me as I turned away from the scene. My whole body felt numb, but I kept walking toward the bright lights of the city. Mindlessly, I slipped the knife deep into a deep crevice hidden behind a building before leaving the alley.

I heard whispers as people pointed toward me, some shying away from me in surprise and disgust. I didn't care, barely even registering the wet liquid trailing down my arms. Somewhere in the back of my mind, the thought of legal consequences flew through my head. My legs continued to trudge forward, subconsciously traveling along the familiar path toward my apartment complex.

The receptionist gave me a weird look as I stepped into the elevator and went up. My hands shook violently as I turned the doorknob, entering the peace of home. Hannah sat on the couch reading papers, not even flinching as I entered. Her eyes briefly widened, but nothing beyond that.

An ugly feeling rose inside me, and I didn't feel qualified to even look at Hannah. I sat on the small seat near the couch and receded into myself. Soon enough, I felt her eyes on me, and I looked up to see her examining my body. I still had scratches from my fall to the ground, and small spots of blood stained my clothes.

She still wouldn't meet my eyes.

# Chapter 6

*July 16, 2103*

· · · · • • · · ·

I PULLED OUT A box of cereal from the pantry while my
small duffle bag hung loosely over my shoulders. As the
letter suggested, I packed light for the trip, limiting myself
to basic hygiene products and clothes. Or rather, *Hannah*
limited me to basic hygiene products and clothes. My original
idea of "light packing" had included two-months' worth of
clothing and food.

I checked the clock once again. It was 5:45, just fifteen
minutes before the letter said that the vehicle would arrive
in front of the apartment complex. I sat down at the table
and looked around the empty kitchen. It made me feel
lonely, though, I should've been used to it by now all things
considered.

When I got home on the Fourth of July, waiting until the
sixteenth was one of the most drawn-out periods of my life.
Every single second felt like an hour as I laid down in my bed,
aimlessly staring at the ceiling, unable to sleep. The image of
Holton choking on his own blood kept flashing through my
mind like a video on loop. *Why did I do that?* I asked myself,
and the question continued to haunt me.

Every day, the news failed to not cover the story. Horrid
images of Holton lying in the alleyway atop a pool of his

own blood surfaced on the big screens across downtown, reporters scathingly tearing into theories on what the small wolf symbol on the ground meant. The first time I saw the news, I thought that my heart had stopped.

*It was the day after the fact. When I came to, it was to the harsh prodding of someone poking something into my side. I slapped at the offending limb and reeled back in surprise when a male voice shouted in surprise.*

*Slowly, I opened my eyes, growling at the person who stood in front of me. "What the hell are you doing this early in the morning? The sun's not even up yet."*

*"Get your head together. It's six in the evening. It's just cloudy outside. Jesus Christ, get yourself off the couch and clean yourself up," Tony scathingly replied with a scowl. "Also, check the news. Looks like one of your Bastard friends lost a screw and went berserk."*

*I heard several footsteps moving away before a door slammed shut. Groggily, I pushed myself off the couch, grimacing when I saw the dried blood caking my arms and clothes. I hastily tore the jacket off my body and tossed it far away from me, the red-stained cloth making me uncomfortable. Reaching out, I grabbed the remote to the TV and flipped toward the news channel, reeling back in surprise at the first thing I saw.*

*It was the dead body of Holton. The image was slightly blurred near the neck area, but the face was unmistakably Holton's. It was lit up on a screen behind two reporters who were shouting furiously at each other. Their voice merely became background noise while my eyes were fixated on the image in a daze. Holton stared back at me, eyes open wide. I shut off the TV immediately, heart pounding in my chest as I took deep, labored breaths.*

*Then, I remembered in detail last night. The red haze, the knife, the sick feeling of satisfaction, everything. I felt like throwing up, bile rising in my throat as the image of Holton once against flashed in my mind. A cold sense of reality settled in my stomach.*

*I was a criminal and not just any kind of criminal. I was a murderer. A Bastard who murdered a regular civilian to boot.*

*I spent the next few days holed up in my room, lying on the bed, trembling. Even the slightest sound made me jumpy, and I wondered how long I'd have until the police would track me down. Five days? Ten? Maybe I'd last until the month before they took me off to a high-security prison.*

*When I checked my email after a few days of silence, the only correspondence that came through was another blip about Camp Daedalus. That was on July 9th. It was the only comforting grace that gave me the hope that they had yet to figure out the culprit behind Holton's death.*

A soft vibration buzzed against my leg. The clock on the lock screen of my phone flashed 5:50. Leaving the half-eaten bowl of cereal at the table, I quickly brushed my teeth before putting my shoes on. One last time, I glanced toward Hannah's door at the end of the long hallway, hoping that she would at least pop her head out to say goodbye. I had no such luck.

Sighing, I opened the door, which beeped as I passed through the doorway. The hallways outside were practically empty since all the other residents were still tucked away in dreamland.

"Ethan?"

I froze and peered back through the doorway. Hannah's head poked out from behind her bedroom door as she yawned and rubbed her hands against her eyes tiredly. Her gaze was glued to the floor. She was still garbed in her nightwear, and her messy bed head stuck out in all directions like a bird's nest.

"Sorry," I sheepishly called. "Did I wake you up?"

"No, I just wanted to see you out before you left."

"Oh."

An awkward silence fell between us. Hannah kept shifting her right hand back and forth from her left arm to her neck as if she was undecided about where to put the limb. To be fair, I wasn't fairing much better. My eyes kept darting from left to right, staring at the walls of the apartment complex as if they were the most interesting thing in the world.

Another vibration from my back pocket made me jump. The alarm that I had set for 5:55 as a final reminder rang from inside my pockets. That snapped me out of the little trance that I had been in. When I saw Hannah still nervously fidgeting, I sighed. Kicking off my shoes, I took a couple of hesitant steps toward her before throwing my arms around her in a tight embrace. Hannah stiffened, then relaxed and returned the hug.

"Be careful," she whispered.

"I will."

She pushed me away and bore into my eyes with a penetrating stare. "I mean it. You have to promise me that you'll be careful."

"I promise."

Out of the corner of my eye, I peeked at the clock on the wall, which was quickly ticking by.

"Ethan-"

"Hannah, I *promise*. Don't worry. I have to go, or I'm going to be late,"

She nodded. "Remember, no matter what happens, look after yourself first, and make sure that you're safe."

I watch Hannah go back into her room, chuckling when I heard a loud thump followed by a pleased sigh as she jumped back into bed. Strapping my shoes back onto my feet, I took a final sweeping look around the small apartment house, thinking, *I won't be back here for another two weeks.* The thought brought up a new wave of trepidation, but I steeled myself. Sliding past the doorway with my duffle bag, I silently closed the door behind me.

I felt light, as if an invisible weight had been lifted off my shoulders.

As I pressed the elevator button to go down, I imagined what the camp would be like. As the small electronic panel in the elevator started counting down the floors, I became nervous. Passingly, I wondered if someone would be waiting for me downstairs.

*14...13...12...11...*

The pace of my heart started increasing. An old grandma next to me shot me a toothy smile.

*10...9...8...7...*

My hands were starting to get clammy, and I rubbed them furiously against my pants to dry them off. An angry guy in a suit was shouting into his phone.

*6...5...4...3...*

Oh, God.

*2...1...Ding!*

As the elevator doors slowly parted, I peered through the gap, expecting just about anything. But no one was standing in the lobby save for the receptionist, who I gave a nervous wave to. I looked down at my watch. It read 6:00 A.M. on the dot. The vehicle should've been here already.

Just as I finished the thought, a black sedan pulled around the corner and stopped in front of the lobby doors. Stepping out, I waited for the driver to come out so that I could greet him with my practiced greeting. Instead, the trunk of the car opened on its own, and I hesitantly tossed my duffle bag into the trunk, nearly jumping as it automatically shut with a click.

As soon as the trunk closed, the back door of the car swung open, showing the somewhat spacious back. I stuck my head in and peeked toward the driver's seat but saw no one there. Relief and disappointment flooded my system. "Sweet, self-driving car..." I muttered.

Hesitantly, I got into the back seat, wincing as my head bumped against the roof of the car in the process. The door automatically shut behind me as I got in. Decor and color were sparse in the car. The entire front seat was occupied by a single driver's seat which was centered in the front row, giving the backseat more legroom. The leather was jet black, and still had a "new car" scent to it.

Suddenly, the car lurched forward and started its journey to Camp Daedalus.

As I shifted around in my seat, something brushed up against my leg. Peering down, I found a familiar looking blue envelope resting on the seat right next to mine with "Ethan Holfstras" printed across its face. The letter inside read,

> *Dear Mr. Holfstras,*
>
> *Camp Daedalus is meant to test your abilities to the fullest and immerse you in an environment where we may best assess your existing abilities and hopefully, foster new abilities that may emerge as a result of the camp. For this reason, the schedule is designed to maximize your time in the training facility and to help this program run efficiently, we are expecting you to read the brochures and information packets that are provided in the vehicle. You should be able to locate*

*them in the pocket behind the driver's seat. Further directions will be printed on the information packets.*

*We look forward to seeing you at Camp Daedalus.*

*Camp Daedalus Administrative Staff*

It wasn't the most welcoming letter in the world. Setting the letter down, I fumbled around with the driver's seat pocket and found the information packets and brochures. All combined, they were around fifty pages worth of reading to do, front and back.

I started with the small little guidebook at the top, and the information inside described how to go about reading all the information within the packet. There was a rule book, ability assessment guide, self-written report, and some basic information and policies regarding the camp in general. While opening the massive rules packet, I sighed.

This was going to be a long journey.

I WOKE UP as a robotic voice announced, "We have arrived at military base 0293. Welcome to Sector 178."

My eyes were still throbbing from all the reading I did during the ride, and despite the nice, long nap that I got, the migraine and nausea persisted. The analog clock at the front of the car read 22:23. I peered outside, and since it was completely dark, I couldn't tell if we were indoors or outdoors. A few moments later, my question was answered. The car suddenly halted, throwing my body forward from the abrupt change in momentum. I heard metal grinding against metal as some gears shifted around before the car started moving downward.

When the car elevator came to a stop several minutes

later, the wall in front started slowly receding to the side, opening like a set of moving wall panels that you would see in fancy ballrooms. It was lined secondarily by a high-security gate, and as the walls fully receded, a blinding light poked at my retinas.

Considering that it was a military base, I expected something more hardcore. Along the lines of my imagination were things like nuclear weapons stashed in one corner of the base, and tanks sitting in another corner while soldiers would be rushing around with their gear on. But it wasn't anything like that. The foyer that I entered looked like a very small underground warehouse. A couple of pick-up trucks were parked near the entrance wall and a guard tower sat directly to my left. A gruff looking man sat at the counter, peering up as the car pulled up to the stop barrier. He glanced toward his left and pressed a button. The barrier swung up, letting the car pass through.

I was engulfed in darkness once again as the car entered a long, dark tunnel. The enthusiasm I had at seeing a military base for the first time continued diminishing as the minutes passed by. I expected much more excitement and movement, but this just felt like any other old, abandoned building.

As my time in the long tunnel closed in on the five-minute mark, a dim light appeared in the distance, marking the approaching end of the tunnel. The sight on the other side of the exit made my mouth drop.

"Now this is what I'm talking about…"

The interior of the base was something that seemed like it was pulled straight out of a movie. It was spacious, shaped like a hollow cylinder that went down three stories. Each floor had a "ring" along the outer wall, which was dotted with entryways that led to different parts of the building. A long, spiraling ramp went down from "ring" to "ring" while steel crosswalks zig-zagged across the center of the building.

The car spiraled around the ramps until it reached the first floor. It was even more impressive than the rest of the building. A large, circular foyer occupied the entirety of the first floor. In the center, a large statue, presumably of someone important in the military, stood. The statue almost reached the third story and it made me wonder how they had gotten it down here in the first place. The nameplate at the bottom read "Tyler B. Whitman."

The floor was lined in pale white marble while darker streaks painted the Republic flag on the ground. All around the circular foyer, there were doorways manned by guards that lead to different parts of the building. As the car slowly came to a rolling stop in front of the sculpture of Tyler B. Whitman, the back doors popped open. My heart started pounding once the sole barrier between me and the building disappeared. Nervously, I stepped out into the building.

The first thing that I noticed was that the building was cold. Almost freezing cold, in fact. It was almost as if the people maintaining the air conditioning had left it on full blast. The second thing that I noticed about the building was the fact that the air was easy to breathe, contrary to the stuffiness that I expected from a facility that was located this deep underground.

With a loud pop, the trunk opened again, and I dug around the back to whip out my duffle bag. As soon as the trunk closed, the car engine flared up again, and it started driving away.

"Now, where do I go from here..." I nervously asked myself.

Near the wall behind the massive statue, there was a large, elaborate gate that was designed in the shape of the Republic's wolf-like emblem. Each curve was lined with glossy gold and black outlines that glinted under the low-lying fluorescent lights.

"Are you looking for something?"

The woman who had called out to me was sitting behind a high guard desk sipping at a cup of coffee. She looked friendly enough.

"I'm here for Camp Daedalus, but the instructions didn't really say where-"

Almost as if on cue, the heavy metal gates drifted open, scraping against the marble floor with a loud screech as a tall, bald man walked out. He was accompanied by another man of shorter stature holding an E-Board tightly against his chest. I shifted around nervously, not knowing how I was supposed to properly address a military officer. Was I supposed to give him a handshake? Was I supposed to bow my head? Was I supposed to salute?

Fortunately, they decided to greet me first. "General Bergen," the bald man introduced, keeping his hands behind his back. "I will be your instructor throughout your time at Camp Daedalus, as you should already know. My assistant, Lieutenant Gordon Korbert, will be here to help assess your progress and develop your regimen throughout your time here." He motioned toward the man behind him, who nodded without looking up.

"You must be Mr. Holfstras. I've heard plenty about your home life. Plenty of prestige and some good connections there. I sure wonder how you managed to evade all of the negative attention and paparazzi coming your way considering the circumstances," he said in faux concern. I saw him glance toward the base of my neck and felt the brand squirming. His mouth twisted into a snarky smirk that disappeared as soon as it formed.

"As you've been briefed during your travels here, your communication with the outside world will be somewhat restricted. At this moment, I'm going to ask for any external communications device you possess. We won't be needing any distractions while you're here. Besides, I'm sure that there's plenty of things that will keep you occupied at this facility."

Before I could interject, Lieutenant Korbert held his hand out, and I disgruntledly handed over my phone. "Wonderful. A compliant person is a successful one, a lesson you should've been taught early in your life. Let's just hope you manage to get it through your head by tomorrow because we've got a busy day scheduled. Speaking of compliance, I'm sure you've read through those pamphlets I provided for your car ride?"

I responded through gritted teeth, "Yes, sir."

"So, you should know the different programs and facilities of Camp Daedalus, though I will guide you throughout the facility to familiarize you with the layout. Follow me. We'll start with the athletic training facility and go on from there. Just put your bag where it is, you'll reunite with it at your dorm room."

I barely had time to process the entire encounter before he and Lieutenant Korbert turned around and started walking off toward a doorway to the side. Hastily, I ran after them. The lighting was a dim white, and the narrow hallway that we entered was lined with doors and large windows, most of them being sparsely occupied office spaces. Further down, the office lined hallway gave way to a large, bustling common space. Stairs led up to different walkways, and shining pseudo-natural light poured in through the massive skylight taking up the ceiling. So far, it was the most welcoming part of the facility, all things considered. Though, the multitude of armed guards killed the warm and homey vibe.

The tour led into several long twists and turns before we ended up in a small, cramped elevator. It was a well-appreciated break for my legs.

"General Bergen?" I timidly started.

He grunted in response.

I squirmed and scratched my cheeks with my index finger, trying to hide the fact that I was nervous. "None of the pamphlets had details of what the camp activities are. I was wondering if you could tell me a little bit more."

"That is none of your business."

"But-"

He shot a baleful glare at me as the elevator paused in its movement and a soft ding chimed, letting us know that we had arrived at our destination. "Let's stop moving our mouths and start moving our legs," General Bergen suggested. His words appeared friendly, but his tone was anything but.

"Sure..."

I quickly learned that General Bergen was not a man of many words. He was one of those people who judged others based on their actions, and seeing how our first interaction went, his opinion of me probably wasn't very high.

"This is the athletic training facility," Lieutenant Korbert announced. "The facility is mainly used for developing your physical capabilities in terms of muscular strength and stamina. Many of our regimens also focus on overall athletic enhancement including increasing hand-eye coordination, increasing general athleticism, strategic mindsets, and some other things as well. We can't go inside right now, but feel free to visit tomorrow."

We stopped in front of a large paneled window which gave a balcony view to a large gym which included a track, a pit of sand, grassy areas with barbed wire, and more. There were certainly things in that facility that I wouldn't mind not getting comfy with.

"You'll be expected to use this facility as much as time allows. After all, just because a person's brain is dull doesn't mean their physical body has to be dull as well," General

Bergen noted. "Moving on, we'll take a look at the Dining Hall..."

So on and so forth, Lieutenant Korbert gave me a full three-hour tour of the military base and the facilities that it included. General Bergen split off from us near the one-hour mark to go do his own work at a different part of the military base. That was one goodbye that I could live with.

Lieutenant Korbert took me to the Dining Hall first, then to the Tech Rooms, Weaponry Maintenance Room, the library, the main office, and some other rooms that I found uninteresting for the most part. Finally, at the end of the trip, Lieutenant Korbert took me to the dorm rooms, which I was somewhat excited about.

We took a long series of twists and turns on the third floor, which I soon realized was where most of the unimportant facilities were. Since most of the cadets lived in combined barracks, I was expecting similar arrangements. But instead, we stopped in front of a single metal door with "300-1" plastered on a plaque to the right of the frame.

Lieutenant Korbert handed me a couple of papers along with a golden key card. "This key card is something you must protect with your life. It will get you into most of the rooms in this military base, including some which are only available to higher-ranking officials. It was created specifically for Camp Daedalus at General Bergen's request. But most importantly, it will get you into your dorm room, room 300-1."

My room was near the far end of the hallway. It was also fairly close to the bathroom, which I appreciated. Lieutenant Korbert prompted me to swipe the key against the lock, and immediately, I could hear several gear-like objects whirring inside of the knob before the door swung open.

The room felt cramped. Although in terms of raw size it was similar to my bedroom at home, something about this room felt suffocating. It felt like a cell disguised as a luxury room. The decoration and furnishing in the room were sparse, the room nearly bare for the most part save for the gigantic screen that was mounted inside of the wall opposite from the bed.

"What is this screen for?" I curiously asked, running a finger down its cool metal body. "I don't suppose it only functions as a TV."

Lieutenant Korbert explained, "This is called the 'Dashboard,' something the military uses. Its main purpose will be to update you on your schedule and provide you daily reports of your performance in our program. Just think of it as your guide and informant into everything that is going on in this building."

"Cool…" I whispered. It was like getting a personal supercomputer.

"In the drawers of the closet to your right, you will find a couple sets of the camp uniform along with accessory items that you may find useful. Get a good night's sleep today. The schedule will start bright and early tomorrow morning," Lieutenant Korbert suggested before leaving.

The Dashboard read 01:36. It was far too late to still be up and running on full steam, especially after the long tour. But before I slept, I wanted to make sure that I understood how this Dashboard thing worked. After sifting through at the guidebook sitting on top of the nightstand and poking around a little bit, I managed to develop a basic under-standing of it. I set an alarm for six in the morning.

Shutting off all the lights, I tucked myself into the thin, black blanket. My heavy eyelids couldn't stay open any longer, and the soft breeze of the air conditioning lulled me to sleep.

# Chapter 7

*July 17, 2103*

· · · · ● · · · ·

A N EAR-SPLITTING RING shocked me out of my short trip to dreamland. The alarm's high-pitched screech was a stark contrast to the soft violin melody of my phone that usually woke me up in the mornings. Unless Hannah woke me up, of course.

I flipped over on the bed, groaning as I held the edges of the pillow against my ears. The noise was still as loud as ever. Leaping out of the bed with head pounding wildly, I jabbed my fingers toward the gigantic snooze button that appeared on the Dashboard screen. My eyelids still felt heavy as if weights were dragging them down, and I had to force my half-functional legs over to the closet where I dug out the sandy brown camp uniform.

Tossing the uniform over my shoulders to hide my wolf-shaped brand, I swiftly paced toward the communal bathrooms located just a few steps away from my room. The charcoal stained Norman door was adorned with a thin metallic label with "Men's Room" written on it. I grasped the handle with both hands and pushed as hard as I could. The door wouldn't budge. I gave it a couple more experimental pushes to no avail. Suddenly, the door swung out toward me, and a couple of chuckling men walked out. My face flushed in embarrassment as I noticed the plate right below the elongated door handle reading, "Pull."

Dashing into the bathroom, flushed with embarrassment, I took a second to register the silence of the room. The bathroom was quite empty, something not atypical considering how early in the morning it was.

The walls were all comprised of navy colored tiles. To the left, a sectioned off area had lines of urinals and stalls while another sectioned off area to the right had rows of curtained-off shower rooms. A furious brushing sound came from next to me. In front of the sink mirror, a lone male, probably around my age, was brushing his teeth while looking at himself in the mirror as if he was looking at the most interesting thing in the world.

"Good morning?" I called out.

The guy froze and turned around to face me, giving me a clearer view of his features. At the moment, he was topless, showing his scrappy physique that left much to be desired. His hair was a dirty blond, presumably dyed considering that a thicket of black was peeking out from underneath the blond waves. The glasses framing his eyes were black with thick, rectangular tethering around the edges. His eyes were a dark brown, but was devoid of any enthusiasm for life, unlike Hannah's vibrant hazel eyes. He merely acknowledged my greeting with a sneer before going back to what he was doing before. So much for a first impression.

Stepping past the stuck-up blond, who I decided gave off the same vibe as Tony, I entered one of the shower stalls and started scrubbing off the dry sweat clinging onto my skin as hot water poured over my body. It felt refreshing after the long night of traveling. After staying under the stream of water for a good length of time, I shut off the shower and dried myself off with a towel. As I put the sand-colored uniform on, I noticed gratefully that the somewhat high collar hid my wolf-shaped brand from sight.

I sat in front of the mirror for another good ten minutes making sure that my hair and uniform were fixed while getting the residue water droplets out of some tight spots. I took my sweet time, hoping to make a good impression on the first day by making myself look presentable.

After everything was in place, I carried my dirty clothes back to my room and tossed them down the laundry chute. The small list of things that I was instructed to bring along was already fitted inside of a small drawstring bag. I glanced toward the Dashboard. The blue-tinted screen sat there innocently, flashing me the time. 06:51. I had to blink to make sure that I wasn't imagining things.

"Goddammit!" I hollered, before frantically rushing out of the door. The assembly room was located on the first floor near the central entrance of the base. That meant that I had to go down three floors, and also, cut across the entire cylindrical building. In nine minutes. That wasn't even considering the fact that "being on time is being late."

The hallways were still mostly empty, though they were starting to fill up with unfamiliar faces as people started waking up. My heart was pounding as I ran, worry coursing through my veins. I didn't want to be the last one to arrive, especially considering the horrible first impression I had made yesterday. I broke into a sprint, practically tripping over my own legs to reach the elevators.

After pressing the down button, I waited and waited, tapping my foot on the ground impatiently. The elevators were moving in slow motion going from the first floor, then to the second before it finally reached the third floor and opened with a ding. I dashed in and mashed my finger against the "1" button, tapping my feet furiously against the ground while waiting for the doors to close. But just before they closed, a hand poked through the tiny gap, and the elevator doors popped open again.

Standing on the other side was the blond boy from the bathroom earlier. His hair was now swept to the left, and a silver watch adorned his left wrist. He was also wearing a sandy-colored uniform that was nearly identical to mine. Frantically, his eyes oscillated from the watch to the elevator doors. When his eyes met mine, his demeanor became calmer. He sauntered in, standing next to the door with his back turned to me. He didn't take a single moment to acknowledge my presence.

The atmosphere inside of the elevator was tense, to say the least. Although he tried to make it subtle, I noticed that he was glancing back at me periodically. It also helped that he was as subtle as an elephant. I tugged at my collar as the air seemed to get thicker as the elevator continued its descent.

After what seemed like forever, the elevator doors popped open, and I dashed around through the winding halls. I eventually reached the "C" section of the building, and I urgently looked for room 131. *111...115...119...124...I'm almost there.*

Suddenly, I crashed into something hard, knocking me to the ground. A splitting pain shot through my head, and I felt lightheaded from the impact, stars swimming in my vision.

"Ow, ow, ow, ow," a female voice hissed.

"Sorry," I apologized, jumping up quickly. I held out a hand for her, which she took gratefully. "I wasn't looking where I was going."

"Don't worry, I wasn't looking where I was going either."

When she stood up, the top of her head came up to my chin. Silky black hair flowed behind her like a waterfall, stopping just above the small of her back. She was also wearing a baggy, sand-colored military uniform although she had tape wrapped around her wrist and ankles.

"Where are you going?" I asked curiously.

"Same place you're going, probably?" she responded uncertainly, looking up and down the hallway with her curious black eyes. "Are you here for Camp Daedalus?"

"Yeah, I am," I confirmed. Holding out my hand, I introduced, "I'm Ethan, nice to meet you. Though, I guess crashing into each other isn't such a good first greeting."

She giggled and shook my hand with a smile, a couple of cute dimples forming on her cheeks. "Selene. Nice to meet you too."

We got into a comfortable pace walking toward Room 131-C. The short walk gave me a small opportunity to learn just a little bit more about her. She apparently liked the oceans, which reminded her of her home, Sector 198 out near the western coast. I had never met someone from the outer sectors before, and my imaginary conjectures of ugly people working in mines were shattered the more I talked to Selene.

She was a nice person. Even though we had met for the first time, she wasn't averse to telling me more about herself. We even had a little friendly banter about the question, "Are hotdogs sandwiches?" before we finally reached the conference room. I opened the door for her, following soon after.

The room was small, just barely large enough to fit a semi-circular table and another desk into the space. A large Dashboard sat behind General Bergen, who was sitting an office chair behind the front desk. He focused a sharp stare on me as I walked into the room. I glanced at the clock which hung above the electronic board. It read 06:58. Good, that meant that I wasn't "late." Technically.

Nine chairs were set out on the large, semi-circular conference table with six of those seats already being occupied by other people. They were all wearing the same sand-colored uniform and stared at Selene and I as we found ourselves seats toward the right end of the table. It put me right next to General Bergen, to my discomfort.

No one was talking. Everyone was seemingly occupied by their own thoughts as they sat there, keeping to themselves. The clock already had counted well past 07:00 and had just turned 07:08 when the door swung open once again. My head swiveled toward the door. I had already guessed who the last person would be but silently prayed for my guess to be wrong. To my immediate displeasure, I had no such luck, and the person standing there was the same blond-headed kid that I had met in the morning.

"I'm sorry I am late," he dramatically announced. His voice was silky, a low baritone voice that just captured you with the way each syllable rolled off his tongue. "I ran into some traffic, General Bergen. It's an honor to be here."

Silence reigned after his entrance. Someone snorted. With a low hum, General Bergen stood up and look toward the newcomer with a heated glare. "If you're so *sorry,* then you can make it up by giving me fifty pushups. Get down!" he yelled.

The newcomer looked panicked, but soon grew angry. "Look here-"

"*Now,*" General Bergen emphasized.

The blond looked like he was having an internal crisis but after looking toward General Bergen once more, he got down and started pumping his arms up and down. All we could hear were his grunts and groans as he started counting from one. The rest of us, minus General Bergen, were watching him maneuver his body up and down until the novelty of watching wore out.

"We are going to begin this orientation," General Bergen announced. The blond was still at twenty.

"Welcome to Camp Daedalus. This is now officially the fifth time we've had to institute this program and bring in children like you to participate. These camps are usually experimental in nature, sponsored by the government."

I tilted my head in confusion.

"That being said, the reason that all of you are here is to hopefully, by some dumb luck, cure yourself of whatever they thought was wrong with you. Is that understood?"

A chorus of mumbles responded to him.

"I asked, is that understood?!" he yelled again.

"Yes!"

General Bergen sighed and rubbed the palm of his right hand against his face. "While you are here, you will be calling me General Bergen. Additionally, my orders will be answered with, `Yes, sir.' Is that understood?"

"That sounds like the dumbest thing in the world. Why would I degrade myself like that?"

I turned my head as a defiant voice came from the back of the room. The blond, who must've just finished his pushups, was now glaring at the General. His condition was looking worse for wear. Sweat was pouring down his face and the uniform was drenched in dark brown near his chest and back.

"Excuse me?"

"You heard me," the douche continued.

"You, who do you think you are?" General Bergen inquired. He looked positively furious. His eyes were contorted into the most baleful glare I have seen to date, and his hands were clenched tightly as if he was prepared to cave in that kid's skull.

"My name is Inthmus Vali," he started in a snarky tone. "The sole heir to Vali Co., from Sector Eight. I'm the-"

General Bergen leaped out of his seat, and before I could register what was happening, he had Inthmus pinned against the wall with his fists clenched around his uniform collar. He threatened in a quiet whisper, "That was a rhetorical question, numskull. I know who you are. A stuck-up little brat who wasted his talents, unlike his father, and landed himself here. You are an actual failure, unlike some people here. Sit yourself down in that chair, and keep your mouth closed. One more insubordination and your father will be getting messages, understood?"

Inthmus' eyes widened in fear as he nodded his head up and down rapidly like a bobblehead. General Bergen roughly slammed his body against the wall one more time, and Inthmus' body was visibly shaking as he picked himself off the ground. "Just wait until my father hears about-"

A threatening glare shut him up.

After releasing a deep sigh, General Bergen stood again at the front of the room and cleared his throat. "Starting from the left end of the table to the right, start introducing yourself. Your name, age, and sector will do."

As they went around the room, I found it difficult to focus and missed most of their names. My attention was fixated on Inthmus, who was squirming in his seat with sweat still pouring down his body. When his eyes met mine, he snorted and turned away.

Suddenly, the room went silent, and I felt Selene nudging me on the shoulders. I snapped out of my trance. Everyone was looking at me expectantly, and I stammered, "U-Um, h-hello. My name is Ethan Holfstras, I'm sixteen years old, and I come from Sector 36."

General Bergen sighed loudly and started lecturing us.

"Camp Daedalus, as I mentioned, is a camp where we're working to develop and refine what you already have in order to make you suitable for the workforce. As you are now, you all are worthless. So, to get the results we want, we'll be working you harder than you've ever worked before. You're here to learn about this camp, not socialize like a bunch of Academy students. Those days are over. Grow up," he spat. His back arched as he stretched in his seat.

The electronic board behind him flashed brightly and switched to a collage of various images displaying the facilities I was shown to yesterday.

"You've seen these facilities, but Gordon didn't explain to you how they would work. We will be doing that today as we go through our standard routine."

The image shifted into a chart with all our faces lined up vertically. A half-filled gauge was displayed next to each of our faces.

"This is your performance analysis. Every day, based on your performance, Gordon and I collaboratively will be assigning your ratings and rankings. Your ratings will change your score which is presented on this gauge. Each of you will start off with your score at 50. Every day we will assign you a score from negative ten to positive ten. That's how you will be scored daily during these two to three weeks. If you ever reach zero, you fail, and you will face consequences."

As General Bergen turned his head toward the board, the screen shifted into a blank column with nine empty spaces. He tapped the title near the top which read, "Final Assessment Rankings Board."

"This is solely for the Final Assessment. At the end of the camp, there will be a final exam of sorts. Information regarding the content of the test will be undisclosed. Every day, we will assign what is called a 'ranking score' separate from your rating score. This will go from one to nine. To calculate the final rankings, your total score will be averaged, so make sure you keep your placement consistent."

He started digging around in his desk and pulled out a large silver case. As he opened it and turned it toward us, I could see nine pristine smartwatches laid out in front of us. Each of them had jet black leather straps with a metallic finish for the body. He briefly explained, "These mirror the Dashboards that you have in your rooms. Keep them safe. They will be your best friend."

As we stood up and rushed toward the front of the room to grab our watches, General Bergen walked toward the back of the room calling, "That's all you need to know for now. The only rule is to obey my words. Also, if I would give a word of advice, it would be to remain cautious. That is all."

After giving us his cryptic message, he left, closing the door with a loud bang.

Immediately, it felt as if an invisible pressure had lifted, and the room was filled with the sounds of people chattering amongst each other. Some of the girls, who must have gotten to know each other early on, started whispering amongst themselves while looking at the Dashboard, which had switched back to the image of our rating point gauges. It was still only around 08:30, and my stomach was growling in hunger.

"Do you want to come and get breakfast with us? Serena and Trace wanted to spend some time getting to know other people," Selene asked. She was motioning back to a small group of two girls.

"Sure, why not?" I replied. Everyone else had started making friends, and I had no desire to become a loner. Ditching the rest of the people back in the room, the four of us navigated back through the winding hallways until we reached the spacious dining hall. Steam was pouring out from behind the counter area as the aroma of different foods assaulted my nose. It wasn't anything close to being a five-star meal, but it was much better than what I was imagining as "military food."

After grabbing a plate of macaroni and cheese, I sat myself down with the rest of the group and started chatting with them. "How about we go around and give extended introductions? I don't feel like I got anything out of that short meeting." I prompted.

"That's because you were spacing out," Selene pointed out.

My cheeks heated up in embarrassment. "Whatever."

"I'll go first!" one of the other girls cheerfully started. "I'm Serena, and I'm hoping that I can work with medicine later! I like to listen to music during my free time! How about you, Ethan?" she inquired.

"Well, my name is Ethan. I'm not really sure what I'm going to do in the future, so I guess that's why I am here," I humorously said. "I like reading too, I suppose, and spending time with my family."

"Do you have a big family?" Serena asked curiously.

I shook my head. "I'm actually an orphan, but my friend, Hannah, who I met at our orphanage, worked hard to make us self-sufficient. So, it's just a small, three-person family. She's also in the medical field and has traveled across the country, so maybe you might've heard of her?" I asked rhetorically with a hint of pride.

"What's her last name?"

"Kamiya."

Serena's eyes widened like saucers. "Hannah Kamiya? No way! She's so pretty and talented! You're joking, right? She's pretty much a celebrity, and you tell me that you *live* with her?"

I nodded hesitantly. Seeing the glint in her eyes, I wasn't

so sure if telling her was such a great idea. Serena fidgeted, hesitantly asking, "Is she okay though? Didn't she get her doctor's certification removed recently? It was all over the news. 'Prodigy oversteps her bounds,' or something like that. I-"

My smile became strained. I saw Selene frantically tap Serena on her arm while pointing at me. Serena's mouth formed an "o" shape before it closed, cutting off mid-sentence. I was grateful and was sure that Selene meant the gesture to be subtle, but unfortunately, she had as much of that quality as Inthmus did.

Serena winced and apologized to me. "Oh, sorry, it was just something that was on my mind for a while. A-Anyways, you mentioned that meeting. I really did find it strange that he left it on such an empty note."

"I think he's just trying to get us comfortable. Getting rid of ambiguity and all that. Hopefully it stays this way," Trace chimed in jovially, taking a bite out of her cheeseburger."

"Yeah, hopefully…"

# Chapter 8

*July 22, 2103*

· · · · ● ● · · ·

URING THE FIRST couple of days, General Bergen led us through a set of preliminary evaluation exercises which included physical tests, cognitive tests, and other specialized career assessments.

The physical exercise was the most grueling. He set up an obstacle course with many different challenges on the grassy area inside of the athletic facility track; it had floating wooden platforms that we had to cross, thin poles that we ran on top of, and a small river that we had to swim across. By the end, my uniform was soaking wet, and my muscles were sore and probably bruising.

Fortunately, the cognitive exercises were not so demanding. General Bergen brought us down to an empty white room with several long desks placed in four straight rows. There were nine thick packets of paper that were spread across the entire room. In the packet, there were several different activities/tasks ranging from detective work, military strategies, accounting proficiency, computer programming, basic logic puzzles, and more.

All the other campers were intelligent, resourceful, and much better than I was. This only made me more confused, wondering what the pre-required traits that people going to this camp had. Thankfully, by some dumb luck, I wasn't overshadowed by everyone. Although most of the other campers were ranking higher than me, I was still able to keep myself in the sixth to seventh range. I only lost twelve rating points during the first three days at camp.

"You stupid maggots! Have you learned nothing from your first days here?!" General Bergen hollered, blowing off my eardrums.

*Until now,* I thought as General Bergen began another long slew of insults. A "tongue-lashing" was an understatement to describe what the furious general was dishing out to us. Once the preliminary tests were over, he started putting us into team simulations, and just now, had just put us through a strategy simulation assessment where we were supposed to cooperate to find a solution in a conflict scenario. But rather than working together, everyone started branching off and making different decisions and of course, we failed.

"For God's sake! How do you not understand yet?!" General Bergen yelled once again, smashing his fists down on the desk. He leveled a murderous glare at all nine of us who had different reactions to his outburst. Serena, Selene, Trace, and this other kid named Carter visibly flinched away while the others remained aloof. Inthmus, being the person he was, sneered at the ground scornfully.

General Bergen raked his hands across his hair tiredly while shaking his head in disappointment. "Thirty-minute break. Meet up afterward at the athletic training center. All of you will be receiving negative marks for this exercise. Now get!"

As soon as we left the room, the blame game started up.

"Carter, you idiot! Why the hell would you choose to toss a grenade out when we were surrounded on both sides?!" someone yelled. I recognized her as the girl who usually took the first-place position in every exercise. Her face was contorted into an expression of fury, her pale white fist shaking visibly.

"I-I don't know Alyssa. I thought that it would be the best choice to clear the area!"

Alyssa got right up into Carter's face who was starting to sweat bullets. He looked as if he was looking into the face of death. "You've been playing way too many video games, you stupid shut-in. This is real life, get a grip. Look at what good your *strategy* did," she accused.

Serena indignantly interrupted, "You don't have to be mean about it! We all made different mistakes on our own."

"Make the correction," Alyssa seethed, jabbing a finger into Serena's chest. "You all made mistakes, not me. If you would've done as I said, then we would've been in a better position to complete that stupid exercise."

Serena swatted the offending finger away with a scowl, and Alyssa snorted. Rearing back, she spat a blob of spit on the ground in front of Carter, then leaned back to spit another in Serena's face. Her icy sapphire eyes bore into my own as if challenging me to say something. When I didn't respond, she scorned, "Stupid losers," before walking away.

Serena wiped off the spittle with the sleeve of her uniform, glaring at Alyssa's retreating back. "I don't know what her problem is! She's just been ignoring us and making fun of us ever since the beginning!"

"Yeah…" I despondently responded.

Selene was still hovering over Serena, helping her get every bit of the insulting spit off her face. Her eyes burned with a fury like the one burning in Serena's eyes. "One of these days, I'm going to make her regret being born," Selene threatened menacingly.

I placed my hands up placatingly. "Calm down, don't waste your life in prison just because of someone like her."

Selene snorted, then lightly smiled. "It was a joke, don't worry, I'm not that petty. But if she does that again, I'll leave a little more than a couple of scratch marks on her face and body."

Somehow, I didn't think that she was joking.

"I'm going to go back up to my room to clean off a little. I'll see you all in a bit," Serena said downtrodden. After exchanging short, awkward goodbyes, we all split off in our own directions. After reaching my room, I flung myself on the bed and stared up at the ceiling, wondering where this camp had taken a wrong turn.

I glanced at my Dashboard. My rating points were sitting comfortably at thirty-eight, probably somewhere around thirty after that exercise. I had a comfortable margin until zero, but since all my points had been in the negatives thus far, the gap wasn't as comforting.

The anxious thought was constantly running in my head. *What if I fail?* Based on the current trajectory, I would probably only last until the middle of the second week. Not only that, but the exercises that General Bergen was handing us daily had only been getting harder and harder.

A beep brought me out of my scattered thoughts. The Dashboard updated in a robotic voice, "At 1530 hours, you are to report to the athletic training facility. I repeat, at 1530 hours, you are to report to the athletic training facility."

Looking at the time, I noted that there were only about twenty minutes before I was expected. I spent the next ten minutes enjoying the brevity of the break until it was interrupted by a soft buzzing that vibrated against my wrist. A low groan escaped my lips as I pushed myself off the bed and stepped out of the room. My eyelids were bogging down wearily from all the mental and physical strain.

Walking at a leisurely pace, I navigated around the empty hallways. Just about when I reached the elevators at the t-intersection conjoining the male and female dorms, a forceful pull brought me tumbling to the ground. My back impacted someone else's, who fell to the ground underneath me. The "assailant" giggled nervously, and apologized, "Sorry, I didn't think you'd fall down like that."

I turned around and saw Serena, who wore a sheepish smile on her face. Standing up, I brushed some of the imaginary dust from my arms and legs and held out my hand for her. "It's fine, just don't do it again. Or I'll sic General Bergen on you," I joked.

"Ooh, scary."

We had a good laugh at General Bergen's expense and walked to the training facility side by side. The short walk was anything but eventful. Although Serena tried to make small talk, I constantly ended up inadvertently shutting down the conversation by stuttering and losing track of what I was about to say. When we finally got there past the embarrassment and nervousness, we saw the rest of the group waiting for us as General Bergen started barking out instructions.

"We are going to start with some hand-to-hand combat training. Afterward, we're going to deviate from the schedule a little bit and do a couple of activities that I planned in response to the utter *disgrace* of a performance this group has been showing," he scornfully spat.

Carter raised his hands, asking, "General Bergen, I thought this was a career training program? Why do we need to go through hand-to-hand combat training?"

He shifted his gaze over to Carter, and sarcastically

replied, "Well, this *is* a military base, Mr. Keeble. Hopefully, by some miracle, you'll develop some general skills as well, but as a *military General*, I am inclined to lead you through a more militaristic training. Does that answer your question, Mr. Keeble?"

Carter nodded fearfully.

General Bergen brushed some imaginary dust off his jacket and guided us toward a raised platform that had been set up in the corner of the large room. "The fighters for the round go up there and fight with whatever skills they have. I know from your records that you, Dylan, have some background in martial arts, so we'll be letting some of the others fight before you go. We'll have a randomizer determine who will be fighting who today."

A small Dashboard mounted on the wall flipped through names before it landed on Inthmus' and Alyssa's name. They both walked up onto the platform, Alyssa with a poker face while Inthmus twisted his lips into a cocky smirk. General Bergen shouted, "If you're ready, begin! We will go until someone forfeits or is unconscious."

Inthmus was standing up straight like a wooden plank with his feet planted on the ground, weight shifted backward with his cocky smirk still adorned on his face. "General, are you sure that I have to fight a girl? This isn't fair, is it?"

I peeked at General Bergen's face to see that it was completely passive, but I had similar fleeting thoughts as Inthmus. The physical matchup wasn't looking great. Inthmus had a good three to four inches on Alyssa and his muscles were slightly more pronounced. Then again, under those baggy military uniforms, it was difficult to tell what was what.

Alyssa started hopping lightly, her balance constantly shifting between her left and right foot. Her left arm was stretched out slightly, palms open while her right arm stayed close to her body in a tightly balled fist.

The two stared at each other for several long, drawn-out seconds until Inthmus moved first. He charged straight toward Alyssa slow as a sloth with a loud battle cry. "Don't blame me if you get hurt!"

As Inthmus got close to Alyssa's personal space, he swung his fist toward her face but missed by a mile as Alyssa ducked her head to the right. Inthmus' momentum carried him a couple more steps forward before he awkwardly tripped on his own feet and fell onto the ground. He quickly jumped up, face flushed red. He charged again with his right fist reared back.

Alyssa dodged his punch again, and as Inthmus continued to throw slow, lazy punches toward her head, she continued to weave in and out of the barrage while her feet lightly danced around the arena. It was graceful, almost like watching a dance routine.

Suddenly, the pace of the fight changed. As Inthmus charged in with another missed punch, Alyssa twisted her core around, reverse roundhouse kicking Inthmus in the back; he was knocked to the ground face-first where he started rolling over in pain.

Alyssa maintained her ready position, still hopping around from her left and right foot as Inthmus slowly started getting up.

"You stupid, dumb bi-"

Inthmus didn't even get a chance to stand up and finish his sentence as Alyssa dashed forward and landed another harsh ax kick on his right shoulder followed by a hard hook kick to his head. He limply crumpled to the ground and didn't get back up.

"Yuzef wins! Get that stupid idiot off to the infirmary," General Bergen announced.

The rest of us, who were in the spectator role, were trying and failing to keep our laughter in check. It was painstakingly obvious who the winner of that fight was going to be from the very beginning, and Inthmus' utter humiliation at Alyssa's hands was just the cherry on top.

Alyssa walked off the stage while some other cadets hoisted Inthmus off on their shoulders and took him into a sectioned off room in the corner of the facility, presumably the infirmary. As she sat down, she directed a condescending look toward Serena and me, as if goading us saying, "Beat that." Serena returned Alyssa's look with an equally cold gaze.

With a loud whirring sound, the little screen on the wall started flipping through more names until it landed on Serena and Carter. Serena stepped up to the platform, and I took a second to glance at Carter. His curly brown hair was frazzled and sweat was already trickling down the side of his face despite not having done anything. The wire-frame glasses he wore was taped near the bridge.

"Are you sure you want to keep your glasses on?" someone asked, and Carter waved them off.

"Alright, begin!" General Bergen yelled, and the "fight" that followed was more like a comedic skit. Serena started off the fight with a charge, landing a weak punch that grazed off Carter's right jaw. He stumbled back, and uncertainly looked down toward General Bergen, meeting his eyes.

"General Bergen-" he started to say but was interrupted as Serena dashed at him and landed a solid punch against his jaw. It came out of nowhere, and I heard an audible crack as Carter's head snapped back violently. He wobbled when he returned to his upright position and looked dazed, tipping from side to side.

"I forfeit!" Carter cried desperately as Serena started charging again.

General Bergen cringed at him in disgust before announcing, "Hotchinson wins! Keeble, get yourself checked out at the infirmary."

When Carter was out of sight, I heard General Bergen mutter under his breath, "Jesus Christ, what the hell is wrong with these kids. Is the Board trying to piss me off right now?"

With a heavy sigh, General Bergen pressed a button on his watch, and the panel started scrolling through the different names before it landed on Dylan's and mine. I glanced at him from the corner of my eyes and saw him doing a couple of warmups to stretch his arms and legs. He looked excited, not worried.

I did a light set of jumping jacks myself before entering the arena floor. Dylan was already standing on the opposite end, eyeing me as if he was trying to get a gauge on my abilities. He was shorter than me, which gave me a slight advantage in reach, but even through the baggy uniform, I could see his pronounced muscles.

As General Bergen hollered for us to begin, I got into a low, athletic stance with both hands out in front of me, balled into fists in a boxer position. Dylan traced every movement I made with his calculating eyes and smirked as if he was amused. He held his hands limply to the side as he bounced around on the balls of his feet. His back was arched, leaned back slightly as if inviting me to take the first hit.

Cautiously, I took a couple of steps forward, pausing periodically to gauge Dylan's reaction. His lips were still crookedly twisted in a condescending smirk as he looked down on me. He seemed so close, right in my range of reach.

Taking initiative, I swung my fist in a wide arc toward his stomach, bending my legs at the knees so that he wouldn't be able to easily swing back at me. But right before my fist impacted, Dylan twisted around and roughly pushed his palm against my back, making me stumble forward a couple of steps. I almost tripped but managed to regain my balance. I quickly swerved around, expecting to get my exposed back pummeled. However, Dylan was still standing in his original position with a bored look on his face.

Trying to catch him off guard, I charged straight at him without pausing and stretched my legs out to kick him in the side. But instead of it connecting, he caught my legs and swerved me around in a circle as I hopped around on one foot trying to keep my balance. As he let go, I tumbled onto the ground while hearing laughter from the spectators who were watching us from the side. I grit my teeth in anger, staring at Dylan who was still smirking with his feet planted in his original position. Putting up a fake smirk, I taunted, "Is that all you can do? Dodge and throw? Maybe you can find a career in wrestling, not fighting."

I cringed at my own insults. They sounded so corny. But to my surprise, Dylan retaliated in a furious voice, "Alright pipsqueak. Let's go."

As Dylan's hopping started quickening in pace and his movements became more erratic, I started wondering if getting him riled up was a good idea. In a sudden spur of movement, he surged forward, invading into my personal space. Before I could react and move my body, a swooping fist came in from my left, digging deep into my stomach. It felt like a hammer crashing into my gut, and it knocked all the air out of my windpipe. Bile rose deep in my throat as I collapsed to my knees. Another unexpected blow to my head knocked me onto the ground, and before my vision blacked out, all I saw was Dylan's cocky smirk.

WHEN I CAME to, the first thing I saw was a blank white ceiling while sounds of grunting and yelling faintly sounded in the distance. My head was still pounding from whatever Dylan had hit me with, and my eyes were still twitching in agony as the overhead lights stung my eyes. Not only that, but my stomach and neck were also still sore from the hits that they took.

"You woke up?"

I turned my head to see an older military cadet glancing toward me with an emotionless expression from the desk he was sitting at. Behind him, I saw Inthmus lying on an infirmary bed, still out cold.

"General Bergen told me that if anyone woke up before the exercise was over, to send him over his way. Get back out there," he lazily said. After his message was relayed, he turned back to the little computer on his desk and started typing away. Hesitantly, I pushed myself out of bed and walked out of the infirmary.

The other campers were still sitting on the side of the arena as Blake and Trace stood on the platform exchanging blows. They weren't anywhere near as good as Alyssa and Dylan were, but they still managed to put on a good show as they swiftly danced around each other. When I reached the rest of the group who were spectating, I plopped myself down in a seat next to Serena who was watching the fight with an entertained look on her face. The short brawl went on for a little longer until Trace, whose black hair was styled into a short bob, put up both of her hands a sign of surrender.

"Blake wins! Alright, that's the end of the exercise. I now hope that most of you realize how lacking you. This is why we have this facility available, which I've been advising you to use. Clearly, many you haven't been taking my advice to heart," he finished with a glare toward me.

I chuckled guiltily, remembering my quick and

embarrassing defeat at Dylan's hands. Out of the group, I was probably one of the only kids that hadn't listened to his recommendation to use the facility every single day. I paid hard for it too.

When Serena finally seemed to notice that I was sitting right next to her, she asked, "Ethan, are you okay? How's your head doing?"

"It's fine," I replied wearily.

Silently, she gave a sweeping look across my head and body, checking over my injured areas. Her "checkup" must've been satisfactory because she turned around and continued to listen as General Bergen talked away.

"We're moving onto another exercise. Come. Vali will catch up to us later." He then guided us out of the training facility and through the twisting hallways. Except, this time, we weren't headed towards any of the facilities that he had shown us during our first moments in the base.

Our destination was the foyer on the first floor, specifically, the sealed off central entryway. The guard posted near the entrance nodded and pressed a couple of buttons, opening the Republic emblem gate. I entered nervously as the already narrow passageway thinned even further as we continued to walk forward.

"Where do you think he's taking us?" Selene whispered inquisitively, and I shrugged, wondering the answer to that question myself. The hallways were getting darker, the lighting becoming sparse. Instead of fluorescent ceiling lights illuminating the hallways in a vibrant white hue, the colors shifted into a dimmer red coming from dull amber lighting.

Suddenly, General Bergen stopped in his tracks and pulled something out of his pocket and turned toward his left. He tapped the object against a thin reader embedded in the wall. Suddenly, the wall started splitting open. Although I hadn't noticed it before in the darkness, a keener second look showed that the wall wasn't solid. It was a tiny elevator door that was designed to blend in with the wall. The car was tiny, probably built to hold no more than five people at a time at max.

"Four people at a time. Any more than that and the system is designed to register it as an infiltration attempt. You'll die," General Bergen warned. We shifted around nervously, looking at each other as if silently asking who the first person would be to go into the mysterious elevator.

"Now!" he yelled, getting impatient.

I hurriedly spilled into the elevator as Serena, Trace, and Dylan scrambled in after me. The doors immediately closed us in. I squirmed uncomfortably, heat rising to my cheeks as Serena's body tightly pressed against mine. To my surprise, instead of rising upward toward the second and third floors, the elevator started descending further down. At the rate that we were going and the amount of time we had spent on the elevator, we must've been at least seven to eight stories below the first floor already.

The trip didn't last much longer. After descending for a couple more seconds, its momentum downward stopped, making my stomach fall uncomfortably. The two panels of the elevator doors drifted apart, parting to a view that I would probably never forget in my lifetime.

The room was *huge*. It was comparable to the size of the foyer on the first floor, and every inch of the walls were lined with wires and monitors which had various graphs and statistics displayed on them. A low, blue light left the room in a shadowy glow, almost to the point of complete darkness.

Six huge monitors filled the entire front wall of the room, each displaying a separate graph of their own. One had a map of the Republic drawn on it with red and blue lines darting across on them; there was also a large red blob near the southern border next to the Republic Capital in former Kansas City. The rest of the border—lining the former states of Texas, Oklahoma, Kentucky, and Virginia—was clean. Another screen showed a world map. The Eastern Federation was blurred out in black while the rest of the world was either lit up in red or green.

The rest of the room was filled with desks, computers, and loose papers. Some desks sat alone with a computer flipping through pages automatically while others had people working on them. There weren't many people, though. At most, five people were working in that huge room from what I could count. Although with the dim lighting, maybe there were more hiding somewhere.

A sudden push from behind me snapped me out of my reverie.

"Ethan stop blocking the way," Serena chided, and with another push, I stumbled out into the room as the others filed in after me. The elevator doors closed on their own. I continued to observe in a trance the various lines flitting across the maps displayed on the screens. Soon, the rest of the group arrived, General Bergen arriving with the third and final group. I noted that Inthmus had also come back.

After corralling us into one spot, he herded us over to the far-right corner of the room away from the front screens. The corner had two long tables set up with nine desktops humming on them.

"Here, I got it all ready for you," a female voice proudly announced.

We all turned our heads and saw a woman, maybe in her early thirties, talking with General Bergen.

"Thanks, Julie," he replied in a monotonous voice, turning to us with his hands directed at her. "This is Julie. She's the head of the Intel Division for this military base and she helped me get this exercise set up for you hopeless children."

She gave us a cheery wave before turning back to General Bergen. "I'll leave you to it, and, be nice to the children. Don't forget, you still owe me," she purred before sauntering off to do her own work.

General Bergen let out a heavy sigh. "Sit down at a computer, there's enough for all of you. I've had Julie set up a very basic defense cybersecurity system on a server."

"It really isn't much more than your average security setup," he continued. "To make it even simpler, all of these systems are on a closed network. A little bit of background in computer sciences or data analysis might be helpful, but this is just a problem-solving puzzle. All of you should think together and act together, or you'll succeed, but fail."

Without explaining his cryptic message, General Bergen then motioned for us to sit in front of the computers. We uncertainly shuffled toward the chairs and stared at the black, empty screens. As the computers started to boot up, the first thing that showed up on screen was the Republic flag as the wallpaper for the home screen. The bright blue glow of the computer screens radiated onto our faces, inviting us to defile it, but I didn't have a single idea of what to do from that point on.

"Begin whenever you're ready. You have two hours," he commanded. General Bergen pressed a button on the server box before walking out of the room to do whatever Generals do in their off time when not babysitting "children."

Immediately, some people started typing away and I leaned back in my chair, trying to see what the others were doing. They were sifting through different menus while one kid down the row was typing frantically. I looked up and down at my computer. There sat a keyboard, mouse, and screen. The concept of "hacking" was foreign to me, having only ever used a phone and a computer to type documents for Academy projects. Taking a deep breath, I grabbed for the mouse and began clicking around aimlessly, trying to get something to pop up on the nearly empty home screen.

*Maybe it won't be so easy.*

The kid on the far end was still frantically rapping his fingers on his keyboard, the loud, methodical clicking filling the air. I saw a small white box up on his or her screen while words rapidly filled up the spaces. The low lighting hid who it was, but they looked far ahead of everybody in terms of completing the exercise.

I, on the other hand, was totally lost. In the end, I spent the whole two hours just observing other people working on their screens while my own remained blank. Once in a while, I tried to open different tabs and property pages, but it didn't yield any fruit. My boredom made the time pass by much slower than usual.

Just as promised, the elevator doors chimed after two hours and General Bergen tramped back into our workspace.

"Your hours are up! Hands off the keyboards and mice!" he shouted, and walked down the line, making sure that everybody stopped working. Near the end of the row of tables, he turned to one of the computers and stared at the screen.

"I'll be checking on your work. There will be absolutely no tampering with your computers from here on. In fact, everyone stand up and wait by the elevator entrance. I'll call you over when I'm at your computer."

We all stood up and stepped back, save for the person at the computer General Bergen was already inspecting. As we shuffled toward the elevator, I was able to see who it was. The frantic typist from earlier was Carter, and General Bergen didn't seem very happy with his work. Without speaking to him, he sweepingly went around each table and looked at each of the computers. He called us all back at the same time with a disappointed look on his face. But toward Inthmus, he directed a hopeful expression.

"Vali, who helped you finish this exercise?"

Inthmus snorted and responded. "No one did. I did everything with my own intelligence. This is one thing that I don't need their help on."

General Bergen sighed with clenched teeth and turned toward Alyssa. "Well, Yuzef, how about you? Did anyone help you finish this activity?"

"Why would I have someone else helping me when I can do it myself?"

"*Disgusting,*" General Bergen spat. He turned his attention to the rest of us and shouted, "That goes for *all* of you! You all knew damn well that I meant for you to work together, yet you struggled on the sections that others would have easily handled for you. I never said *all* of you had to finish, did I? I said, work together!"

He let out a low groan and dismissed us. "Get the hell out of my Intel Division. Go to your dorm, and I'll have Gordon do the analysis on this exercise. If you don't understand simple words such as 'work together,' then you're worth nothing to the country, worth nothing more than a bag of flesh and bones."

Silence fell upon the room, the only audible sounds being the whir of computer fans and the light buzz of all the screens. Carter's chair lightly squeaked as he stood up, his boots clicking on the concrete floor as he slowly shuffled past us. He pressed the button on the elevator, which was luckily free access from this end, and walked in as it arrived. Selene, Serena, and I shuffled in after him, heads bowed in defeat.

"That sucked," Serena noted, and I scoffed. That was the understatement of the century.

Retracing our steps through the narrow hallways, we were back into the first-floor foyer. We broke off into our own little groups and headed toward the dining hall. Sitting around a circular table, we ate our food silently. Fear probably wasn't the right word to describe the atmosphere that hung over us. It was more so tense and weary if anything. Many of us still had bruises and welts from the exercise in the arena.

Serena tried to start up some small talk, but it was merely filler for our minds. It went in one ear and right out the other. Although I knew Serena meant well by trying to keep everyone's mood up, her voice was becoming grating to listen to. I quickly gobbled my food and snuck away from the attempted social engagement, and instead decided to retreat to my room for some alone time. But I didn't even make it out of the dining hall before Blake intercepted me. His short, black hair was greasy, clinging to his head like a mop.

"Can I help you?" I asked, not really in the mood for fun and games.

"No, the question is, can *I* help *you*," he said cryptically. I was about to walk away when he got in front of me and held his hands out in front of him placatingly. "Wait, wait, wait. How about this. What if I told you that there was a way that you could make phone calls to the outside from here?"

That piqued my curiosity. Being away from my phone for days had killed me on the inside, and I missed the outside world. "I'm listening."

He grinned mischievously. "How about we go on an adventure?"

# Chapter 9

*July 22, 2103*

· · · · ● ● ● · · ·

"ARE YOU SURE this is okay?" I asked hesitantly. As soon as I accepted Blake's "offer," I followed him, trusting that he would make smart decisions for whatever he was planning on doing. After all, despite his lighthearted attitude, he had been placing within the top three for every exercise. But now, slivers of doubt entered my mind about his prowess and this "adventure." Specifically, I was worried about the guy's maturity levels.

"Yeah, it'll be fine," he reassured with a grin, glancing up and down the long hallway. "As long as we don't get caught, we have done no wrong. I think."

"You *think?*" I hissed, and backpedaled, fully content on leaving this plan behind. But Blake stopped me with a firm grip on my arms.

"Let go," I warned.

He grinned and pointed toward a door just to the right of the t-intersection we were standing in. "You see that? That's the secondary intel room. General Bergen showed you that on your first day here, right?"

"Yeah," I replied, not seeing where he was going with this.

"Well here's the important part. That room has an

*untapped* phone that can call anywhere in the country. You want to call your parents? Boom! You want to call your girlfriend? Double boom! You want to call up a-, well, you probably shouldn't do that, but you get the idea," he pitched with a dramatic tone. I could literally see the glint in his eyes. "What do you think?"

I nibbled at my fingernails, thinking it through in my head. "What about the people that are working in there?"

"Out for dinner."

"Security systems?"

"Non-existent."

"Patrols?"

"Also non-existent."

I sighed, curiosity and desperation guiding me to slowly buy into the idea. "How much time do we have?"

Blake glanced down at his watch and whispered a couple of numbers to himself. "Around twenty-five minutes. Twenty-seven to be exact, but let's be on the safe side. Regression calculations don't always turn out to be exact."

I nodded. "What do we have to do?"

"I'm glad you see it my way, friend," Blake victoriously said, grinning from ear to ear. He pointed a finger at the door. "Since it's your first time, you can have as many minutes as you want, under twenty minutes, of course. Just go in there, find a bright red landline phone, and dial whatever number you want. Just make sure that you use the *red* phone, not the other ones."

"Why? What do the other phones do?"

He grimaced. "You don't want to find out."

I shuddered, imagining all the possibilities. Blake looked toward me expectantly, and I nodded. Stealthily, we walked over to the door labeled, "Intel Division B." Blake popped the door open and dashed in quickly. Meanwhile, I waited outside nervously, sighing in relief when his head popped out just seconds later. "Alright, we're all good. I'll keep watch, you dial those numbers."

Nodding, I exchanged places with him, quickly dashing into the room as he came out. I looked around in awe. Although it was nowhere as big as the other room in the basement, this room had an artistic quality to it that the other room didn't have. In the compact space, the blue, green, and red glow from the computers and server towers reflected off the metal panels, creating various shapes and patterns that repeated across the entire room.

On a desk in the far corner, I spotted the red phone that Blake had been talking about. Nervously, I reached my hand out toward it, heart pounding in my chest. Just as I was about to touch it, I stopped. *Why would he help me?* I wondered, doubt creeping into my mind. Blake didn't even know me. Once again, I stared at the phone that was sitting on top of the desk. Why was it there? For what purpose?

*He's trying to trap me, get me expelled,* part of my mind told me. Warning bells were tolling inside my head, telling me to get out of the room as quickly as possible. But the curious side of my head kept me rooted there, drawing me toward the phone. The temptation pulled on me like a siren's call. Eyes squeezed shut tightly, I slowly grabbed the phone off its mount, half expected sirens to go off, signaling my expulsion. *This is how I go, I guess.*

But nothing happened, and I sighed a large breath of relief. The dial tone was ringing through the earpiece, and reached out to dial, "284-162-8138."

The calling tone of the phone rang repeatedly for a minute, but no one picked up. Immediately, the line cut off, changing to a dull, flat-pitched dialing tone. Cursing, I frantically dialed the same number again, waiting impatiently as the calling tones kept buzzing in my ear. I was losing hope by the second, but suddenly, the tone was cut short, and a soft alto voice asked, "*Hello? Who is this?*"

"H-Hannah," I whispered jubilantly, my heart soaring in joy at hearing her voice. "It's me, Ethan." It was so good to hear her voice again after a full week of being away.

"*Wait, who is this? Ethan? Why does your voice sound so hoarse?*" she asked worriedly.

"Just a lot of exercising. Damn, it's so good to talk to you again. How have you been? Anything interesting happen while I was gone?" I asked eagerly, wondering if I missed anything big.

"*Watch your language. But no, nothing's been going on. It's all same old, same old. I finally got back with one of my colleagues that I had been working with and started on a project together. Some important government stuff, you know?*"

"Wow," I breathed. "That's amazing. I'm sure you'll do great!"

She giggled. "*Thanks a lot. How are you calling though, and why didn't you call earlier?*"

"T-They decided to let us call back once," I lied. It flowed off my tongue like sandpaper grating on wood. "But I don't have my phone because they also took that away. Sorry."

If she had caught onto my lie, she didn't let it show. "*That's great. Hey, I have to go really quick because I was just about to go into the research lab, but if you're able to, call back whenever you can, okay?*"

"Yeah, I'll do that. Bye, Hannah."

"*Bye.*"

The dull flat-pitched dialing tone marked the end of the call. Cautiously, I set the phone back down on its switch hook and tip-toed out of the room. Blake was still waiting outside of the room, looking up and down the hallway. When he saw me coming out, he grinned. "Let's go talk somewhere else."

Talk?

I let him lead me back toward the bustling common space that I had seen on my first day here. It was completely empty, which also left the couch seats unoccupied. Blake plopped himself down on a green one-seater, becoming one with the soft, bouncy cushions.

"So," Blake asked, wiggling his eyebrows. "Who'd you call?"

I deadpanned, "I only called my...sister. Don't read too much into it."

Blake pouted while twirling himself in circles in the seat. "Man, that's boring. That was a once-in-a-lifetime opportunity and you decide to call your sister? You're a bummer man, a real disappointment."

I shrugged. "I do me and you do you. Thanks for showing me that, Blake, really helped me get out of my funk."

"Pleasure doing business with you," Blake said, giving me a mock salute. "Don't overuse it though. Don't want them catching on if you know what I mean."

"Yeah, for sure."

Spirits slightly lifted, I went back through the hallways toward the elevators, going up to the third floor while Blake stayed in the common space. As the elevator doors opened, I heard a door slam shut around the corner with a bang. When I peered into the hallway, curious, I heard some *colorful* language that was coming from one of the rooms. I noted with mild amusement that it was Carter's unique high-pitched voice.

After keeping that moment recorded in my mind for future entertainment, I went into my room to lie down, though I noticed an update to my schedule on the Dashboard:

*2100 hours: Training Facility.* Blake's little adventure had taken nearly an hour, maybe two if counting the little talk at the end, which gave me little time to rest before the next activity, but it had been worth it.

When 20:50 struck, the Dashboard reminded me to leave the room in a robotic voice. I threw on a new uniform that wasn't dirty and stained with blood and jogged down to the training facility. No one else besides General Bergen was there. He was standing in the middle of the track, muttering to himself. As I stood next to him, an awkward silence fell between us. "What is this exercise going to be about?" I asked, hoping the lighten the air.

He didn't respond. Instead, he continued to mumble to himself while kicking at the ground. Occasionally, his jaw would clench, and he would stare at the ground murderously, making me back away a little bit. That man had some issues.

Soon enough, the rest of the group started filing in. They looked a lot more relaxed than they had been before. Serena was chattering away with Selene and Trace while the others were standing there silently. Carter was the last person to hobble in at the last second before the clock struck 2100 hours.

As if on cue, General Bergen straightened his back in attention and turned toward us. "This is the last thing you'll do today, or forever, depending on what you make of the experience. Follow me."

General Bergen led us away from the track, back toward the secluded corner where the arena was set up. Collectively, we watched General Bergen stop and stomp his feet on the ground several times, a loud thump resonating every time his legs dropped to the floor.

For a second, I thought that the man had possibly gone insane. But as he continued to stomp on the ground, I reeled back in surprise when I heard a metallic clang. General

Bergen grinned before bending down to slide his fingers *underneath* the floor to lift a small panel out of the ground. A hole with a thin ladder going downward hooked to its walls appeared, like an entrance to a sewer. I noticed a very natural, earthy smell coming from the small hole.

General Bergen explained, "This ladder leads down to a simulation facility that is set to mimic a forest environment. Since we're all the way out here in the desert and can't get greenery naturally, we developed it artificially and designed an environment that mimics a forest. We'll be going down there to do a survival training exercise which will be the last thing you do for... today. Depends. Get it moving."

One by one, we went down the ladder, the smell of forestry getting thicker and thicker with every rung that we climbed down. Soon, I reached the ground, and I hopped off the ladder, staring in awe at the environment that I found myself in. He said that they had "mimicked" a forest, but it was practically the real deal. Thickets of branches and leaves filled my vision as far as I could see in the dark, and I could feel the soft dirt sinking underneath my combat boots. A breeze gently blew, rustling the branches in sync like an orchestrated symphony. A loud clunk snapped us back into reality.

*"Testing...testing...okay, everything seems to be in order,"* we heard General Bergen say. All of us could hear him, but none of us could see him. *"As I said, this is a survival exercise where anything goes. There are traps, animals, natural hazards, and various things that are placed inside of this forest. What you're looking for is a small hut, which will have another set of ladders that lead back to the training facility. You have unlimited time to finish this exercise. Good luck and let's hope all of you make it out."* His voice cut off, and I was seriously hoping that the last part was a joke.

In the darkness, we could barely see each other's faces,

let alone identify who we were standing next to. But it was clear that no one was wearing a smile. A high-pitched voice wailed, "What are we going to do?! I wasn't born to be in this kind of environment." Somewhat unsurprisingly, it was Inthmus, and one didn't need to look at his face to know that he was already at wit's end. We watched as he started climbing back up the ladder. Moments later, consecutive metallic bangs rang out from the ladder shaft before it went silent. "Dammit, it's locked!"

Collectively, we sighed before warily sizing each other up. We hadn't had much interaction outside of our little friend groups and being in this situation wasn't going to change that anytime soon. Alyssa first stepped up and growled, "I don't need any of you with me. We'll split up, then holler or something if you all find the hut."

Blake rebuked, "Splitting up is probably the worst thing that we can do right now. All our previous exercises have been about teamwork and making sure that we trust each other. What's to say that this one is any different?"

"Well, yeah, but teamwork doesn't mean anything if I'm going to end up carrying every single one of you to the end line, does it? Maybe you'd be useful and trustworthy, but I sure as hell won't be trusting *him* any time soon," Alyssa scathingly finished before pointing her finger at Inthmus.

"Point taken, but still, we probably shouldn't split up."

Alyssa irritably tapped her foot against the ground. "What's the point? Even if we do stick together, we won't be working 'together.' These idiots will just end up dragging us down with them," she bit, turning to leave.

"Then at least take one person with you," Blake protested in panic.

"Fine, Dylan, come with me," Alyssa conceded, sighing as she seemingly realized that this arrangement was the best that she would get. "But you all are going to figure out who takes *him*." she venomously spat, pointing at Inthmus.

We all looked at each other nervously, hesitant to step up. I watched Serena hook her arms around Trace and Selene. "We're going together!" she announced, and I felt my heart sink. I was coming to terms with the fact that I would have to lug Inthmus around when Serena added, "I'm also taking Ethan!"

My heart soared, and I sent Serena a grateful look.

"Alright, I guess I'll have to take him," Blake dejectedly muttered, a defeated look on his face. Alyssa gave him one final look of pity before taking Dylan and disappearing behind a grove of high bushes.

"I guess we should go too," Serena called, motioning for us to leave. After giving Blake and his group a wave, we started walking into the forest, selecting a different course from Alyssa's group.

Five minutes later, Serena complained, "Why'd you choose this route?!"

The path in front of us was thorny, thick branches with talons clawing at our clothes and skin. I, being in the front of the group, was forced to continually move the offending limbs to the side in order to continue forward. I could barely see beyond ten feet ahead of me.

"How are we supposed to find one stupid hut in this darkness?!"

"Maybe you can *smell* it out Serena, or some kind of echolocation with that screechy voice," Selene joked.

"Maybe you can stuff it, Selene."

It was amusing to see the two girls go at each other, but Serena did bring up a good point. The forest was unbelievably *dark*. Although there were several oddly placed fluorescent lights that provided artificial lighting, without a sun or moon, the forest floor was shadowy and enveloped in a shroud of darkness. Furthermore, the fluorescent lights were placed high up beyond the tree branches, so only the faintest light trickled through. The atmosphere was only made eerier by the elongated shadows that the tree branches drew on the ground.

"Let's just keeping moving," Trace encouraged. "I'm not getting good vibes from this forest."

Serena clearly wasn't feeling the same trepidation that Trace and I were and hopped on that opportunity to start making fun of Trace. "You're such a baby Trace. Nothing is going to happen to us. This is supposed to be a camp to help us become better right? I highly doubt they'd do anything that hurts us. This is all just training," she jubilantly commented.

"Yeah, but remember what happened in the arena?" Selene remarked, grounding the group back to reality. "Ethan almost got a concussion with the way that Dylan kneed him in the head. But General Bergen didn't do anything to stop Dylan, right?"

The subject of conversation suddenly shifted, and they stared at me as if they were expecting me to say something about the whole situation. I raised my hands in surrender and shrugged. "I don't know...no pain, no gain?"

Serena, Selene, and Trace collectively rolled their eyes and continued walking forward.

"Let's keep moving. The sooner we get out of here, the sooner I can take a bath and go to sleep. Ethan, start clearing those branches," Selene ordered, and we finally started making slight headway again through the thicket of trees. I meekly followed Selene's instructions, clearing branches to the side as the girls followed. Unfortunately, every inch was lined with barberry plants, and their spiky thorns clung to my clothes, making it nigh impossible to clear them off to the side. Moving forward even a single inch made me feel like

I was trying to maneuver through an obstacle course. Thin red lines appeared on my exposed arms each time a thorn scratched my skin.

"Wait, stop," Selene called, and I halted my movements in an uncomfortable position. My foot was stopped midair, trapped in between two branches of thorns, and my arms were twisted in odd angles to the side to avoid a long, limp tree branch that was close to tearing into my left arm. I tried shifting around, hoping to get into a more comfortable position.

Someone slapped me in the back, sending my legs straight into the branch of thorns. The row of thorns dug into my ankles, the tree branch also leaving a long gash along my arm. "Ow, who pushed me?!" I growled, and two arms latched onto my torso and pulled me back.

Stumbling, I turned around to see the girls pressing their index fingers pressed to their lips. "Shhh," they sibilated simultaneously. "Listen, can you hear it?"

Ignoring the blood pounding in my head from irritation and frustration, I strained my ears and kept silent, listening. "I can't hear anyt-"

"Shhh," they chided again, and I grit my teeth. Reluctantly, I closed my mouth and started listening for whatever they were hearing. This time, although it was faint, I could hear it. It was soft, nearly inaudible, but it was quite clear to anyone who was listening for it. A soft burbling came from beyond the wall of leaves and thorns. It was the sound of water.

Eagerly, I started pushing the branches and thorns to the side with renewed vigor.

"Wait, don't-"

I didn't get to hear the end of whatever Selene was trying to say because my foot got caught an inconspicuous hole in the ground that tipped me over. My face was getting closer and closer to the thicket of thorns and branches. "Oh, fu-"

The thorns whacked my face and left long gashes across my cheeks. Or rather, my face whacked the thorns, which left long gashes across my cheeks. Howling in pain, I gently held my two hands in front of my cheeks, softly dabbing my face with my index finger starting with the forehead, then my cheeks, my nose, my mouth, and my chin, hissing as the injuries stung with every touch.

Muffled laughter erupted behind me. Selene held her two hands against her stomach and coughed, "I told you."

Groaning, I pushed the remaining thorns and branches away, a bit more cautiously this time. Eventually, gaps started emerging from the wall of green and I could see rocks and fallen logs sitting nearby a river of clear water. Scattered flashes of pulsing yellow lights from bugs dancing in the sky illuminated the bank of the river in a gentle glow.

As the last of the branches were cleared away, Selene, Serena, and Trace excitedly dashed over to the banks of the river, staring down at their reflections in the crystal-clear water. They stroked their hands in the water experimentally, cooing in pleasure as the cool sensation washed over their skin.

"Ethan! Come wash your wounds in the water. It'll hurt less," Selene suggested, beckoning me over. I could think of ten different reasons why washing exposed wounds in a potentially contaminated river would be a bad idea, but since it didn't appear to do anything harmful to the girls when they dipped their arms in, I figured that it would be okay, by some twisted logic. Besides, in the grand scheme of things, eliminating the short-term pain was probably more important than worrying about a potential infection down the line.

Sitting next to the girls, I experimentally sank my hands into the water, wincing as the water seeped into the small scratches on my hands, reigniting a new wave of stinging. When the pain diminished to a dull throb, I slowly sank the rest of my arms into the water, sighing in satisfaction as a spreading chill washed over my arms. The nerves on the surface of my skin tingled as pleasure washed over me. Taking my arms out, I whipped them around in the air a couple of times, flinging the water droplets off. Rolling up the pants of my military uniform, I let my legs sink into the cool water, enjoying the refreshing feeling it gave.

On that bank, the four of us spent seemingly hours just reveling in the peaceful atmosphere. The moment was perfect, almost serene without a fault. Serena, Selene, and Trace were still enjoying the novelty of waving their arms through the water as the soft, pulsing glow of fireflies lighting the dark sky trapped the area in a cozy atmosphere.

But as soon as that thought passed through my mind, a harsh, icy breeze started blowing in from nowhere, and droplets of murky rain started falling from the sky. *Drip, drip,* the sound echoed, and an alarmed shout of panic pierced through the night air.

# Chapter 10

*July 23, 2103*

· · · · ● · · · ·

As soon as the strangled cry rang out, Serena, Selene, and Trace started running toward the sound before I could stop them.

"Wait! Don't go off on your own!" I yelled, chasing after them. When they disappeared into the forest, they became invisible as the low-hanging branches covered them with their green blanket, and the lighting grew dim once again. I continued to follow them along the river, and the stream continued to get thinner and thinner.

Soon enough, I passed the river source and was dashing through the dark forest. A grove of drooping evergreen trees lined the small trail that I was running alongside, but the three girls were now completely out of sight. I frantically called out, "Selene! Serena! Trace!"

I came to a slow stop, panting with my hands on my knees as I strained my ears to listen, hoping that they would signal back. A low veil of white fog coalesced around my ankles and the surrounding area, impeding my vision. I couldn't tell where the next row of trees started and stopped.

"Ethan!" Serena's faint voice called.

Her desperate cry came from my left, and I ran toward the

voice which led me off the trail and into the woods. Although the surrounding area was still dark, I could still make out the pale, blond hair that reflected the small amount of light that filtered through the umbrella of branches. Several more figures hidden in the darkness were also standing next to her.

"Come quickly!"

As I rushed over to them, I finally saw why they were being so frantic. They were hovering over Blake, who was lying on the ground face down with a nasty looking wound near the base of his spine. Someone at least had the good sense to press a piece of clothing on the wound, slowing the bleeding.

"General Bergen! We need help!" Serena started shouting, and I was almost hopeful that the exercise would be called off. But Serena's voice merely echoed in the forest until it dissipated. The sound of crickets chirping replaced Serena's plea for help, and her choked sobbing soon came after.

I watched in silence as Trace worried over Blake while she gently held his hand in her own. She was muttering soft words of comfort as she tried to keep him awake. By the second, I could see the strength leaving Blake as his eyelids fluttered open and closed rapidly.

"Do something!" Trace shouted at Serena, who was trembling while on her knees beside Blake. We all uncertainly glanced at each other, unsure about what we could do in this situation, and I asked gently, "Didn't you say you were part of the Medical Sciences track Serena? Can't you do something?"

She shook her head frantically while droplets of tears started forming in the corner of her eyes. "I-I didn't really do well in my classes. If I could get something to stop the bleeding and cauterize the wound, maybe I could do something about it, but without an actual medical kit, I can't help him!"

I exhaled in disappointment as Serena continued to

desperately press the red-stained cloth against Blake's wound. Carter and Inthmus, who were also present, cast their eyes down toward the ground, apparently not knowing what to do in this situation. Although, I saw out of the corner of my eyes that Inthmus was more or less apathetic about the whole situation.

"What do you have on you guys?" I tiredly demanded from those not tending to Blake.

They jumped in surprise, then started digging through their pockets. Inthmus and Carter turned out with mostly blanks while the girls handed whatever they had to Carter. He juggled around the items and recited, "We have a couple of cigarettes, a wad of cash, and some other little trinkets like gum and stuff, but I don't think that's going to help. Inthmus also managed to snag a bagel from the dining hall."

The joke at the end was slightly tasteless at that point, but I somewhat minimally appreciated his attempt at trying to lighten the mood. Unfortunately, everyone was still solemn and in a state of panic. Blake's strength was fading out by the second, and the wound wasn't getting any better.

"If only we had some Etonic plants at hand…" Serena wished.

The Etonic plant. Hannah had shown me that when we were fourteen years old and wandering the forests on the outskirts of Sector 78.

"That's the 'miracle plant', isn't it?" I asked.

Serena jumped as if surprised. "How do you know about-, of course, Hannah, right?" she said with a glint in her eyes. "She's probably taught you a bunch of other cool stuff," Serena added with envy.

I nodded blankly. "No, not really. But go back to what you were saying. What about an Etonic plant?"

Serena wistfully sighed. "Never mind. There probably

aren't going to be any around here since this is an artificial forest. I don't know, maybe we can't help Blake after all…"

I growled. "What the hell are you talking about? We have to at least try."

I turned to the others, who had been watching our banter go back and forth like a ping-pong match. "We need to try and find an Etonic plant. Maybe it'll be here, maybe it won't, but this is the only chance we have. Because if not…" I trailed. The others nodded.

"What does this look like?" Selene asked.

"It's almost like poison ivy. They have similar shapes, but the difference is that Etonic plants have white spots on the underside of the plant. So, make sure you're careful when you're searching. Serena, keep adding pressure to the wound while we're searching."

She nodded briskly with a frown but continued to apply pressure to the wound. Blake continued to groan softly. That was good. There was no chance that he'd survive if he lost the will to live. As everyone dashed away, I commanded, "Serena, keep talking to him. We can't have him losing his grip."

I ran off into the forest, looking for the elusive little plant Hannah had shown me all those years ago. It'd been two years since I'd seen one, but I still remembered the jagged shape of the plant and the dotted underside that looked like a constellation.

An icy gust of wind was still howling across the forest, the rain pattering down on the trees. As if to make our job even harder, the downpour came down harder, decreasing my visibility further. I could barely see a couple of feet in front of me. It must've been at least ten or twenty minutes after we had split up, and I still hadn't heard the shouts of jubilation that should've accompanied the discovery of the plant.

Suddenly, my foot caught on something hard, making me trip and fall to the ground. A rough, oblong object slammed into my forehead as my face impacted the ground. My right foot felt like it was on fire, my ankles throbbing along with the pounding in my head. I limped onto my feet, hopping a couple of times on my left to regain balance.

"Of all times…" I growled. When I tried to move forward, each hop on my left foot made my right foot sting as if knives were digging deeper into it. Hesitantly, I took another cautious step forward, only to curse as all my strength dissipated from my legs and my face was reintroduced to the ground. My head was practically swimming, and flashes of light and stars started filling my vision. I had barely managed to tilt my head upward, avoiding taking in a mouthful of wet dirt.

Through my eyelids, the world was blurring in and out of focus, and I could feel the grip on my consciousness fading away as my head swirled. Three crashes to the head in a single day couldn't have been good for my body. But before I succumbed to the darkness, I caught something on the edge of my fading vision.

At first, I thought that it was just the stars from the impact that was filling my vision, but as I blinked several times to wash out the rain obscuring my sight, I realized that the specks of lights weren't from dizziness, but were small stars painted against a green canvas. There, growing near the underbrush of a small bush, was a small little plant with three leaves. The leaves were sharp and spiky as if little thorns were growing straight out of the leaves. White stars adorned the underside.

My eyes widened as big as saucers as I mustered up all the strength that I could, and shouted, even as the edges of my vision turned to black and I couldn't even think any longer.

"I found it! I found it…. I found…it."

All the strength left my body and my face fell onto the soft dirt beneath me.

WHEN I CAME to, the first thing I noticed was that I was on someone's back. The rhythmic ups and downs as the person moved bounced my head around from side to side, increasing the pain I was getting from my migraine.

I begged whoever was carrying me, "Can you drop me off?"

The person stopped abruptly, making my forehead bash against the back of their head. A sudden shock ran through my body, and abruptly I was lifted off the person's back and was set on the ground.

"Ethan! Are you okay?!" Serena screamed, and I held back a wince as her loud shouting practically shattered my eardrums and worsened my migraine.

I held out a hand toward her, waving her down. "Please, not so loud," I implored, holding my right hand against my head. It was still throbbing from the impact with the tree root and the light filtering in through the gaps in the canopy of trees stung my eyes. A warm, welcoming breeze replaced the icy winds from last night. It still had nothing on the actual sun and the warmth that it provided, but it was a close second. I took a glance at my watch. 08:23 A.M.

"How long have I been out?"

Carter answered, "Give or take seven hours. We found you out there all busted up, laying right beside the Etonic plant and cradling it as if your life depended on it." He smirked as he patted my shoulders. "You got lucky. If your hand had been to the right just a few more inches, you would've been grasping at a hand full of poison ivy."

Last night's events slowly came back to me and I looked around, searching for the wounded man that I had gone through all that suffering for. "Where's Blake?"

Carter pointed behind him. Inthmus, who was generally silent and broody, turned around and on his back, Blake was snoring away. His face, normally twisted in some variation of a mischievous expression, was calm, his head tilting lightly with every breath. I peeked at his lower back where the grievous wound was yesterday and saw clothing tightly wrapped around the wound. "How's he doing?"

"He's exhausted. You really saved him. At the very least he won't be dying on us any time soon. We just need to give him some time to overcome the exhaustion and the shock a little bit," he sighed while scratching at his neck. "It's not every day that a sharp log punctures your back."

"What happened?" I questioned. It was something that had been nagging at my brain since the evening, but it didn't seem appropriate at the time since everyone was panicking.

Carter sighed and sat down on a fallen log, shaking his head while looking down at the ground woefully. "It's not a pretty story. Right after you left, we followed a thin trail that brought us through an open section of the forest. It was a pretty pleasant trail and because of that, maybe we had our guard down."

Inthmus snorted from where he was standing just a few steps away, and Carter smiled morosely, kicking at a small stone next to his foot. He continued, "I was the one that fell. We came upon a small ravine that went maybe twenty or thirty feet down. The cliffs were rocky, and the only way across was a thick log that ran across the ravine. Of course, we would've gone around if that was an option, but it was stretching as far as we could see. So instead, we decided to take our chances. Blake and Inthmus suggested we go down the ravine and climb back up the other side."

"So, where the hell did the puncture wounds come from?" I growled impatiently.

"If you let me finish," Carter shot back irritably. "I was about to say, I didn't want to take that route down. I wanted to take my chances with the log." He sighed loudly before standing up to stretch his arms and legs, which I noticed was also riddled with scratch wounds.

"So, while Blake and Inthmus was heading down the ravine, I got scared and decided to go across on the log. It was all going great, and I kept my balance fairly well until I got to the middle. Then-"

Carter shivered started breathing faster and faster, hyperventilating. My eyes widened in alarm and quickly placed my hands on his shoulders, looking right into his eyes. "Carter. Carter! Breathe, man! Deep breaths."

His shoulders shuddered once more before his breathing started returning to normal. "The log collapsed. The rest were already in the middle of the ravine and managed to catch me, but the splinters that rained down from the log caught Blake in the back as he was covering Inthmus. I grabbed him and started running alongside the path at the bottom of the ravine until we reached wooded areas again. The storm last night started picking up, and that's when we called for help."

That was a hell of a story. "What about Alyssa's group? Have you seen them or heard anything from them?"

They timidly looked at each other before shaking their heads. "We haven't seen them since the start of the exercise last night. They've been out there alone for half a day. I haven't heard a single thing from them. But I'm sure they're doing fine."

"Yeah, probab-"

Suddenly, the air shifted. All the sounds around us deadened. The trees, the wind, the insects, everything. It was replaced by a soft metallic clang that kept ringing periodically out from afar.

"What is that?" Trace asked nervously. The sound kept ringing throughout the forest unnaturally, each toll sounding slightly louder than the one before it. We all waited with bated breath, and I strained my ears, trying to identify the sound. *Clang, clang, clang.* The resounding noise was as clear as a bell.

The air shifted again. All the sounds of the forest, which had deafened for a while, came back, but the metallic clang kept calling out to us, persisting with its methodical toll.

"S-Should we check it out?" Serena asked timidly.

"Isn't this the way that people get killed in horror movies?" Carted asked nervously.

*Thanks for that morbid thought,* I mentally said. The tolling was slowly getting softer by the second and was almost becoming inaudible. "Do you think we should check it out?" I called, and the opinions were split. By the second, the sound was dissipating, and people were reluctant to go. When I saw that they couldn't make the decision, and the sound was almost fading entirely, I forced an executive decision upon them, urging, "We're going. Let's check it out."

The walk to the source of the noise took a good thirty minutes, the periodic clangs becoming louder and louder with each step that we covered. To our left and right, a thick wall of spiky evergreen tree leaves blocked our vision. The sound felt like it was coming from right near us, the sound resounding against my ears clearly. Soon enough, the packed tree line thinned, and light started entering through the spacious openings in between the trees.

The packed straight gave away to a lush clearing of green grass that came to our hips. There, in the center of the open clearing, was a small wooden hut. Two people were sitting around the small wooden porch near the front. A long, pipe-like construct jutted out from the top like an extended chimney. As we got close, we finally found the source of the clanging noise. Alyssa, who was holding a large metal pole, was banging it against the concrete foundation of the hut which made the crisp toll that we had been hearing for the past half hour.

Once Alyssa finally saw us, she sighed loudly, dropping the metal pole onto the ground. Her face and body were drenched in sweat, and she was lightly panting in exhaustion. She remarked, "What the hell happened to him?" She was pointing at Blake who was still resting on Inthmus' back.

"Had an issue with a gigantic splinter. He should be fine now. We managed to find some Etonic plants and got it applied onto his wound," I replied. Alyssa whistled admiringly and went over to Blake to check his back. She slowly rolled back the hem of his shirt and looked at the wound.

It didn't seem as bad as it was last night. The bleeding had completely stopped, and the flesh had already started to mend back together. Putting the healing properties of the Etonic plant and the pressure applied from the clothing had done miracles for the wound. Alyssa nodded her head before turning back to us. "Who was the one that did the rush job on this idiot? This is some clean medical work. Although, you should probably still get up quickly and make sure that he gets checked by an actual professional."

She stepped up onto the porch and pointed at the long tube sticking out of the ceiling. "It has another ladder thing like the one that we just got off. You all can, I don't know, carry Blake up there or something," she said. Before any of us could respond, she was already inside the hut, and I could hear the soft clacks as she made her way up the ladder.

Our little climactic journey in the forest ended—in an anti-climactic fashion in my opinion. As we climbed up the rungs of the ladder, the thick scent of the forest faded away, replaced by the clean air of the military base. As we opened the panel and filed out, we came out from the center of the track and saw General Bergen standing near the entrance as if he had been waiting for us the whole time. His face showed no emotion, and he beckoned us over.

Personally, I only felt mild annoyance toward the stone-faced General, but some of the other campers, specifically Trace and Serena, had some words to say. Trace, the first to speak, angrily asked, "What was that exercise supposed to do?! Were you going to just let Blake bleed out?!"

"You *were* warned," General Bergen shot back, justifying himself. He sweepingly gazed at all of us. "Since your *friend* here, a term I still loosely use to describe your relationship, wanted to know, I will remind you of your purpose at Camp Daedalus."

From out of his pocket, he took out one of the brochures that we had been given during our car ride to Camp Daedalus. He also pulled out the pink contract form that we had signed. He flipped open the brochure and read, "This camp was established in order to foster cooperation with the hopes that campers may find new opportunities to develop skills necessary for entrance into the workforce, and possible entrance to the U.R. Military."

Flipping the brochure shut, he glared at us. "I don't think you all understand your positions. If you had not been given an opportunity to come here, you would be out on the streets right now, digging food out of trash cans. You were *rejected* by the system. So here we are, the government provided an opportunity for you to possible enlist in the *military*, yet the nine of waste it all because of your worthless self-pride. Do you even think about the hundreds, no, *thousands* of students who are out on the streets right now because they weren't given this opportunity?"

"We healed Blake and found the Etonic plant together," Inthmus countered, and we all nodded in agreement.

It was the wrong thing to say. General Bergen's face twisted into a sneer and he spat, "Yes, you *found* the Etonic plant. First, you shouldn't have had to go look for it in the first place if you would've taken care of each other and maybe Mr. Tyson wouldn't have had that kind of injury in the first place. Second, do you really think that Holfstras, who I might add, was the only person who came up with an actual solution without being an absolute idiot, would just *trip* over something at random?"

I mulled over that thought. When I tripped, I did have the passing thought that the tree root was oddly placed. General Bergen continued, "In that forest, I control everything from the outside. The weather, the landscape, the bugs and animals, the plants, *everything.* Even when I created a perfect environment for everyone, you managed to end up with *this.*"

General Bergen's face was getting red, and he waved the brochure in his right hand in front of us. "During your time here, even with one of the most goddamn advanced military bases in the country and its resources at your disposal, you've used this opportunity to do *nothing.* Gossiping. Arguing. Relaxing. The government didn't sponsor this damn program so that I could come to babysit lazy teenagers in doing nothing!"

He took a deep breath before taking the brochure and crumpling it up. Tossing it on the ground, he rammed his boot down on the ground to crush it. "No more," he whispered. "You-" he said, pausing as he raised a shaking finger toward the far wall of the training facility. "-will be going out there. Outside of the military base, outside from all the comfort, outside from all the guidance, and outside of any interference. You will relearn the meaning of survival."

We stood frozen as General Bergen's furious words pierced us like hot knives. My legs were shaking, and I found it difficult to stand. Helplessly, I watched as General Bergen straightened his back and leveled a glare at all of us. "One week. There will be no structured programming for one whole week. Then, we will see if you have earned a chance at redemption."

# Chapter 11

*July 30, 2103*

· · · · · • · · · · ·

"WHAT DO YOU mean Carter's been expelled?!" Blake growled angrily.

"Have you ever picked up a dictionary in your life? It means that he will no longer be participating in this camp."

After the survival training exercise, we all had the week to think about how to prepare for the "real experience" that the enraged General vowed to send us on by the end of the week. He had said that the week would be free for everyone to do whatever they would like, but clearly, that wasn't the case. On the Day of Judgement, exactly a week after the survival exercise, General Bergen had called us to meet down in the foyer first thing in the morning to give us the news that Carter had been expelled.

"Where is he now?" Blake seethed, and General Bergen didn't dignify his question with an answer. He merely fixed Blake another annoyed glare before turning his back on him.

"He's been sent away from this camp. That's all I can and will tell you."

Out of the corner of my eyes, I saw Blake's face becoming flushed deeper by the second in anger. He opened his mouth to say something, but General whirled around, interrupting him with a sharp, condescending remark. "What part of this is surprising? On the very first day of this camp, I explained that anyone whose points dropped below zero would be expelled. That was the established rule. Just because there was no organized programming, you think that we haven't been keeping tabs on you?"

General Bergen invaded into Blake's personal space, breathing right down his neck. "He spent the week in his room, doing nothing, only leaving occasionally to do a few exercises. Mr. Keeble decided to waste the opportunity that he was given. If you have a problem with my decision, we can toss you out as well. Is that what you want?"

The muscles around Blake's mouth and jawline tightened, and for a fleeting second, I thought that Blake would do just that, pack and leave. However, I was relieved when Blake despondently responded, "No, sir."

"Good. Take a little bit of time to rest yourself. *Some* of you deserve it. I will call you when it is time to leave. The final exercise will be beginning soon," General Bergen commanded as he made to leave.

I caught the last sentence that he said and called out, "What do you mean final exercise?"

General Bergen froze as the rest of us stood at attention. Slowly, he whirled around on the balls of his feet, meeting our inquisitive stares. "It's exactly what I mean. This will be your final exercise before we decide what to do with you all. For your sakes, I hope that you all do well."

"Didn't you say this would be a chance to earn our redemption?" I questioned, now thoroughly confused. Deep in the corner of my mind, a shred of fear started picking away at the confidence that had been building throughout the week.

I had been training like none other. I had even gotten

Dylan to help me out during my training to work on my hand-to-hand combat skills. Although most of the training sessions ended up being time for Dylan to beat me up, there were moments of "genius," as Dylan liked to call it, that emerged.

*It was around three days since the beginning of the "break." Three days since I started working with Dylan on combat training. He landed a hard hit on my head, something that he seemed to have a habit of doing. It put me on the ground, panting, exhausted, and out of breath. When I got back up on my feet after the small unsolicited break, my mind was in a haze. I couldn't form fully developed thoughts, and the edges of my vision darkened. Suddenly, my mind felt clearer than it had ever been before, and my muscles felt rejuvenated.*

*My body took an unfamiliar stance and charged at Dylan. Everything that he did I could see as if he was moving in slow motion. The right hook that he was throwing, the left knee he had prepared in case I duck from the hook, and his twisted core, preparing for a back kick. Instead of dodging, my left arm blocked the hook, my right arm looped under his left leg, and as I tossed his leg to the side, making him lose balance. My whole body twisted like a tornado in a hurricane kick and the flat of my boots landed right on Dylan's face.*

*He fell onto the ground like a tree being cut down at its base. When he got back up, he looked dazed and was holding out his arm to steady himself. He turned toward me in shock. "Dude, what the hell? I didn't know you could do that."*

*The haze slowly faded, and my tunnel vision disappeared, going back to normal. I muttered, "I didn't know I could do that..."*

That was four days ago. Since then, the phenomenon had only happened one more time, but I could never get it to willingly work for me. It didn't bother me though. I didn't like the limiting feeling that the tunnel-vision state gave me anyhow.

That was the main reason for my protest. I stared at General Bergen, hoping that he would answer my question. All the beatings that I endured throughout the week were not going to be put to waste.

"This *is* your chance at redemption. It will be the final test to determine whether you have accomplished the goals of this camp. If you have, then good for you. There will be further instructions afterward based on your performance. Maybe you'll be sent back to your sector, or maybe there are greater things waiting for you. But if you fail, well, let's hope you don't fail," he finished ambivalently.

With those final words, he left the foyer through the central passageway, which I realized was the path to the most secretive rooms in the base. Silence followed his departure and we looked at each other. Blake was still red from fury. Without another word, he stomped away toward the dorms.

The rest of us, now reduced to seven, nervously stood around the atrium.

"That stupid idiot," I heard Alyssa mutter. "Absolutely useless to begin with." She dragged Dylan and toward the athletic training facility while Inthmus scoffed and went back up to the dorms. He had dark bags under his eyes and looked exhausted.

"When did Carter leave?" Serena asked.

"I would assume some time during the evening. But that's strange. I would think I could've heard the gates opening to let the car leave the military base even if I was asleep," Selene mentioned with a quizzical look on her face. Her eyebrows were scrunched up, mind straining in thought.

"Don't think too hard," I joked. "You might hurt something up there."

But I looked at the ground wistfully as well. Although I couldn't claim to be a very close friend to him, I still did have some sort of a bonding moment.

*It was one of the rare times that Carter had come out of his room to do a little bit of exercise. As I went over toward the weight room, I saw Carter struggling to do some pullups on the high-hanging bar next to the dumbbell racks.*

*"Hey, man," I awkwardly called out. "What are you doing?"*

*He raised his eyebrows at me. "What does it look like."*

*My face burned in embarrassment. "Right."*

*Carter landed back on the ground with a thud, and sat down on one of the benches, quenching his thirst with some water from a bottle. He grabbed at the collar of his uniform, fanning it while trying to cool off. I watched dispassionately until a small streak of black near the base of his neck made my eyes widen. The small tattoo on my neck squirmed.*

*"You too?"*

*Carter whipped around toward me, eyes wide when he saw my gaze fixated on his neck. He clamped his hand down on his collar, glaring at me. "Don't you say another word," he said, voice trembling.*

*"Hey, calm down," I placated, pulling at my own collar. I showed him the black Republic emblem on the bottom of my neck. "I would've never guessed."*

*He sighed, lying down the bench despondently. "I don't like talking about it. It's not easy being 'a literal waste of space' in the inner sectors."*

*"Which sector do you come from?"*

*"Seventeen," he muttered with a faraway look. "They'd always beat me, sometimes starve me, or just chase me around for fun. I always had to live off food that came off the streets until someone was kind enough to pick me up off the streets. Still ended up here, though. Same story for you?"*

*"Sort of..." I replied hesitantly. Being treated poorly was a reality for us, something that we accepted, but never to Carter's degree. "How are you still sane, man?"*

*He shrugged. "Some miracle. But you should see what they do to people like us in the Core Sectors. I heard they literally use us Bastards as slaves."*

*"But it's outla-"*

*"And you think that those stuck-up high-brows would care about stupid laws? Laws that they create and own?"*

*I thought back to Inthmus with his arrogant attitude, carelessness, and indifference for others. "I guess you have a point."*

*"Here's my advice for you, Ethan. Stay away from the Core Sectors, or you won't like what's coming to you."*

*"I will, thanks."*

Although Carter had been useless, in the most respectful way, in all other ways, his advice had given me much to think about. It had put a damper on my motivation for a while, but I was saved by the others, who constantly kept me occupied. Although I wouldn't go as far as to classify everyone as best friends, Serena, Selene, Trace, and I spent time together over the break. I also tried getting to know some of the other people at the camp like Blake, Dylan, and Alyssa, but wasn't all too successful. Blake was friendly enough and gave me the time of day as did Dylan, but my attempt to befriend Alyssa had turned out to be a disastrous venture.

*It was Saturday, nearing the end of the week-long training break. I was standing on top of the makeshift arena in the training facility working with Dylan who wanted to try and bring back my "tunnel-vision state."*

*"Come on 'Squeak! You're supposed to be trying to hit me, not avoid me!" Dylan taunted, wiggling his fingers at me. He had a frustrated look on his face and sighed despondently as he whacked away my last palm strike toward his sternum.*

"You seem to be making lots of progress," a sarcastic voice interrupted. It was Alyssa, but instead of wearing the sand-colored uniform that was part of the camp kit, she only had on a gray sports-bra along with tight, skin-fitting shorts.

Dylan sighed, "I guess, but not as much as I would've liked."

"How about I fight him? Then we can gauge how far he's come!" she said excitedly. I would've almost believed that her offer was one of kindness had she not been sporting a malicious grin on her face.

"I-I don't think-" Dylan started.

"Alright! What are you waiting for? Get down here Dylan!" she commanded while pulling herself up to the ring. Dylan visibly deflated, then reluctantly got down from the raised platform, shooting me a concerned glance. He stood and watched from the sidelines, nibbling at his fingernails.

As she stood across from me, bouncing around from her left and right foot, I was sweating bullets despite the chilliness of the facility. I started remembering the time she had destroyed Inthmus in front of everyone and wondered if I was in for a similar fate. Settling into a low stance, I waited. Alyssa looked amused if anything. Her cocky smirk never wavered while her eyes bore into mine with a calculating look, as if trying to find the best way to humiliate me.

"Are you ever going to start moving?" she taunted.

I charged forward with my fists up defensively. As I got closer and closer, I reared back a fist and let it fly toward her face. She ducked out of the way, moving in to land a solid punch against my stomach. Before I could even react, she kicked the back of my kneecaps from behind, bringing me to a kneel. Her legs wrapped around my head, and in just seconds, I was lying on the ground with my head trapped between her thighs in a suffocating chokehold. On the side, I could hear Dylan groaning in disappointment.

*"Do you give?"*

*I grunted, latching onto her legs in an effort to break myself off the hold, but to no avail. Alyssa's hold only tightened, further blocking off my airway. "Fine! Fine, I give!" I choked.*

*The crushing force on my neck and head lifted, finally letting me grasp at a breath of fresh air. I coughed and wheezed several times, trying to gulp up as much oxygen as possible while Alyssa clicked her tongue from where she stood. From my fetal position, I saw Alyssa turn toward Dylan and mock, "Come on Dylan, either you're not doing anything as a teacher, or you've found yourself the most useless student on the planet. Which is it?"*

*Dylan snorted, "He's just a little rough around the edges. You haven't seen him when he's serious."*

*"You keep telling yourself that. Whatever, I'm going. Have fun with your 'Squeaks' for all I care."*

*As Alyssa sauntered off to a different part of the training facility, Dylan came up to me, and complained, "Come on, man. You're making me look bad in front of her. You could've done so much better than that."*

*I ground my teeth in anger and looked toward Alyssa's retreating form.*

*I decided that I hated that girl.*

Admittedly, some people were easier to talk to than others. For example, Selene and Serena were more open people, while Trace was a little more closed off. On the other hand, people like Blake didn't have that kind of problem. He just exuded a natural friendliness and openness that let people get comfortable with him. That's why it was so surprising to see Blake explode the way that he did with General Bergen just moments ago.

"-do you think, Ethan?"

Everyone was looking at me expectantly, and I rubbed

the back of my neck, embarrassed. "Sorry, I didn't hear what you said. What was the question?"

Serena sighed in exasperation. "We asked, what do you think about this whole situation? With Carter, the upcoming survival exercise, everything."

I thought deeply. It was a question that had been plaguing my mind for a while but didn't find a good answer for. "Well, we can't do anything about any of that now, right? I mean, we're still just kids in their eyes and don't really have much power. Carter disappeared in the middle of the night, so maybe they just wanted him to not get embarrassed. As for the survival exercise, I'm honestly just hoping that I got through it in one piece," I finished nervously.

Everyone nodded in agreement and with that sentiment embedded in our minds, we separated off towards our own dorms to get more sleep. I figured that the moment was best spent resting since it was still six in the morning. I was still dead tired from the whole week. My muscles were sore and the mental stress from anxiety didn't help either.

Lying down on the bed, I drifted off to sleep.

I AWOKE TO the incessant buzzing of my watch. The little black box was vibrating like crazy, the screen flashing from black to blue as small strings of text flew across the screen, reading, "Survival Exercise Pre-Meeting, 1200 hours." I looked at my watch, confused. Meeting? General Bergen hadn't mentioned anything about a pre-exercise meeting. Was this for everyone? The meeting was scheduled to take place in one of the rooms that were within the central entryway of the atrium, and my heart skipped a beat in nervousness.

I glanced toward the gigantic clock that came with the

Dashboard. It was already 1130 hours, just thirty minutes before the meeting, and I was a mess. While I was sleeping, my clothes had gotten sweaty from the musty heat, my hair was tousled every which way, and overall, I looked like a caveman.

I jumped out of bed, landing in a pile of my own clothes that were neatly stacked near the base of my bed. Well, they weren't so well stacked anymore. Grabbing a cleaner set of the bland uniform, I dashed toward the bathroom. When I opened the door, this time, it was a lot livelier than the first time that I had entered. Several older military cadets were going about their daily business and one familiar face stood out amongst the crowd.

"Hey Inthmus," I apathetically called. We hadn't really gotten friendly at all during the past week. Hell, I wasn't sure if *anyone* had gotten close with Inthmus yet. Though, his tendencies to act like an arrogant bastard had somewhat decreased.

"Hey," he replied.

An awkward silence fell between us as the chatter of other military cadets and running showers overshadowed our own voices. A soft buzzing from my wrist thankfully interrupted the awkward moment. "Sorry," I told him. "I have to shower. I'm trying to get ready for the survival exercise. I'll see you later?" I questioned. For a moment I wondered if I should ask him about the meeting but thought better of it. There were better people that I could ask about something like that.

I moved past him, ignoring the slight flicker of his eyes toward me, and took a quick shower and made my way down to the foyer. In front of the entrance to the central hallway, I faced a different guard from the woman from my first day. He was sitting at the security desk with a bored expression. It was ten till 1200 hours.

"Do you have a key card for entry or a request for audience?"

I was sure that I had left my golden key card in the room and didn't know what the second thing was. The guard shot me an intimidating glare as he saw me fumbling around with my words. Timidly, I asked, "What is a request for audience?"

The guard's glare became even more venomous. "If you don't know what that is, then you probably don't have it. Leave, kid. As I've said repeatedly, without special permission, this place is off-limits to campers like you for a reason."

"Again?" I questioned. "Have people tried getting in here before?"

He didn't dignify my question with an answer and went back to his own work without even giving me a second look. I nervously glanced at my clock which was speedily counting down to 1200 hours. I panicked. There wasn't nearly enough time to go back upstairs and grab my keycard. I spoke up again, desperately asking him, "I've been called to a meeting by the General. If I don't get in right now, I'm going to get in trouble."

The guard snorted. "Good one, I haven't heard that one before," he chortled. The man even had the gall the swing his two legs onto the table in front of him and stare me down with a condescending glare. "Just go back to your room. I'm not letting you in without the proper authorizations."

"He's with me," a deep voice growled, and I whipped around to see a thin, lanky man standing right behind me. He had a tight, form-fitting suit on and was holding a silver briefcase in his right hand.

The guard, who was previously half-lidded and sitting with his back slouched against the office chair, suddenly shot up in a salute. "Hello, Dr. Collers! What brings you here today?"

*Dr. Collers?* I thought. The name sounded familiar, but I just couldn't put a finger on it. I watched as Dr. Collers continued to converse with the guard. "Nothing pleasant I'm afraid. One of the more recent developments that we were making hasn't been going so well, so I'm here to update the General on that. I told...Ethan here to wait here for me. If you would kindly let us through, that would be great," he finished with a pleasant smile.

"Y-Yes, of course!" the guard stuttered, and with a press of a button, the emblem gate drafted open, leading to the dark central hallway illuminated by fluorescent lights. Dr. Collers motioned for me to go in first and I obediently followed, feeling Dr. Collers' presence right behind me as I entered the small enclosed hallway. Looking down at my watch, I found that I still had around five minutes to get to the meeting.

I turned around to face the tall man who was garbed in a brown suit with thick-framed glasses. When he saw me looking at him, his brows rose, and he asked, "Don't you have a meeting to get to?"

Some of the light in his eyes seemed to have died as soon as he entered the hallway, and he didn't seem to be as friendly as he was before. He glanced down toward the base of my neck but didn't comment. I answered, "I have a little bit of time left, and it wouldn't be right to just leave before saying thank you. Dr. Collers, I've heard your name before, but I can't place where-"

"Perhaps you've read one of my works?" he jabbed, cutting me off. His eyes softened, and he held out his hands in a placating gesture. "I apologize if I come off as rude for the moment, but I have something urgent to get to. One of my... underlings, so to speak, made a large mistake in a research project I was doing. So, I'm in a little bit of a hurry to amend the mistakes that she made. If you'll excuse me," he deflected. I watched as he stumbled down toward the far end of the small hallway and dashed into one of the narrower hallways lit by amber lighting.

What an interesting man.

I wanted to question him just a little bit more. His name was like a little rash that needed to be scratched until you were satisfied, and I was so close to figuring out where I had heard his name. I glanced down at my watch and sighed. Unfortunately, it seemed that the questioning would have to wait since the meeting came first.

The room was at the end of the first hallway that I entered, room C111. A small metal door with a small knob was the only entrance to the room. I leaned my ear against the door, hearing nothing from the room. Nervously, I looked to my left and right down the hallway to see if anyone was coming. I grasped the handle and opened the door slightly. I peeked my head through the small gap and sweat nervously as General Bergen met my gaze. His stonily looked at me and questioned, "What are you doing? Come in and take a seat."

I teetered in and closed the door behind me. The room was set up quite simply. A long desk sat in the middle of the room across its length. General Bergen sat on one end near the electronic Dashboard in the front while another chair was set up on the opposite end.

I hustled over to the empty chair and sat myself down. As soon as the meeting started, I was expecting General Bergen to fire away with his cold comments, but interestingly, he didn't say a single word. He simply sat there, watching me from the opposite side of the table. Every time I tried to meet his gaze, his piercing stare would make my eyes subconsciously drift back down to the table, unable to hold eye contact for more than a couple of seconds.

"You've used the week well," he started, and my back straightened in surprise.

"T-Thank you?" I uncertainty replied, and the General guffawed amusedly, a peal of full-blown laughter coming from the depths of his throat. A small ball of annoyance started fluttering up from inside me at hearing the General laugh, but I elected to stay quiet. He settled down a few seconds later.

"I haven't had such a good laugh in a while. But in all seriousness, you've come a long way since you came in here a week and a half ago. I've seen some of the stunts that you pulled in the arena during your free week. Some of those moves were impressive," he gushed, and I thought that I heard a hint of pride in his voice.

I kept my silence.

He started settling down from whatever emotional high he had just gone on and leveled a blank stare at me and spoke. "Let's get down to business. I called you down because you have a separate objective from the others during this survival exercise. Your goal is to win."

"Win?" I asked.

"Yes, win. Emerge victoriously, come out on top, secure the bag, atta-"

"I understand what the word win means General Bergen. But I don't understand how I can 'win' a survival exercise. If it's anything like the last one, I'm sure there's going to be a singular goal?" I wondered, and the General sighed while tapping the desk with his fingers.

He continued, "This is a *you* mission. Separate from the rest of the group. I'm sure you'll figure out the parameters of this survival exercise once you get out there, but nonetheless, while the overall objective is the same, you will only pass if you manage to win the challenge, do you understand?"

I didn't. "I still don't understand how you 'win' a survival exercise."

"You'll understand soon enough," he muttered as he stood up. "I've been disappointed many times throughout this training camp. Everyone appears so complacent with their weaknesses that they've given up on trying. This is unacceptable. There is a reason why this country puts its faith in a whole generation of teenagers and children to lead it in its future. I will not accept this country going downhill because some of them decided that it's not worth it to try."

Out of his pocket, General Bergen pulled out a stick of cigarette and a small lighter. He struck the flint wheel and stuck the cigarette in the small flame. The packed tobacco burned with a small red flare flashing with every breath that General Bergen took. He exhaled deeply, releasing a long puff of smoke into the room.

"There are people that need help in this country. You all are people who can help those people in this country. That is why I cannot bear to see people with talent waste it because of some laziness," he whispered, taking in another puff of smoke. I stayed silent, watching as General Bergen continued mulling in his thoughts.

"What do you think creates a society? An effective one?" he asked, staring at me with curiosity hidden deep in his eyes. His brows were raised expectantly as I fumbled around for an answer.

"You can go now, Ethan. You will understand what your mission is once we begin the survival exercise. Prepare for the journey. Bring lots of water," he commanded.

I stood up and walked toward the door, coughing a couple of times when the smoke hit my nostrils. Opening the door, I slipped out, but before I could close the door, General Bergen said, "Remember, Ethan. Trees without branches cannot bear fruit."

"Yes, sir," I answered. At the time, I didn't understand what he meant by those words.

# PART 2:
# Lost Wolf

· · · · · • • · · · ·

# Chapter 12

*July 30, 2103*

· · · · ● ● · · · ·

"**I**S EVERYONE READY?"

"Yes, sir!"

All of us were decked out in our own gear. To begin with, we all started with the same basic survival kit: military uniform, bottles of clean water, hygiene products, and things like that. After the short and confusing pre-meeting, General Bergen called everyone down to the military storage room as soon as the clock hit 1500 hours and had us line up in random order.

"This is where we'll be using the rankings that have been determined throughout the camp based on your performances in the exercises. Your ranking will determine what additional supplies you get on top of your basic kit," he announced and motioned to a long table sitting behind him with eight bags on it.

"I will announce your rankings starting from the lowest to the highest. Get your bags and go to the van sitting in the atrium. Do not open it until the exercise begins." The stony-faced General pulled out a small little sheet of paper from inside one of his pockets and called, "From bottom to top, it's Inthmus, Ethan, Trace, Selene, Serena, Blake, Dylan, and

Alyssa. That's the order. Get your bags and head over to the van."

He left us to our own devices and left the room. Animatedly, we walked over to the long table of bags and experimentally started lifting them up and down to see if we could figure out what these bags held. I couldn't hear much in mine, but I could hear metallic clinks and jingles coming from some of the other bags that people were holding. My bag was somewhat weighty, but not enough to suggest anything big hiding inside of it.

When I saw the others, some of them looked like they were struggling under the weight of their own bags. *I wonder what's in them,* I thought. My mind shifted back to the side-mission General Bergen gave me several hours earlier. *Would it help me if I stole some of their items?*

When we went back into the atrium, a long, white van was waiting for us in front of the massive statue of Tyler B. Whitman. The "man with the massive marble beard", as we liked to call him sometimes. General Bergen was already waiting for us in the driver's seat of the van with the backseat doors popped open.

"Get in," he commanded, and one by one, we scrambled into the back of the van which was lined with three rows of long four-seaters. The very front of the car, housing the driver's seat and the passenger's seat, was separated from the rest of the car by a thick wooden panel.

As I pulled myself into the cramped car, I cringed as a musty scent hit my nose. The further back I went, the worse the smell got. It was as if the car had been left without care for decades. Serena and Trace also sat in the back row with me, complaining about the smell.

As soon as the last person, Blake, got in, a cadet leaned his head into the van and handed Blake a two-liter bottle of a creamy liquid along with eight cups. The engine started revved up with a violent shudder, and General Bergen called to us, "Every one of you, take half a cup and drink up."

The cadet was still looking into the van as we passed around the large bottle and cups. Under their careful watch, we all downed half a cup of the liquid. I initially expected it to taste like medicine, but to my pleasant surprise, it tasted just like water.

"Did everyone drink?" General Bergen called.

"Yes, sir," the cadet replied.

"Good."

The back door slammed shut, and soon, the van lurched forward in broken strides and drove along the spiral ramp going toward the third floor. We passed through the dark tunnel and got back into the elevator. My stomach lurched as the vehicle started moving upward, and for ten minutes, all I heard was metal grinding against metal as the car elevator traveled to the surface. There was no small talk, no excited jabber. It spoke for how all of us were feeling at the moment. Nervous.

Soon, the car stopped its ascent abruptly, tossing my head against the roof of the car. I frowned. It was still dark in the car. I could feel myself being carried forward by the moving wheels, yet the window remained dark, keeping me trapped in a dark void. Hesitantly, I leaned over Trace and ran my finger across the window. I recoiled away. The surface felt rough, almost like the bark of a tree. It seemed as if the windows had been replaced by thin wooden panels that were placed in the grooves instead of glass. The darkness continued to increase my anxiety about the upcoming mission as my heart began pounding harder and harder against my chest.

Slowly, but surely, my eyelids started feeling heavy, the weight forcefully shutting my eyes. Everyone else was feeling the same. Serena's head lolled against my shoulders while Trace was leaned against the car window.

"Goodnight, and see you later," General Bergen called, and finally, I succumbed to the exhaustion that suddenly overcame me.

WHEN I CAME to, my skin was sizzling from the dry heat, and a bright light burned my retinas. The first thing I saw was a tall archway made of multiple layers of stacked orange colored stone. Small brittlebushes and flowering weeds decorated the base of the little archway along with the cacti and dead bushes that dotted the desert landscape. A small mountain range could be seen in the distance. Not a single man-made landmark, such as a road or a sign, could be seen as far as I could tell.

To my left and right, Serena, Selene, Trace, and Inthmus were still out cold while Dylan, Alyssa, and Blake were huddled around a small sheet of paper. They barely even noticed me walking up behind them, peering over their shoulders reading the short letter that was written on the page.

*Survival Mission Objective: Return to the Military Base*

*You are dropped in an unknown location in the Sonoran Desert. Find your way back to the military base. Your watches acting like trackers, so don't even dream about abandoning the mission and heading for the sectors. The punishment for such an act will be on par with being a traitor to the country. Use the resources you have at your disposal, and good luck.*

How they interpreted the message didn't matter to me because everything quickly became clear. The objective that General Bergen gave me during the pre-meeting now made sense. Warily, I eyed the others to gauge their reaction, and they didn't seem all too concerned. Blake and Alyssa both had calculating looks in their eyes as they continually skimmed the paper repeatedly as if it would give them a clue.

"Any thoughts?" I asked, and they twirled around in surprise.

"You're awake?" Alyssa asked.

"Yeah, so what do you think about this?"

"Nothing much yet," Blake responded with a loud sigh. "We just woke up too, so we haven't had enough time to plan this whole thing out either."

"We'll wait until everyone else wakes up," I suggested, and the two squirmed uncomfortably, but didn't say anything. It took nearly thirty minutes for everyone else to wake back up. During that time, Alyssa and Blake kept digging into the message, looking for clues while Dylan and I helped get everyone up to speed.

Soon, we were all huddled in one large group.

"Maybe we could follow his tire tracks back?" Selene suggested, and at face value, it seemed like a good idea. General Bergen, by mistake or by intention, had left a thin tire track imprinted in the sand following the van's movements back toward the base.

Alyssa interjected, "Tire tracks will disappear after a while. Especially considering the wind and how far he drove us out, they're not going to be on the ground during the entire trip. Since he took a lot of twists and turns along the way, that might end up getting us lost when the tracks disappear."

Despondently, we kicked at the ground and put our heads together, thinking of ways to find our way back. I wasn't exactly sure what was going on in everyone's heads, but personally, my heart felt like it was sinking deeper and deeper into my stomach. It felt chilling, as if the blood pumping through my veins had suddenly become several degrees colder.

"What about our watches?" Blake suggested. "Are those still usable to call or make heads or tails of where we are right now? Can you check, Ethan?"

I glanced down at the sleek black watch strapped tightly on my wrist. It stared back at me with its time flashing off and on with a blue glow. I gently tapped my finger against the screen, but nothing else happened. "Nothing," I reported.

More disappointed looks rounded the group.

"Does anyone have anything in their bags that might help?" Blake hopefully asked, and we collectively took our backpacks off our shoulders. Inthmus eagerly started digging into his bag, yet the rest of us just stood there like statues, nervously glancing at each other.

"Guys?" Blake called.

I took the weighty bag off my shoulders and started looking through its contents. There wasn't much. It was just a small survival kit that included a multifunctional swiss knife, several boxes of matches, a long strand of thick, black rope, and what appeared to be a small square piece of tarp folded up.

There wasn't much in the others' bags as well. The best thing that turned up were handguns inside Alyssa, Dylan, and Blake's bag. Picking up the small, rectangular swiss knife in my hands, I tossed it up and down experimentally. The small device was jet black, a thin metallic coating running along all four inches. It was weighty, not necessarily ideal for certain situations, but it looked sturdy at first glance. I continued to mess around with it a little bit, popping open the various functions of the knife. There were pliers and blade knife, a half saw, several can and bottle openers, along with some other accessories like nail filers. I stowed it away in the small pocket on the sleeve of my left arm, making sure that I could easily take it out with my right hand quickly and smoothly. Just in case.

Blake rekindled the conversation after he looked through his bag. "Let's see if we can gather materials that will help us. First, let's talk about essentials. Does anyone have extra food or water?"

Selene and Trace nodded. They dug around their bags and pulled out a couple of ration bars and some non-perishable canned foods. Selene mentioned, "We also have a little bit more water. Nothing fancy though."

Blake sighed while scratching the back of his head. "I guess we'll have to take what we can get. Moving on, second, is there anyone that has shelter? Maybe like a tent or something? If not, we're going to have to just sleep on the sand."

"I have a small tent," Alyssa bragged. "But I don't plan on sharing it with any of you anytime soon."

It didn't seem like things were going so well. All the kits seemed to be prepared for individuals, thus, there was a severe lack of supplies to be shared, and most certainly, these supplies wouldn't get everyone through for long.

"Okay," Blake started. "There's that. What about navigational tools? Does anyone have anything that could help us find our way back like a map or compass?"

"I have a compass," Dylan chanted.

"Does anyone have a map?" Blake called, desperately hoping that someone did.

No one raised their voice, much to his disappointment. "I guess that was hoping for too much. We'll have to work with what we have. So where are we going to go from here?"

"I'll lead a group."

We turned our heads and saw Inthmus pointing to himself with a confident grin on his face. That was a big surprise, considering his less than favorable reaction to the first survival exercise.

"What?" Blake incredulously asked, but Inthmus' cocky grin didn't waver a single bit.

"I can lead the group. I've traveled a decent amount with my dad, so finding our way back should be a piece of cake," he boasted. "Besides, there's no guarantee that you'll do anything but a piss poor job at leading us anyways."

"*He* of all people will not be leading me for this," Alyssa hissed, and I saw Dylan nodding along from the corner of my eye.

Inthmus growled, "What's your problem with me? Ever since the first day, you've been a cold, stuck-up harridan that believes the world owes you something."

Alyssa knocked him down to the ground with a punch to the face, seething, "The world *does* owe me something, for taking *everything* away from me. Dylan, let's go!"

"Alright," Dylan lazily called.

Alyssa hoisted her bag onto her shoulders, and after giving Inthmus another good kick to the ribs, she started walking away without another word. Dylan heartily waved goodbye before waddling to catch up to Alyssa, who was furiously marching away at a brisk pace.

Selene whirled on Inthmus, accusing, "What the hell Inthmus? Why would you say something like that? You've done nothing but antagonize people ever since the beginning of camp. What's the matter with you?"

"That's it," Inthmus fumed. "I'm going to find my way back to the military base first, and you'll all regret not listening to me. Are you coming with me, or not?"

I saw him give a sidelong glance toward Trace, who had remained silent ever since we were dropped off in the desert. She timidly grabbed onto the strap of her bag and walked over to Inthmus' side as he grinned victoriously.

"Trace," Selene asked in disbelief. "What are you doing?!"

"I'm going to follow him. You all know that I've been the outcast of your little group anyways. All of you spend so much time together, and even though I'm there sitting right next to you all, I feel so distant."

"And *he* is going to change that?"

"Yes, he will," Trace curtly finished.

"Are you stupid?! What made you want to follow that worthless, perverted, arrogant filth?"

In return, all Selene got back was an emotionless poker face.

"Let's go, Inthmus," Trace called, walking away without another glance back. Inthmus followed her, turning back to stick out his tongue mockingly. I stuck out my middle finger and flipped him off.

As a parting jab, Inthmus yelled, "Have fun with that little bastard! Maybe you can find some use for him!"

My body froze, blood turning to ice. I vaguely heard Selene and Serena yelling back at Inthmus, but my mind was swimming with questions. Did he find out that I was a Bastard? Or was he just making a general comment? I saw him walking beside Trace and remembered the purposeful glance he had shot me when he said that. He knew.

"He's such an idiot," Serena frustratedly growled, and I nervously glanced around to the rest of the people that remained, wondering if they had caught onto the nuance of Inthmus' insult. Fortunately, they were still hung up on the fact that Inthmus had left with Trace. With that, our large group, which had originally started with eight people at the get-go, was now down to four: Blake, Serena, Selene, and me. Looking at them, my confidence wasn't rising. Blake looked as if he was going through a mental breakdown and was curled up in a ball after seeing the brawl, and Serena was comforting Selene, who was sobbing uncontrollably under the shade of the stone arch. I could practically see the proverbial rain clouds hovering over their heads.

"Blake," I called. He didn't respond.

"Blake," I called again. His arms and legs twitched, and I could tell that he heard me.

"Blake!" I shouted in his ear. This time, he flinched violently, lashing out his fists toward my arms. I narrowly dodged it, and sheepishly grinned is his irritated eyes met mine.

"What do you want?" he growled. "Can't you see I'm going through a crisis here?"

"Not to be rude, but we don't really have time for that. Everyone that is going to leave has already left, which means that we need to keep moving so that we don't die out here."

Blake lifelessly kicked his feet against the ground, a cloudy expression forming on his face. It seemed so wrong. "What do you suggest we do? We don't have a single thing that can help us find our way back to the base since Dylan took the compass, and all we have is food and water."

"We have to try something, though," I pleaded. "Can't we follow the tire tracks and see where they lead us?"

"Do whatever you want."

I waited for him to add anything, a suggestion of what we could do, or something of use, but he remained silent. His eyes were devoid of hope and life, and his posture lacked strength.

"Serena! Selene! Can you come over here for a moment?"

I shouted. Serena whispered something into Selene's ear before bounding over to where we were standing.

"What's up? Selene will be here in a second. She's...well... you know."

I nodded morosely and waited for Selene to come over. Her face was a mess. Tears were still streaking down her cheeks, and the skin around her eyes was puffy and red. Every once in a while, she let out a choked sob.

"I know it's been a little rough, but we have to move forward," I encouraged. "We'll follow the tire tracks as far as they lead us, then we'll decide where to go from there. As we move, ration the amount of food and water you take in. We could be out here for as short as three days, or as long as a week. Please, don't lose hope."

There was nothing notably different about them even after my speech, but I smiled lightly as I saw their posture straightening as some form of life re-entered their eyes. As the sun began to shift, preparing for dusk, the hill and space under the archway were illuminated in a golden light. In the distance, I could see two groups of people moving in separate directions. They were marching along, making progress toward who knows where.

"Let's go," I suggested, and with all our belongings shouldered on our backs and our hope renewed, we set out into the open expanse, hoping that fate would smile down upon us on our journey.

# Chapter 13

*July 30, 2103*

· · · · ● ● ● · · ·

"SO, HOW ARE we going to sleep tonight?"

Once we hit the road, the hours had flown by quickly, the expansive desert not leaving much for entertainment or visual pleasantries. I led the group through a two hour stretch of walking with occasional ten-minute breaks in between. My legs felt like they were going to fall off. The sun was nearly hidden behind the rising horizon and the orange glow faded, giving way for the consuming night sky. I glanced down at my watch. It was 2044 hours, just about time for the nocturnal predators to start coming out of hiding.

"Let's get on top of that plateau and camp at the top. Alyssa was the only one with a tent, so we'll have to make do with a night under the stars," Blake suggested, while Serena and Selene groaned.

"Can't we sleep down here?" Serena pleaded. "It'll be so much easier than having to climb up all the way on top of the plateau."

Blake shrugged while giving Serena an indifferent "do what you want" kind of look. "If you want to sleep with the scorpions and snakes, be my guest. Just don't come calling for me when the desert hounds carry you off to their underground den and keep you for a late-night snack."

Serena's protests quickly died after that. Just as the sun was about to fully disappear around the Earth's bend, Blake found a sizable plateau that we could use as howls rang out in the distance. It wasn't tall, maybe around twenty to thirty feet above the ground. There were multiple jutting rocks that could easily be used as a foothold or handhold.

The top of the plateau was flat, covered entirely by a thin layer of yellow sandstone. While the others were setting up camp with the tarp I had given them, I peered out into the expansive darkness as the moon bathed the plain of cacti in an ethereal glow. In the distance, I could see a small pack of desert hounds rushing after a pronghorn. The stars were glowing brightly in the sky, twinkling mirthfully.

Something else also flickered near the horizon, like a star on the ground, out of place from its heavenly formation. Squinting, I gaze into the distance, seeking the small flicker once more. For a second, I wondered if I was seeing hallucinations, so I rubbed my eyes vigorously. But when I looked again, the small flicker of light was still there. The casted glow was white, shining brightly, contrasting with the darkness of the cave which served as its backdrop. But the glow was minuscule, and I only had the luck to catch it because I had been looking in the right place at the right time.

Curiosity ignited, I eagerly rushed to the others who were starting to get comfortable on the flat plateau. "Does anyone have binoculars or anything of the sort?" I gushed, and they perked up.

Serena started digging through her own pack and pulled out a pair of binoculars. With a flick of the wrist, she tossed them to me. I gripped it in my right hand but panicked as the smooth metallic barrel slipped out of my grasp. Fortunately, I was able to catch it before it tumbled down the plateau.

I turned around and grinned sheepishly, cringing as it was met by dull stares from the three who were sitting on the ground. Turning back toward the desert, I held the two lens holes against my eyes, training the small device toward the small flicker of light in the distance.

The image was a little bit blurry, but as I started adjusting the little knobs on the sides, the identity of the flickering light became clear. It looked like it was an overhead light for a building of some sort. Although it was still too far away to be seen for certain, I saw the faint outline of a small, warehouse-like building sitting inside a cave embedded near the base of a plateau in the distance.

Excitedly, I beckoned Blake over to where I was standing. He groaned and lazily walked over to me. "What is it? We were having a good conversation going over there."

Without saying another word, I shoved the binoculars into his hands and directed his eyes over toward the building in the distance. His breath hitched, so I figured that he must've spotted the small light and the building as well.

"So? What do you think?" I eagerly prompted.

"What even is that?" he whispered. "The building looks ridiculously small. Though, there might be some supplies in there that we could use. But that's like, twenty, thirty miles away. How the hell did you spot that?"

"Would you believe it if I told you I was looking at nature when I found it?"

"Hell no."

I shrugged my shoulders and sat down in between Serena and Selene. "Either way, that might be our ticket to getting more resources for this trip. It's definitely a detour from our original trail, but I figure that it might be worth a look, right?"

Blake started scratching at his imaginary beard while in deep thought. Under his breath, he muttered, "But that might compromise our original trail, and we might not be able to find it again. At the same time…"

It was almost like watching him fight an internal battle with himself. If we weren't in a life or death survival exercise, I might have laughed at him. Maybe. Suddenly, his back straightened, and his head shot up from where it was hanging previously. He stopped scratching at his imaginary beard.

"Alright, we'll go toward the building first thing in the morning. Let's get a good night's sleep, then we'll start heading there first thing in the morning. If we're lucky, we'll be able to get there by late in the evening tomorrow."

He seemed positively proud of the plan he had made although it was me that found the building in the first place. But for now, I let him have his little triumphant moment of glory and the two girls clapped away at his dramatic demonstration.

We let Serena and Selene settle down on the tarp that was laid on a flat portion of the plateau while Blake and I just took to lying down on the solid rock structure. It was slightly uncomfortable compared to the beds that we had been treated to back at the military base, but it was still good enough to sleep on.

Wishing each other goodnight, we fell asleep, and oddly, even though packs of desert hounds howled in the distance as they caught their prey, sleep came easily to me.

# Chapter 14

*August 1, 2103*

· · · · ● · · · ·

THIRTY MORE MINUTES of walking in the blazing heat, and we'd be at the building. I wasn't sure if this exercise was intentionally designed this way, but putting eight sixteen-year-olds in the Sonoran Desert during the summertime was pure sadism. General Bergen wanted us to suffer. Badly. It was only the third day, but calluses and blisters were already forming on the balls of my feet.

"When are we going to get there?" Serena complained, fanning her face with her hands. Sweat was pouring down her head as her feet dragged behind her.

"Serena, stop complaining. You asked that thirty *seconds* ago. We'll be there soon," Blake replied, annoyed by the constant pestering. He also seemed at wit's end, exhausted.

"Well, I'm *sorry*, but I'm annoyed that we've been walking for the past day and a half without finding anything interesting," Serena pouted. She began kicking up the sand, riling up a cloud. Selene, who was standing right behind her, walked right into it and erupted in a fit of coughing.

"Serena, stop that! You're getting dust into my hair!"

Serena obliged. Fortunately, the rest of the short trip was quiet, which gave me time to scan and take in the small building that we were arriving at. Just as I had seen two nights before, a large fluorescent light was dangling at the top of a tall lamp post next to the entrance: a single metal door stood between us and the inside of the building. It was dented in several places, but the knob handle was still intact.

The building itself wasn't that impressive, however. It was about the size of the room that we were given at the military base, and the exterior wasn't in a very good condition. The paint on the concrete was chipped off, and the metal layering was rusting. Parts of the roof appeared to be caved in as well. Even worse, I could hear the insects buzzing around in there even at this distance.

We looked at each other nervously while Serena and Selene looked at the building more in trepidation than excitement. Blake shrugged and started pulling at the doorknob. My heart throbbed in anxiety with every hollow thud that sounded as the door rattled in its frame. The building was locked.

"Shouldn't we knock?" I suggested, and Blake looked at me as if I was stupid.

"Look at the building. Do you think we should knock?"

"Good point."

After a couple of rougher shakes, the knob handle broke off while the door remained lodged in its frame.

"Jesus Blake, how much force did you pull the thing with?" Serena admonished.

He looked scandalized. "I wasn't expecting the whole damn thing to come off. I was trying to get the door open!" he exclaimed, throwing the broken handle on the ground.

Blake eyed the door and walked a couple of steps back. After taking a deep breath, he dashed forward and rammed his feet against the door near the strike plate. It shuddered but didn't budge. Only a small dent in the metal remained. Repeatedly, Blake continued to kick away at the door, the frustration showing on his face as his repeated attempts weren't getting anywhere. But finally, on his seventh try, the door creaked, and the frame itself fell with concrete dust flying every which way. A gathering of flies and other bugs started buzzing around like an angry swarm as they flew away from the building through a large hole in the ceiling. Carefully, we took the downed door and gently leaned it against the outer walls of the building.

The first thing that I noticed about the little place was the putrid smell. It was as if someone had intentionally filled an entire room with rotten eggs and other spoiled food. Clearly, no one had ever thought of checking back into this place. But besides that, the interior was quite uninteresting. There were two long desks lined up along the far back and left wall with an old computer that was completely caked in dust. The rest of the room was filled with filing cabinets with papers peeking out behind closed drawers except for the massive mound of debris in the middle of the room.

Blake walked in, and I half expected the floor to cave in underneath him. This place clearly hadn't had very much upkeep—if any at all—over the past few years. I took a deep breath of fresh desert air before following suit. Our boots clacked on the floor as we approached the desks sitting in the back.

There were multiple binders that were stacked on top of each other, and a quick flip through them revealed a collection of uninteresting information. It was full of budget reports, utility usage, and some other boring things that were laid out in rows upon rows of numbers. All the other documents were the same. Occasionally, there would be something about an experiment project, but the pages were torn apart to an extent where it couldn't be read. After maybe half an hour of sorting through the papers, the desk was cleared, exposing the dust-covered surface of the metal.

I faintly made out the outline of a large frame that was screwed onto the surface of the desk.

"Stand back," I warned. Taking in a deep breath, I blew a stream of air at the desk, riling up a cloud of dust. Wincing, I coughed a couple of times, waving away the cloud before looking through my teary eyes at the image inside of the frame. Even though the glass was still dusty, it was clear what we'd found: a map. Something that we had been hoping for since the beginning.

"It's a map," I announced in awe.

The others began animatedly shuffling toward the desk, the dust settling just enough to see the rough outlines drawn on the large sheet of framed paper. Just to the left of the center was a box labeled "Headquarters." Strewn across the map laid other buildings and landmarks. There was no visible scale, but at the very least, the map looked confined to just the nearby desert area.

"There. That's where we are," Blake suddenly declared. A finger slid onto the map, pointing at a small square located near the edge of the left border.

"If I have some time, I might be able to figure out where the military base is based on my calculations," Blake promised. "Can you leave me alone for a bit? You can scrounge around a bit more to search for supplies if you want."

We all nodded in agreement and left Blake to study the map while we explored the room. I started opening the small drawers on the other desk, hoping to find some kind of secret compartment. The other two split off to opposite sides of the room to scan the filing cabinets.

I blew at the desk, sending dust and a few loose papers flying into the air. This one was much less orderly than the other, and better matched the theme of the rest of the room: disorganized. It seemed like whoever had last been there meant to clean up but left in a hurry. Checking over the documents revealed nothing. They were pretty similar to the other boring reports that were scattered across the room: legal papers, pamphlets, and other documents. Frankly, it would be far too boring to actually read through them, so I just skimmed them over.

After shuffling through several stacks of papers, my hand froze on a crème-colored half sheet of paper that looked worn and torn. It was formatted very differently from the others, the clear differentiator being the half of a fading watermark labeled "CLASSI-" plastered onto the edge of the pages. The title at the top of the page read, "The Second Advent Project," but the rest of the page was missing. The other sheets of paper in that group were also torn up and folded, one even slightly chewed. The thought of what might have lived in this building made me shudder.

"Hey, are you done?" I called to Blake.

He looked up, shaking his head. "I'm starting to doubt myself. I don't think we're where I thought we were. I'm close to figuring it out, but there are so many buildings here with labels on them, so it's hard to pinpoint which one we're at. The direction almost matches up, but this plateau is way too close to the building to match. In fact, the whole scale of this map is skewed. It keeps on changing its ratio of inches to miles. It feels like we're really close to everything on here, but take that with a grain of salt."

"As long as we have a general direction of where to go, we'll be fine. Try to figure that out before anything. Do you need me to do anything?"

He started scratching at his imaginary beard again. "If you can figure out the label or name for this building, that would probably help."

I nodded in understanding before moving over to the binders full of report papers. They had various utility records, but the title showed different names for the building identification section on every single page. They were always two-letter labels followed by a number. NW-2, NW-1, NE-7, SW-12, and so on.

"Hey, Blake, do you know which direction we came from? Cardinal directions, I mean."

"No," he grumbled. "I was thinking the same thing you were, but Dylan had our only compass."

"Drat."

Silently, Blake continued to maneuver around the map, trying to figure something out. I gazed around the room, sifting through several more binders full of reports. On a whim, I left the building scouting around the outer perimeter. I looked around the doorframe, wondering if there was any kind of plate that would indicate where we were. To my dismay, the walls of the building were covered in sporadic patches of sand that covered up large portions of the concrete. Gently, I brushed some of the sand away from around the doorframe, and the wind gently blew away the dislodged sand, making it slightly easier to see. There, near the right edge of the doorframe, was a small metal plate caked in sand. I blew at the plate, sending the loose grains of sand away. *NW-3* it read.

"Blake!" I hollered. "NW-3!"

"Got it!"

I walked back into the room and saw Serena, Selene, and Blake all hovering over the map, their faces pretty much pressed against each other side by side.

"Is that good or bad?" I asked.

"Good and bad, more like," Selene responded. "All the bases are pretty much equidistant from this one building in the center called the 'Headquarters'. Beyond this system of buildings, the map doesn't show anything else."

"So, it's simple right? We have to go to the Headquarters," Serena chimed.

"Right…" I muttered hesitantly. "Blake, what do you think?"

"We don't have much of a choice, do we?"

"That's true."

Blake opened a couple of drawers of the desk we stood around and pulled out a thin screwdriver. He started unlodging the screws near the edges of the frame.

"What are you doing?"

"Trying to take the map out, just give me a second."

Just minutes later, he had the frame unscrewed from the table. He flipped it around and started undoing the screws that attached the mounting board to the frame. When it came off, he gently scooped the map off the glass, cradling it as if it were a newborn baby.

"Alright, I'm ready. Let's go," he said. "This place smells like death. I don't think my nose can handle this anymore."

"My nose couldn't handle this the moment we stepped in," Selene joked.

As the last person leaving the building, I grabbed the door and set it leaning against the open entryway. It stayed still, loosely lying in its original place. I sighed a breath of freedom and relief. It felt so much better to breathe fresh air rather than inhaling the toxic scent of rotting food and death.

"This feels so much better," Serena cooed, stretching her arms and legs.

Blake ignored her. "Alright, now that we know where we have to go, let's start moving. We need to make as much progress as we possibly can. Based on the map, it should be at most a two-day walk from here to the Headquarters. Maybe even a bit shorter if we can move faster. This is good, this is really good." For the first time during this trip, there was something positive to look forward to.

"What about the original route with the tire tracks? Won't we lose it?" Serena pondered.

Blake looked at her. "We have four days' supplies at minimum, six maximum. I'm not confident in gambling on our supplies lasting us until the end of the trip if we followed the tire tracks. We can't afford to risk anything right now. This is the desert. It's basically life or death," he responded.

We all nodded in agreement. Silently, Blake signaled for us to follow him as he led us toward the "Headquarters."

# Chapter 15

*August 3, 2103*

· · · · • • • · · ·

THE ROUND DOME of the building roof became visible over the peak of the hill as we continued to march forward. Its architectural style was almost Greek-like, except for the fact that the building was covered in a gray metallic sheen rather than pure white marble. It was much larger than the small room that we had found back in the desert—almost ten to twenty times bigger. Additionally, the building was surrounded by a single parameter of barbed wire fencing with warning signs hanging off it.

With rocks softly crunching underneath our feet, we approached the single gate that was on the path to the front entrance of the "Headquarters." It was already open, the steel fencing limply twirling around the gate joints. A guard tower was placed to the left of the pathway, but when I peered in, it was empty, the table and computer inside covered in a thin sheen of dust.

"What do you think we should do?" I asked, and the others looked at each other uncertainly.

Blake pushed forward and stepped past the gateway, sighing in relief after he made it through. I rolled my eyes. It was almost as if he was expecting to get electrocuted or something. He continued forward until he was standing right in front of the main entrance, and I looked back at Serena and Selene who shot uncertain glances at each other. Shrugging, I followed and stood next to Blake who was eyeing at the heavy metal door.

He asked, "You want to do the honors?"

"Nah."

He shrugged, then placed both of his hands on the doorknob. With a grunt of effort, he twisted the knob, and pushed at the door, only to find it locked, just like the other facility.

"Of course it's locked," Blake sighed, taking several steps back.

I hugged the left side of the doorway as Blake charged at the right door. He slammed his foot against the cold metal, right below the knob. When the door didn't cave on the first kick, he kept kicking at it until it finally came undone on his eighth try. As the door burst open, flying around the hinge, a loud boom resounded along with a loud male screech. Curiously, I looked in to find a sight that I was not ready for.

The room itself was designed fairly similar to the other facility. All four walls were covered in discolored blue paint, which had chipped away in some parts. Lining the walls were marble tables that were shoulder height, decorated by computers and papers which were strewn out in every direction. It was almost like how banks were set up. In the center of the room, a large pillar stood with a single door attached to its frontal face.

There, in the middle of the room, was the source of the screech. It was a pair of people. One was lying on the ground on top of a small cloth with blood pouring profusely from a wound on the legs while the other was looking towards us with sand caked all over his body and face.

"Well, look at what the wind brought in," the person said with faux, arrogant confidence.

"Inthmus?"

He jumped to his feet, mocking, "You all said that I wouldn't be able to find my way, but look now! I found my way here before any of you did! Even this dumb skank slowing us down didn't stop me."

I glanced to the side and saw Selene's eyes widening in recognition before she rushed past me and kneeled before the injured girl, who was lying down on the ground. "Trace! Trace! Can you hear me?"

She let out a low groan, shivering.

"What happened?!" Selene screamed, marching up to Inthmus. She was furious, her glare frosty with tears brimming the edge of her eyes.

Inthmus' smirk didn't lessen one bit. "She was being stupid, that's what happened. If she wouldn't have gotten in the way like an idiot, she wouldn't have gotten bitten by those desert hounds."

"What?"

"Some stupid desert hounds decided that I'd make a good meal and pounced at me. She got in the way, taking the bite instead."

Selene stared at Trace in disbelief. "So, she was trying to save you?"

"No, she didn't *save* me. She got in the way. I would've been fine either way."

Selene pounced. She knocked him down to the ground with a hard tackle to the body and straddled him, landing punch after punch on his face. "You...absolute...waste...of...space! Trace is worth ten, no, hundreds of you!"

I froze, transfixed by the spurt of blood that poured out

from Inthmus' nose and mouth before the shock wore off. Frantically, Blake and I rushed over to pry Selene off Inthmus. She was kicking, struggling, and screaming with righteous fury burning in her eyes as she glared at me, a shattered look in her eyes. My heart ached as I saw the endless streams of tears running down her face. "Why? Why are you defending him?"

"Because there are more important things to focus on. He'll get what he deserves. Go tend to Trace, she's not gone yet," I placated. Selene sniffed and leveled one last glare at Inthmus, who still smirked despite his bloodied face, before kneeling at Trace's side, gently rubbing her hands while whispering words of comfort. Serena sat on the other side with a small medical kit, trying to figure out something she could do.

"Ethan," Serena called with a concerned look on her face. "It's not looking good. She's lost a lot of blood. Her breathing is really shallow, and her body temperature is dropping."

"Do something, anything! Stop the bleeding!" I yelled.

Blake put a hand on my shoulders. "Calm down, man."

I took a couple of deep breaths, muttering, "Sorry."

Serena seemed conflicted, and she bit at her fingernails with a worried look on her face. After a short while, her face fell, and she shook her head. "I can't do anything. Not with what we have right now. There's nothing we can do to close to wounds completely, and I can't deal with the infection either. I would need a legitimate facility to work on her in order to patch the wound."

Any hope that Trace had of recovery appeared to dim by the second. "How long does she have?" I solemnly asked, and interestingly, Serena smiled.

"It's not like she's at risk of immediate death. She's lost a lot of blood, but the bleeding has slowed enough that it isn't the biggest problem. I'm more worried about the desert hound infection. But those take a long time to deconstruct the internal organs, so she has maybe a week. If we can get her to a hospital fast enough, she's still got a chance."

"That's good to hear," I muttered.

"Yeah, she still in danger though, unfortunately."

I sighed in relief, rubbing my eyes in exhaustion. "Alright, nothing we can do now that we're in this mess. Let's move her over toward the back and set up a camp. We can look through some of the supplies here later. "

"Ethan, maybe...maybe you have something that can help?" Serena asked hopefully. "Hannah must've taught you a bunch of cool stuff that you can use in these kinds of situations, right?"

Irritated, I growled, "No, she hasn't. I'm not her. I don't have the extensive knowledge that she does. Maybe you can ask for her 'pearls of lifesaving wisdom' if you ever meet her."

"I wasn't trying to..." she started but trailed off and looked down at the ground guiltily.

Unbelievable.

"Whatever just work on moving Trace to the back. I'll try to work with Blake to figure out what we can do from here on out and how to deal with...him," I finished, pulling Blake away from Selene and Serena.

He looked at me with his brows raised. "What was that all about?"

"Don't worry about it for now," I waved, seeing his confused look. "More importantly, we need a game plan from here on out. We can't just decide to hop from building to building. We'll set up camp and get ready to sleep. But after that, we need to plan. Is that good with you?"

He nodded, giving a sidelong glance at Inthmus. "Sure thing. I'll work with Selene to get the tarp and stuff set up.

You can start looking through some of the documents in the building if you want. Or, I guess you have a different problem to deal with..."

"Yeah."

Inthmus was still sitting on the ground with a smirk on his face. He didn't look remorseful in the slightest for the comments that he made before, but he also didn't try to move at all. He just sat there, silently. I glared at him angrily, but he showed no response.

"Actually," Blake started. "Maybe you should let me take care of him. Don't want you doing anything irrational."

"No, I've got this."

"No, you don't," Blake said curtly. "There's only four of us, six of us now. We can't afford you doing something reckless. Go set up the tarps and the camp, and we'll figure out a plan after that."

"Blake, you know I-"

"Ethan," he interrupted. "Come on."

I gave a sidelong glance to Inthmus, then spat at his feet. "Fine. Make sure he understands his place, though."

"Of course."

Reluctantly, I walked over to the far back corner of the room and pulled out the large black tarp out of my bag, draping it over the cold marble floor. The fabric flapped limply before settling down, covering the ground like a second skin.

"Hey. Need any help?"

I jumped in surprise and turned around to see Selene laughing softly as she saw me jump. "I didn't mean to scare you," she teased. "I was asking if you needed help, not trying to kill you."

"Don't do that," I warned exasperatedly. "What about Trace? Weren't you taking care of her? Is she doing okay?"

Her face visibly deflated. "Yeah, she's doing fine. We moved her over to the back."

Way to be a mood killer.

"C-Can you help me get the rest of camp set up?"

"Sure!" she beamed, and on the inside, I sighed a breath of relief.

For the next hour, Selene and I got into a comfortable rhythm fixing up some makeshift beds, getting some food prepared out of the limited things we had, clearing away some of the papers, and occasionally checking back on Trace.

"Thanks for helping out Selene," I thanked gratefully. "That would've taken a lot longer had you not helped along."

"No problem. It was fun watching you struggle to move those stacks of papers anyways."

"Hey!"

Selene started laughing, a clear, crystalline sound coming from deep within her throat. Her smile and laughter were genuine and contagious. I started laughing along with her, grasping at my stomach as it heaved up and down uncontrollably.

"Thanks for the laugh, I'm going to check on-"

"Blake?"

"Dylan?"

I whipped my head around, eyes darting toward the front of the room. In the doorway, a tall figure was leaning tiredly against the doorframe. The guy's entire body was layered with a thin sheen of dusty sand, and he was carrying someone else on his back. Only when I took a closer look, did I recognize the man to be Dylan.

He looked exhausted. His face was a pale white, and he was breathing heavily, body posture sagging as if he would collapse at any moment. Alyssa's body was limply lying on his back, and she didn't look any better. A trail of dried blood streaked down her face, her hair was disheveled, and several elongated scratch wounds marred her arms and legs. "It's a surprise seeing you all here. How did you guys find this place?" Dylan asked.

"That's my question. Where did you go after you left?" Blake asked curiously.

"It's a long story. C-Can you please help? Alyssa lost a lot of blood, and she isn't feeling too good. Anything will help, really! Bandages, water, anything!" Dylan desperately cried with increasing volume, glancing behind his back. Alyssa violently coughed, her whole body shuddering in pain.

Dylan collapsed onto his knees, Alyssa's body rolling off his back limply. Selene and Blake immediately dashed over, helping bring Alyssa toward the middle of the room, laying her flat on the floor in a recovery position. "P-Please," Dylan pleaded again.

I was conflicted. My body had forgotten, but in my mind, the memories were crystal clear. I still remembered the time Alyssa held me in a suffocating chokehold, spat at me, and berated me. Even as she looked a couple of steps from the doors of death, I only saw the arrogant, prideful, uncaring girl that she was.

A hand softly patted my shoulders. "Ethan," Blake warned. "She's still one of us."

Once again, my gaze drifted to the ground, where Alyssa limply laid. Dylan's pleading eyes looked up toward me, his weak gray eyes pleading desperately. I clicked my teeth. "Fine, do whatever you want."

I watched in silence as Blake ushered Serena over from Trace and explained to her the situation. Serena nodded and pulled out a bottle of saline solution, gauze pads, medical tape, and large bandages. Methodically, she began at the legs and started rubbing the saline solution against the wound with cotton pads. Every time that Serena made contact with the wounds, Alyssa would hiss, curling into a fetal position.

"What the hell happened to you two?" I asked Dylan, who was getting treatment from Blake. Fortunately, his wounds were only superficial, nothing life-threatening.

"We made a mistake," he sighed, rubbing his hands through his greasy hair. "We thought that we might be able to survive through traveling in the night, but we were wrong. As soon as nightfall hit, we were ambushed by a pack of desert hounds."

"How'd you get away?"

"We both had guns as a part of our pack. Nothing special, though. We managed to nab a couple in the head, and they ran off after that. They still got a good slash at us though," Dylan finished, glancing toward Alyssa's wounds with a downtrodden expression.

I shifted around nervously, not knowing what to say. What was I supposed to say, sorry? That didn't sound right though.

"Are your injuries okay?" Blake asked, glancing at the scratches which were now bandaged.

"Yeah, they only sting a little bit."

The air got uncomfortable, descending into an awkward silence. I sat on the cold marble floor, watching Blake and Serena tend to Dylan and Alyssa. Selene sat on the sidelines, making sure that Serena had room to work. After what seemed like forever, Serena stood up and stretched, shoulders and back popping after staying in one position for too long. A soft orange glow was being cast through the high windows near the top of the four walls surrounding us.

"I'm going to sleep, Blake," I said, standing up. "Goodnight."

"Yeah, goodnight."

I retreated to the corner of the room, laying on the cold, uncovered marble ground. The sound of Selene laughing along with Blake and Dylan about something lulled me to sleep.

I WAS RUNNING. The dream was all too familiar, having seen it repeatedly for the past year or so. But at the same time, it was different. Instead of the gray cityscape and pitter-patter of rain, the open expanse of the desert was spread out in front of me. The land was barren and flat, an unfamiliar setting compared to the plains filled with cacti that I had gotten used to.

A low growl came from behind me, and I whipped around, my eyes meeting the hollow red eyes of a desert hound. This was the first time that I had seen one up close. Although scary at first glance, the more I looked at it, the less I became afraid of it and the more I felt awed by its presence.

Its red fur was sleek and expansive, like an ocean of red. The two crimson orbs held intelligence which I had never seen in any other animal before. The ground shook under its powerful, confident steps. I slowly began to reach my hand out toward it. I wanted to touch its coat of fur, just once.

Suddenly, its peaceful, intelligent eyes turned ferocious, its jaws attempting to pincer my arms between its rows of jagged teeth. Panicking, I retracted my arms and backtracked as it began to growl. It started taking slow, calculated steps toward me, and all the color drained from my face when out of thin air, more desert hounds started appearing, flanking the original. Now, one had turned into twelve, and they were all growling at me.

Everything went dark. The sky had turned black, and the light from the sun had been snuffed out. Slowly, the desert hounds started picking up their pace toward me. I backtracked faster and faster until finally, my heart couldn't face my anxiety, and I ran. I turned around and ran away from the hounds as fast as I could as they were chasing me, howling like rabid beasts.

How long it had been since I had run this hard? For minutes, all I could hear was their howling and pounding as they chased after me. Suddenly, I felt a sharp pain shooting through my legs as one of the desert hound's teeth sank into my calves. They caught me.

I WOKE UP with a jolt, cold sweat trailing down my forehead.

"Ethan, are you okay? You were screaming," Selene asked worriedly. Her eyebrows were pinched together in concern, and I registered her soft hands pressed against my back, holding me up in an upright position.

"Yeah, I'm fine. Just a bad dream."

"Are you sure?"

"Yeah," I reassured. "Don't worry, it just…happens sometimes."

She nodded, but I could still see the concern in her eyes.

I looked around the room. Everyone else was still fast asleep, the deep glow of moonlight filtering through the small windows near the roof. A low campfire that had been set up at some point near the entrance was crackling softly. It was serene, almost as if we were out in the woods on a peaceful camping trip.

A low growling interrupted that thought. Selene's head also perked up in alarm. "What was that?" she whispered.

"I don't know."

Holding my breath, I listened intently with my ears cracked open, but couldn't hear anything. It was quiet. Almost too quiet, in fact, as if someone had put a dampener on nature's sounds. The bugs, which had been buzzing around all night before, were nowhere to be seen or heard, and an ominous wind blew against the building walls. But after a couple of minutes, standing there in trepidation with sweat pouring down my palms, I sighed in relief. It must've been my imagination, fear carrying over from my dream.

But I heard it again, the low growling sound coming from outside the building walls.

"Wake up guys!"

One by one, they jolted up, rubbing their eyes groggily. They congregated near me, confused, and in some cases, irritated.

"Are you stupid? What the hell are you doing in the middle of the night? Practicing for the circus?" Inthmus scathingly insulted.

"You're the last person I want to hear that from," I shot back. "Stop acting like you have any rights in this group."

He looked like he wanted to retort or even lash out at me, but a single threatening glance from both Blake and Dylan shut him down immediately.

"Ethan, what is this about?" Dylan asked. He was standing up, propping up Alyssa who was now conscious again. Oddly, she didn't meet my eyes. Her gaze remained fixated on the ground while a veil of pale blonde hair hid her face. I made a mental note to ask Dylan about her odd behavior later.

"Be quiet and listen."

For several seconds, the group held silent, listening.

Inthmus complained, "I don't hear any-"

A kick to his back prematurely ended his complaint. For several moments, I quietly listened as did everyone else. After the one-minute mark passed by, I started losing confidence but stiffened in alarm as multiple low growls came from the other side of the wall. Everyone else's postures also became rigid.

"No, no, no, no, no…" Alyssa whispered, clutching tightly onto Dylan's uniform until her knuckles turned white. Her whole body was trembling as she shook her head from side to side. "Not again…" she whispered fearfully.

Dylan whispered comforting words in her ear, to which Alyssa started visibly calming down.

"Blake, I'll boost you up to the window, and I want you to tell me how many there are out there. Also, if there's anything abnormal, let me know of that as well," I suggested. Climbing up one of the filing cabinets, I held my palms against each other and made a foothold that Blake could use. With a heave, I hoisted him high enough to see through the window.

He started counting, muttering, "One, two, three, four, goddammit."

We did the same with each wall, going around to the left, front, and right wall before coming back down to meet with the group.

"How many, Blake?" I asked, nervous about the answer.

"Around twenty. Twenty-three to be exact."

That didn't bode well.

"B-But, as long as we stay inside, we should be fine, right?" Serena reassured, seemingly more to convince herself than the rest of us.

Selene pointed at the door, being the cool voice of reason. "Look at that door and what poor condition it's in. Especially after you all kicked it in, the frame is loose. I had Dylan put it back in its place, but it's not going to hold for very long if the desert hounds start pounding away at it multiple at a time. We need to start preparing, making barricades, and creating a contingency plan just in case they do manage to break in."

"What do we need to find?" Serena timidly asked.

Selene glanced around the room. "Anything heavy. Although they're fierce, desert hounds have lithe bodies which shouldn't be able to plow through anything with considerable weight."

"We can use these," Blake said from one corner of the room. He was standing next to the large filing cabinets which were sitting in a neat row along the right wall. Grunting, he tried to lift one of them up, but only managed to get it slightly off the ground before he dropped it. "It's pretty heavy too."

"Ethan, Dylan, Inthmus, can you go help Blake stack the filing cabinets against the door?" Selene asked. Dylan gently laid Alyssa against the back wall, who kept on grasping at Dylan like a child reaching for their mother. He gently whispered in her ears, making her calm down.

"Why should I help, exactly? I say let them in and we can kill them once and for all," Inthmus confidently said, much to Selene's chagrin.

"If you want to be hound feed, then be my guest and leave before we start blockading the door," she threatened ferociously. "If not, get your ass over there right now!"

Inthmus jumped at the sudden shouting, and scrambled over and started pulling at the filing cabinets. I grinned and shot Selene a thumbs-up before hustling over to help Blake as well. The four of us together lifted the heavy filing cabinet and laid it down against the door frame. It barely stretched across to the outer edge of the frame, holding in place.

Something softly impacted against the door, shaking the loose doorframe a little bit.

"Hurry!" Selene cried in a frantic voice, worry starting

to cloud over her face. With each blow against the door, the frame was shuddering, the metal slowly caving in with each crash. My muscles were protesting, screaming as I continued to drag the heavy cabinets over toward the door.

Right as the door was seemingly about to cave in, we got the second cabinet stacked on top of the first. Soon enough, working with Blake, Dylan, and Inthmus while Serena was looking after Trace and Alyssa, we got all four of the filing cabinets stacked up against the door. It barely reached the top of the doorframe.

We waited with bated breath as the desert hounds continued to slam against the door and sighed in relief when the makeshift barricade held firm. Several sets of light steps moved away from the door. I exhaled, falling to the ground, exhausted. My muscles were aching from carrying around the heavy cabinets while my heart pounded from all the adrenaline. I hate to imagine what would've happened if they had gotten through. Sweat was already seeping through my military uniform, drenching the front and back while my hair stuck to my skull as if it was glued.

Sitting there on the ground, my mind was blank. I was starting to think that the timing of my dreams were no longer coincidences. The first time, probably not. The second time, possibly. But three times?

But I didn't have much time to mull over those thoughts. Just as everyone's adrenaline was seeping out of their systems, we heard several loud, pounding footsteps approach the door before something hard slammed into the wall of filing cabinets. If the last several pokes had been small bombs blowing against the wall, this was comparable to a nuke. The noise was thunderous, shaking the entire door frame and then some.

"Dammit," Dylan cried, biting his fingernails. He darted up, as did everyone else, and cried, "Ethan, Selene, Inthmus,

Blake, get more heavy objects to barricade the door. Serena, keep an eye on Trace and Alyssa and make sure that nothing happens to them."

"What will you be doing?" Inthmus asked, and Dylan turned around with a mischievous grin. "I'll be loading up the guns."

Before any of us could ask him what he meant, he dashed off towards the campfire, and started digging through his bag as we all ran to do our respective jobs. We found a couple of old computers that were just collecting dust, so we hefted them up, and stacked them behind the wall of filing cabinets. Just as we were about to put the last desktop on the stack, the barricade shuddered again, sending the stack of computers crashing down to the floor. Each collective barrage of hits against the barricade became harder and harder, and I could see the filing cabinets scraping against the floor as they starting to drift back.

"What the hell is making this noise?" I asked worriedly. "There's no way a single desert hound is creating this much force."

Just as I finished, another hit pounded against the door, shoving our barricade further back. I threw myself at the stack, desperately trying to force it back into place. It was a last-ditch attempt, and I was trying to draw up a backup plan before my body and the barricade gave in.

I peered back into the room, desperately looking for anything that could bail us out of the situation that we were in. My gaze shifted over to the door embedded in the pillar in the center of the room, which we had glossed over for the past couple of hours. Hope.

"Blake! Get the door in the pillar open! We need another plan just in case they break in!" I shouted, and he nodded, charging toward the door, kicking at the door frame.

"Idiot! Try to find a key first. If we cave that one in too, they'll be able to come into that door as well!" I shouted irritably. He froze in his tracks, and scrambled over toward the desks in the back, searching.

Meanwhile, the pounding was getting even harder and harder. It felt even worse than General Bergen's physical training exercises, the time that Dylan beat me during the arena exercise, and the time Alyssa beat me down combined.

"Any luck?!" I hollered.

"Just a second!"

My muscles were straining to hold back against each blow, and unsurprisingly, I was *losing*. With every consecutive blow, the filing cabinets were shifting back further and further, and now, there was an increasing gap between the cabinets and the doorframe.

"Found it!" someone jubilantly shouted. I heard the scratching sound of keys entering a keyhole just as another blow, the hardest yet, pushed me back another inch.

Hesitantly, I turned my head around and peered into the room we had just found. Nothing about the inside of the room was impressive. It was like a little storage room, maybe for a janitor. There were a couple of cleaning supplies propped up against the wall along with several canisters of liquid. Though, there was also a rack of handguns that didn't really seem to fit in along with the cleaning supplies.

"Get in!" Selene shouted, waving everybody in. I grimaced as another hard blow to the cabinet pushed me back another inch. Listening, I heard the soft steps of the desert hound moving back, and in a desperate toss-up gamble, I dashed out from where I was standing and rushed into the janitor room, just as the stack of filing cabinets came tumbling down.

"Close the door!" I shouted at Dylan, who was now holding a small R-MP submachine gun across his chest.

He didn't budge one bit. Instead, he tossed me the submachine gun and ran out from where he was standing near the entrance.

"Keep them at bay! I'm going to get Alyssa!" Dylan cried, dashing toward the back of the room.

I cursed Dylan for his lack of foresight and held the R-MP stock against my shoulders, eyeing the desert hounds through the small iron sights along the top of the gun. My breath hitched as they finally started filing in. There were so many of them, and that wasn't the scariest part. It was what came in last. The thing was *huge*. Towering maybe about two to three feet above the other desert hounds, it looked more like a lion than a desert hound. Its body was massive, and its aura just screamed "alpha."

"Inthmus! Get Trace!" Dylan desperately called from the outside.

Selene, Blake, Serena, and Inthmus were all still huddled inside of the small janitor's closet, shivering in fear as they stared at the pack of desert hounds that were now starting to trap us into a small semi-circular blockade.

"Inthmus! You heard him!" I shouted angrily, and he started shaking his head, his whole body shaking in fear.

"N-No way I'm going out there with all of them there bastard. Don't tell me what to do!"

I grit my teeth angrily, blood pumping through my veins at twice the speed with adrenaline coursing through my body. "Go! Now!"

"No!"

"If you don't go, I swear to God-"

"Swear to what? You gonna kill me or something? You'll be dead then even if you get out of this mess cause you're a bastard!" he taunted in a fearful voice.

A haze of red overcame my vision as I stared at Inthmus

in disbelief. The situation was now desperate. Dylan still hadn't come back, and the desert hounds were now starting to close in. My heart felt like it was going to explode. I didn't know what to do. *Do I start shooting? Do I go out there myself? Do I close the door?*

As the desert hounds took another slow step forward, on a move motivated by fury, I whipped around and pointed the barrel of the gun straight at Inthmus' head. "I swear to God if you don't go right now, I'll shoot a bullet through your head! Get your ass moving!" I cried in a crazed frenzy. With the desert hounds slowly approaching across the room, I couldn't even think straight at this point. I shivered in fear looking over at their rows of sharp teeth which glinted in the moonlight, just waiting to tear off my neck.

"Well?" I repeated.

Shaking, Inthmus started standing up. A growing wet patch formed near his crotch. His legs were shaking, and he collapsed back onto the ground. "I-I-I can't. S-Screw you!"

I shot a bullet on the ground right in front of him. "Move, *now.*"

The desert hounds had made it nearly halfway to the central pillar, and Dylan still hadn't come back yet. Inthmus, who was shaking now more than before with a pale face, staggered up to his feet, and dashed out of the room, hyperventilating. I heard the desert hounds growl as Inthmus' limping figure made its way around the corner. Cautiously, I trained the gun back toward the desert hounds and they paused as if sensing the threat of the weapon I was holding in my hands.

Suddenly, one of the hounds pounced prematurely, breaking away from the semi-circular formation of the group. Panicked, I shot rounds upon rounds of bullets, nearly going through five before I hit the one pouncing at me. The stray bullets flew every which way, only finding one more target to claim as a kill.

"Dylan!" I shouted desperately as the desert hounds started growling aggressively. Their bodies laid low, ready to pounce. As if he heard my cry, Dylan hobbled around the pillar corner, with Alyssa's flailing body cradled in his arms. He gently passed her over to Selene and Serena, who were still watching dumbly, shivering in fear.

"Ethan, close the door," Dylan commanded.

I shook my head, grasping the gun tight enough for my knuckles to go white. "No, there's still two of us out there."

"Ethan, close the door."

"No."

Another desert hound leaped at me, and I let another fury of bullets reign down upon it, the small metal capsules flying in every which direction. Their growling became more predatory and aggressive, and they started moving forward in more methodical steps, picking up the pace.

"Ethan-"

"No, I can't! I won't. I won't. I won't," I muttered, vision crossing as I focused on the incoming predators. The gun was now trembling in my hands, my whole body shaking along to its rhythm. My legs felt like jelly, but they stayed rooted in their knee-locked position. Another two desert hounds pounced, and I slammed my finger against the trigger, letting the bullets fly. I never took my hands off the trigger, even when the magazine ran out of bullets and started dry firing.

My breath hitched as the desert hounds pounced toward me, coming closer and closer with their maws glinting in the light. It almost looked like they were smiling, looking forward to their next meal. Suddenly, I felt someone pulling me back as a hand darted across my vision and grasped at the door handle.

"No, don't-"

The door slammed shut with a large whoosh of wind as several desert hounds crashed into the other side soon after. I heard them retreating away from the door, and for minutes on end, I continued hearing hoarse screams of pain that echoed through the four walls of the janitor's room. Then, there was a brief silence, before a chorus of howls filled the night air.

The gun I had in my hands clattered onto the ground, and my legs finally gave out. As I sat on the ground, I curled up into a small ball and started sobbing.

# Chapter 16

*August 4, 2103*

· · · · ● · · · ·

T HE SOUNDS OF choked sobbing echoed in the small room for minutes on end. In the corner, Serena and Selene were trying to console each other, holding each other's hands while Serena cried into Selene's shoulders. Their eyes were puffy and red, cheeks flushed red with clear trails running down their cheeks; they cried until they went to sleep, leaning on each other by the wall. In another corner, Blake was resting while Alyssa laid on Dylan's lap as he stroked his hands through her blonde locks.

I cried until I could no longer bring myself to cry any longer. My entire body felt drained—emotionally and physically.

"Dylan, why?" I growled, disappointment and anger filling my veins. "You *knew* that Inthmus would've made it through."

"There was no other choice," he sighed. Dylan also looked haunted, and it reflected in his dead eyes. "Just one more second and the desert hounds would've made it in. Then, we'd all be dead, just like them."

"But we could've-"

"No," he cut sharply. "We couldn't have done anything.

Face the facts. We did all we could but still failed. They're not coming back…"

I grit my teeth. Blood pounded inside my head, heart throbbing, and I was ready to just beat Dylan to a pulp if nothing just to satisfy my anger and grief. But I couldn't bring myself to do it, because I knew that he was right. Dylan had made the best choice in that situation, saved the most people, yet this was the outcome we got.

That realization didn't help, though. My head was still throbbing from all the tears I shed, and my face felt numb. The sounds of Inthmus' pained cries from hours before was still ringing inside my head, over and over again like a broken record on loop.

"We could've saved more people," I repeated in a soft whisper. My voice felt weak, and I knew deep down in my heart that there was no truth behind my words. They were mere empty hopes. Dylan looked at me in pity but didn't say anything. He just continued weaving his hand through Alyssa's hair as she dozed away. As she slept, her face was settled in a peaceful smile, lips slightly ajar. It was a complete one-eighty from her pained look last night.

"What happened to her?" I asked, a question that I had meant to ask before all hell broke loose. "And what makes you care for her so much?"

He hummed in thought, and after a while, explained, "I think she broke. She's not a very open person, and she had a somewhat…difficult home life. Not many people gave her love, and it was made worse by the fact that she lived in a harsh environment in the outer sectors. Maybe the shock from the desert hounds was the last straw. Don't tell her I told you this though."

I nodded. "But why? Why do you care about her so much? Didn't you just meet her recently?"

He shook his head, to my surprise. "Not really. Alyssa used to live in Sector 213 when she was younger, but a foster family took her in, and she moved to Sector 66 later on. I met her there at the Academy. We weren't close at all, though."

That was surprising. I had gotten the impression that everyone at Camp Daedalus was from different sectors across the country. Her story sounded familiar though, as I thought back to Carter. "Why was she treated that way, though. Was she a…?" I trailed.

Dylan caught on to what I was saying. "No, no, no. She wasn't a Bastard child. Just someone who was dealt a bad hand in life."

"Oh."

For whatever reason, I felt my heart sink in sadness when I heard that. Although I should've been happy, I suddenly felt a lot lonelier than I had been just a few seconds ago. I peeked back at Dylan, who was looking at Alyssa with a fond expression on his face.

"Hey, I'm going to go to sleep. Wake me up when the others start to wake up," I said.

"Alright."

SOMEONE GENTLY SHOOK me awake, and I opened my eyes to see Blake's face inches away from mine, peering down at me. "Hey, everyone's starting to wake up."

I nodded to him gratefully and pushed myself off the cold ground. "What time is it?"

"Somewhere around ten in the morning. You really slept like a rock."

The atmosphere in the small closet was a lot less teary

and sad compared to a few hours ago. Instead, it was replaced by dullness and bitterness as last night's events and the cold reality settled in. Serena was still curled up in a tight ball with her head stuck in between her legs. In comparison, Selene looked a lot better. Her face was still puffy from all her crying, but her eyes were a lot less hollow, and there was a small spark of life.

"How is everyone doing?" I asked. Stupid question.

Mumbled groans and incomprehensible noises came in response. Dylan was standing up, his ears pressed against the door of the storage closet while Blake went up and down the rack of handguns, picking each one up experimentally.

"Are there any that we can use, Blake?"

He didn't respond, continuing to lift and set them down in silence. After a while, he picked out three guns and tossed one to me. "Yeah, there are about three that are usable. You take one, Dylan, grab this one, and I'll carry another."

I fumbled around with the gun as I felt the sudden weight in my hands. Experimentally, I ran my hands over the smooth body, and for some reason, it felt natural in my hands, unlike the bulky R-MP from last night. I looked at the gun and back toward Blake skeptically. "Are you sure?"

"Who else can wield a gun right now?" Blake asked rhetorically. "We need to get moving as quickly as we can. I pray to God that our supplies out there are still intact because if not…"

I didn't need him to finish the sentence to know what he was implying. "What the situation out there Dylan?" I asked, watching his mouth dip into a frown.

"I can't hear anything," he said worriedly. "Everything seems quiet out there, but that's also what's making me nervous."

His hand rested on the brass knob of the door. "Have the guns to fire, just in case."

A soft metallic scratched echoed off the walls as Blake pulled back the slide, loading a bullet into the chamber of his pistol. I mimicked him and held the small handgun at eye-level. Dylan nervously gulped and slowly turned the knob of the door. A short, soft click resounded as the door unlocked, and the door scraped against the floor in a high-pitched screech as it swung open slowly.

I wasn't sure what to expect, but what I saw nearly made me puke. Dylan immediately closed the door with a heavy pant, glancing back toward the girls. If they had seen any part of what was outside, they didn't give any indication of it.

"Alright, Blake, stay in here. Ethan and I will go through the rest of the supplies and bring whatever is left back here. They don't need to see all of that," Dylan commanded. He acted confident, but his voice was trembling as well.

Blake nodded briskly, his face green.

Dylan glanced at me and nodded. He opened the door slightly, leaving a small gap so that we could fit through, and quickly slammed the door shut behind us. I glanced to my right. A large crimson stain was splattered next to the pillar, leaving a large mark on the floor and close wall. Several sets of red paw prints drew several lines toward the entrance and led outside.

"Ethan," Dylan snapped when he was my dazed expression. "Let's hurry up and get everything we need."

I nodded sharply, and while Dylan went over to the supply bags near the entrance, I moved toward the back and dug through the bags that were in our camp. Fortunately, all of them were still left intact, the inner contents undisturbed. I hoisted the four bags onto my shoulders, stumbling due to the added weight.

"I'm done here!" I shouted to Dylan. "How about you?"

From the front of the room, Dylan nodded. "I'm also done. Is everything still intact for you?"

"Yeah, how about you?"

"Same thing, none of it's damaged. We got lucky."

I grimaced and nodded. "Yeah…"

We congregated back near the entrance of the pillar and knocked twice against the metal door. "Blake, we're coming back in."

With the six bags on our shoulders, we dashed back into the room. Blake's head perked up, and he gave a sidelong glance to the girls who were dumbly sitting in the corner. "Are we in the green?"

"Yeah, somehow," Dylan replied. "How are they doing?"

"We're doing fine," Selene muttered mutely with a frown. "Serena's still in a little bit of shock, but she can start moving whenever you need her to."

I was going to tell her that she didn't need to push herself, but I looked into her eyes and saw a firm determination hiding the mountain of sadness she was feeling. Nodding, I turned to Alyssa, who was now awake. "How are you feeling?"

"I'll be fine," she curtly replied.

I gave her a second glance and nodded. "Alright, we're going to have to move out soon, so just be ready." She nodded, then returned to staring back down at the ground as Dylan looked at her, concerned.

Tiredly, I raked a hand through my hair, sighing in exhaustion. I wasn't sure what I was supposed to do in that situation. Did I comfort them? Lead them on? Fortunately, Blake made that decision for me.

"Hey, I know this is all a little shocking, but we need to move on. If not for ourselves, then for them," he said, downtrodden. "They wouldn't have wanted us to mope around like this. They would've wanted us to move forward."

His short speech was a little cliché and abrupt but still lit a rejuvenating fire under everyone. Some semblance of strength returned to Serena and Selene as they stood up, as did Alyssa. Dylan warned, "It's a little bit...disturbing out there. Do you think you'll be okay?"

Alyssa and Selene nodded while Serena looked uncertain. Seeing this, Selene whispered a couple of inaudible words into Serena's ear, to which she nodded in response. Selene moved around behind Serena and gently cupped her hands over her eyes. "Is this okay?" Selene asked. Serena nodded once.

Dylan looked around the group once more, nodding as he only saw resolute expressions. He grasped the door handle and opened it. As soon as Selene and Alyssa saw the crimson stains on the ground, they balked and made silent vomiting expressions as they walked past it. Dylan immediately made a beeline toward the exit, and I was following him until something caught my interest out of the corner of my eyes. I leaned in toward him and silently whispered, "Hey, I just saw something over there by the cabinets. Lead them away from here, and I'll catch up."

He raised his eyebrows curiously but didn't protest. I nodded to him in thanks and broke off from the group toward one of the fallen stacks of paper that had become dislodged from the filing cabinets. As I was sifting through the fallen papers, Dylan made it out of the entrance, leaving me alone in the building.

The stack of papers itself was not what interested me, but rather, it was what was written *on* it. A red watermark, this time in full print, marking "CLASSIFIED" was inscribed on the pages, and a large printed title on the front page spelled, "The Second Advent Project."

When I flipped through the pages, I gleefully found images upon images of diagrams that had long blocks of text that explained them. Eagerly, I stashed the packet into my bag before running out, having acquired what I stayed behind for.

The others were already far away, gathered near the gateway at the edge of the facility. Serena, Selene, and Alyssa were sitting down on the ground tiredly while Blake and Dylan were talking in hushed whispers. As I got closer, Dylan curiously asked, "What kept you?"

I pondered telling them, but instead lied, "There was something that caught my eye. It wasn't what I thought it was though. Just a bunch of stupid papers."

Dylan looked at me skeptically, and I prayed that he didn't delve into the issue further. Thankfully, he dropped it. If he had caught onto the lie, he didn't say anything to indicate that. He turned to the rest of the group, and asked, "Where do you all want to go from here? We don't know where we are with respect to the military base, and we still have about four days of supplies left."

Serena and Selene shrugged, while Alyssa didn't give any response.

"I think I know a place," Blake suddenly announced. He was scratching his imaginary beard.

"Well?" Dylan prompted. "Spit it out."

Blake dropped his bag down on the ground and started rummaging through it. Gently, he pulled out a large, rolled-up sheet of paper which I recognized as the map from the small building we went to three days ago. He unfurled it out in front of us, and flattened it down on the ground, pointing, "Look at the very edge over there, near the northern section of the headquarters."

I only saw several buildings dotted there on the map. "This doesn't help," I chided.

"No, no. Look *closely.*"

Humoring his request, I took a second look toward where he was pointing his finger. It was literally on the edge of the map, right up to the start of the elegant map border, but to my surprise, there was a small rectangular box that almost seemed like it had been added as an afterthought. A long, faded inscription read, "Transitional Facility."

"It says something about a 'Transitional Facility'. I don't know what that is, but it's marked quite explicitly here in this map," Blake started eagerly, tapping the map with his fingers. "Judging by the patterns that these people have made in their mapping, I'd say it's another building for sure. Even if it's not, it'll get us closer to the edge of the desert, meaning civilization. They don't just call it a transition for nothing, I'd assume."

"Have we just given up on the exercise?" a voice interrupted. We turned around to see Serena who had a worried look on his face.

"Are you serious? We've been put through all this and all you're thinking of is the damn exercise?!" Dylan angrily growled. Serena's expression dropped as she stared at the ground nervously.

"T-That's not what I meant," she corrected. "There are consequences for abandoning the exercise, right? T-That's what I'm mainly worried about. Being a traitor...that's execution, isn't it?"

We exchanged silent glances between each other. She did raise a good point.

Dylan angrily started, "I don't care if abandoning this damn exercise has a consequence. If we try to keep going as we are, we're going to die, and that'll be the last damned consequence you'll ever face."

"I disagree," Blake shot back, shaking his head. He added, "Not because I agree with General Bergen and this exercise, but the last time we failed a survival exercise, he sent us on another one. There could be worse waiting for us if we fail."

I watched them banter back and forth until Dylan and Blake both stared at me expectantly. "W-What?" I questioned, nervously looking back and forth between the two.

"What do you think?" they chorused, and I froze.

Stammering, I responded, "Why are you asking me? Ask Selene and Alyssa before asking me."

Alyssa shook her head. "No comment."

Selene held her hands up in surrender. "I'll say that I agree with Dylan for this one."

That brought the argument back down to an equal footing. Blake and Serena wanted to try and find their way back to the military base while Dylan and Selene wanted to move forward. I considered the pros and cons of making each decision. First, a definite con for sticking with the exercise was death. There was no way to know whether we were going to find the military base before our supplies inevitably ran out. On the other hand, the Transitional Facility was close enough that we could probably make it on our current reserves. That made it an easy decision.

"Alright, let's go," I called, to their confusion. "Let's go to this 'Transitional Facility.' Sorry Blake, but Dylan is right. We have no idea if we're going to be able to make it through until we reach the military base on the supplies that we have right now. I'm not going to bank on a probability game when it comes to dealing with our lives. Also, we don't even know if this transitional facility is out of bounds for this exercise."

He nodded solemnly, even though he looked disgruntled

about my decision. "Alright then, lead on man," Blake said bitterly.

"Sorry man. Let's go," I called. Everyone stood back up with their bags hanging off their backs. They still looked tired, their legs dragging behind them as they walked, but I didn't have any choice but to push them forward. I led them up a hill near the back of the headquarters in silence, trying to get as far away from the facility as I possibly could.

Although I didn't let anyone know, the screams that I heard during the short minutes in the evening were still ringing inside of my head, driving me crazy. It was like an itch that continuously clawed at my mind, trying to tear me apart. When I looked ahead, all I saw was the boring expanse of desert, so my attention was easily shifted toward the sound, which screeched in my ears like a death toll.

The long hours of marching through the desert was procedural, marked by nothing but passing cacti and occasional scurrying animals. We were on an escape mission, to survive and get the hell away from the memories of the headquarters. That also meant that the journey was unbelievably boring since much of the walk was in pure silence. We didn't talk a lot because everyone knew that once the floodgates opened, the conversation would become inevitably shift toward the events the night prior. Though, around 1400 hours, someone found a reason to talk.

Serena's shrill voice screamed in surprise, "Oh God, what is that?"

I turned towards the group, all looking toward something in the distance. Their trail of sight led to a bloodied carcass lying half-buried about a hundred feet to the right. They were so affixed onto the sight, and they couldn't tear their eyes away from it even when I called out to them, "Hello, can we please keep moving?"

The large creature was torn apart from its stomach,

dried blood splattered on the ground around it. Flies were swarming around its carcass with an angry buzz. Personally, I didn't understand their fascination. Yes, it was gory, but we had more important things to do. Most of all, I didn't want to waste time gawking over it, but a few people decided to break formation and approach it anyways.

"Hey, it's a pronghorn! I didn't know these things lived in the desert!" exclaimed Blake, trying to further lighten the mood. Perhaps I had misread the situation. If anything, they seemed more interested rather than disgusted.

"Well, they've lived in the desert for a long time, actually. They've just moved much deeper into the desert because of people. It did them really well too," Alyssa noted sarcastically. "Since they're almost extinct now because of other invasive species and predators."

Despite the morbidity of the information, a few giggles and exhales of exasperation arose from the group at the irony of what she'd said. I could almost feel the heavy atmosphere being lifted a little bit. "Alright campers let's keep chugging along, but keep up the factoids. They seem to be popular in these parts," I encouraged, which was met with some giggles.

Passingly, as we continued to walk, I noticed that the landscape had changed. The flat desert plains filled with cacti gave way small sand dunes while Dylan's compass was directing us toward a particularly large dune in the distance. All the while, small chatter continued in the group behind me, and I chuckled every time I heard the crude jokes that would be popped in occasionally. Despite my desire to join in, I kept my eyes and focus on the road ahead, keeping a lookout for anything of significance.

"How are you holding up?"

I turned to see Selene, who had broken off from the rest of the group and approached me with a small smile. "I guess

I'm doing fine. It's only been what, one or two hours since we've left after all."

"That's good, we don't want you burning out too quickly," she joked.

Although I don't think I showed it outwardly, I appreciated Selene's efforts to make small talk. The continuous chatter that was happening without me was making me feel a little excluded and lonely.

"How is everyone else holding up?" I curiously asked.

"They're doing fine. A little bit thirsty, but Dylan's keeping them going with a little bit of encouragement."

"Good. How about you? After...you know."

Her smile dimmed a little, and she responded, "It was a big shock. Trace was one of the people that I became best friends with during the camp, but now she's just gone. I haven't really decided what to feel about it yet. Right now, it's just a dull pain throbbing in my chest."

I walked beside her, not really knowing what to say. An uncomfortable silence fell between us as I racked my brain on how to answer her. The silence extended on for too long, and I remained mute, failing to answer her. We just continued to walk in sync, not saying a single word to each other.

That brought us to the top of the dune I had my sights set on. Unfortunately, I was met with a less than desirable view. A rough, rocky terrain lay ahead, covering much of the horizon. It went on for miles, and it was directly in the path that we needed to take. I turned back toward the rest of the group and asked, "What do you think? Stop here or move on?"

"Well, it certainly doesn't look good, does it?" Dylan examined. "But at the same time, we don't really have a choice. We've been through worse. Pull out the map again?"

I turned to Blake who fumbled around in his bag and

rolled out the long map. Blake peered over my shoulders and looked toward the small area we were walking into. After a couple of minutes of hums and snorts, he exclaimed, "Well, at least it's looking good. See, the rocky terrain ends just over there. Once we reach it, we'll be home free. In a manner of speaking."

"Alright, then we'll continue moving toward that direction," I paused and pointed towards the rocky landscape. "That's going to be one hell of an obstacle. I don't know how long it'll take us to get past there, and I sure as hell don't know how long it'll take us to get around. We have two choices then, we can go through, or go around.

"Going through adds some level of danger, especially if we're tired. It's tall and bumpy, almost mountainous. Though, there's probably a higher chance of having a water source there. On the other hand, going around is slower but safer. We've been walking desert for long enough that we know what'll be waiting for us. The problem would be our supplies and trying to stay on track. I can't guarantee I can keep track of our location without any notable landmarks. So, thoughts?"

Immediately, Serena had her decision made. "I want to go around. This rocky terrain doesn't look too great," she said nervously. Her eyes were scanning the area with fear and paranoia.

"I disagree," Alyssa countered in a low tone, speaking up for the first time in a while. "It might be risky, but dehydration is a lot riskier. If we try to go around, it's the same risk as trying to continue our mission. We'll never make it."

Selene nodded and agreed wholeheartedly, to my surprise.

"Alright, I guess we're moving forward," I called. My next goal was just to find a suitable, flat area to camp for the night. Though it wasn't yet very late, setting up camp would be difficult in the region we were walking into, and I wanted to prioritize finding a safe location. Especially after yesterday.

The desert quickly transitioned into stonier terrain. As I looked around, I had the fleeting thought that the combination of sandy rocks, clays, and distant structures really made it feel like I was in some kind of ancient desert civilization. I was simply leading my tribe on a hunt for materials or food. Though that was the last situation I wanted to be in, having to search for supplies in this wasteland.

I turned back to see how the others were doing. Though the chatter had died down quite a bit, they, for the most part, still seemed optimistic. Well, I could say that for everybody except Serena. Selene, and surprisingly Alyssa, were still consoling her with their arms wrapped around her shoulders. She seemed to be lost in her own world, her eyes almost empty. She wasn't at all the happy self she had been before, nor did she show any signs of it. Though it was to be expected after that large shock, it still seemed very out of place.

Then, I noticed the condition of everyone else. They weren't fairing very well. Although I had given plenty of time for people to rest during the day-long trip, I could tell some people were getting tired, especially after a mostly sleepless night. Their legs were visibly shaking, and their eyes twitched in exhaustion. It was only about 1900 hours, but we'd already had a rough enough experience that I was willing to put the lost time behind us.

Luckily, we only had to traverse about another mile of the rocky terrain before we came across a choke point where we decided to rest. Ahead of us, a ravine was carved into the ground, a large drop several hundred feet deep, likely crafted by an old, dried-up river that ate away at the soft sandstone. The bottom was clouded by a mysterious shroud of darkness, invisible to the naked eye.

There was a bridge spanning the gap not too far away, as

well as several rock features. It was almost like a small clearing in a forest, though instead of trees we were surrounded by sand and stone. It felt cozy enough, though, and it was almost like our own private getaway.

"This looks like as good of a place as we're going to get." I turned and walked closer to the group. "Let's rest for a while and set up our camp. We can eat and sleep well before tomorrow, but tomorrow is going to be a long walk."

Mostly everybody nodded back and broke, sitting on rocks or deciding to lie on the sand. This area had enough rock formations that were flat so that everyone could have their own private space, too. I approached Selene, who was sitting at the top of a tall rock formation and was staring off into the horizon. She must've seen me approaching because she started talking to me.

"This is some mess of a situation we've gotten ourselves in, isn't it? When I got in the car to go to Camp Daedalus, I sure didn't expect to be lost in the desert, being led by someone who I'd never met before."

"We're not bringing that up anymore, Selene. I can agree, yeah, it's really been hectic, and I never expected to see myself here. But we're going to make it out of here, trust me," I responded.

She turned her head to meet my eyes. "I believe in you."

Those four words made me feel more confident than before, some of the previously existing uncertainty washing away. My heart felt more at ease, and a tingling sensation went up my arms. "Thanks."

We sat together on that rock for some time, silently staring up at the slowly darkening sky. I wouldn't have minded staying there forever, just sitting there enjoying nature had Blake and Dylan not called, "Ethan! Help us set up camp!"

Selene softly laughed. "You should probably go help

them. I'll help Alyssa watch Serena a little bit. Now shoo," she teased.

"You-, I-,"

"*Go,*" she chided with soft laughter.

I snorted and stood up to go and help Dylan and Blake but looked back one last time. Selene's hair, which was now disheveled from dry sweat, blew in the breeze loosely, and her pensive black eyes stared up at the sky. In a burst of inspiration, I stammered, "Selene, i-if we do manage to get out of this, w-would you mind hanging out later? Maybe when we're back in the sectors."

She looked surprised, but smiled nonetheless, "Ethan, we *are* going to get out of this, and of course, I'd love to."

I grinned, then went over to help Dylan and Blake who saw my face and wore a pair of grins themselves.

"Well someone looks peachy," Dylan joked, wiggling his eyebrows.

"Shut up."

Blake gave a silent message to Dylan, who nodded. In chorus, they chanted mirthfully, "Ethan and Selene, sitting in a tree, K-I-"

"Piss off!"

# Chapter 17

*August 5, 2103*

· · · · ● · · · ·

I FOUND MYSELF BACK in the headquarters, straddling the doorway of the janitor's closet as the desert hounds continued to pile into the room. A peek behind me made my heart race. Instead of the small janitor's closet, I saw an endless drop that went on for miles on end, and I was standing right on the edge. My hands were empty, and I didn't see the R-MP that had saved my life before anywhere in sight.

I waited and waited for the desert hounds to charge at me, bite at me, or do something, just to end this dream. Instead, they just stood there in a semi-circular formation as the "alpha" stared at me with its pale crimson eyes.

*"You're a lost child,"* a voice rang. The low baritone voice was powerful and commanded authority, it's reverberating voice filling the nearly empty room. Somehow, I knew in the back of my mind that was the "Alpha" hound's voice.

"No, I'm not," I shot back angrily.

It snorted. Before my eyes, the other desert hounds turned their backs and faded away while "Alpha" continued to stare at me. My collar tightened around my neck in a suffocating chokehold, and I felt as if "Alpha" was digging into my soul. *"What else do you call a child who does not know his friends, does not know his enemies, and also does not know himself?"*

"That makes no sense," I protested, still trying to get over the shock that I was talking to a desert hound. A dream one at that. "I have friends, I have no enemies, and I know who I am."

A deep rumbling sound came from the depths of "Alpha" throat, and I grit my teeth as hollow laughter rang through the small space. The ground below me began to shake until the laughter subsided.

*"Your answer proves my point."*

"Then tell me," I rebuked. "If you know the answers, then tell me!"

Somehow, I felt the disappointment that "Alpha" was feeling, and it made my heart burn in anger. Yet, I felt like I was missing something, a vital piece of a puzzle that just didn't click.

*"Figure it out yourself."*

Suddenly, the ground below me started shaking, and the entire cliffside started breaking apart. The marble floor of the headquarters started crumbling into fine little pieces, falling into the dark void behind me.

*"You will never amount to anything because you do not know the way. You do not know how to accept yourself and move on from the past."*

"What the hell does that even mean?!" I growled. Everything was fading into a pale red as my blood pounded inside my in rhythmic pulses. "What the hell are you?"

The ground beneath me shuddered once more, and I lost balance, feet slipping on the sharp edge of the cliff. My heart was pounding, shaking my entire body along with its panicked beats as I started falling backward.

The last thing I heard was reverberating laughter. *"You still do not understand? I am..."*

I JOLTED UP to my feet as a loud scream followed by sobbing pierced the air. When I opened my eyes, I hissed in pain as the morning lights burned my retinas. The sound was coming from far away, maybe just a couple of hundred paces to my left.

"Ethan, Ethan, wake up!" a panicked voice shouted. Someone's hands grasped my shoulders and shook me roughly. "Ethan, now!"

Through bleary eyes, I sat up and saw Blake's panicked expression. That rang alarm bells in my head. Blake was rarely panicked. "What the hell is going on?" I asked. "It is another desert hound attack?"

"No, it's-"

"Serena! Serena!" a screeching voice sobbed. To my left, I saw Selene crumpled on her knees as Dylan held her in a tight embrace, gently rubbing her back in small circles. Dylan met my eyes and shook his head solemnly.

"What happened?" I asked Blake, who had his eyes downcast.

"Maybe it'd be better if you saw for yourself."

Blake pointed a finger toward the ravine that Selene was kneeling in front of and felt my heart sink. Trembling, I pushed myself toward the edge of the cliff, and leaned over, staring down at the hundred-foot drop. What I saw almost made me vomit and I turned my head away, eyes closed on sorrow and regret.

At the bottom of the ravine, the morning sun illuminated the ravine floor, and I saw Serena lying there, arms and legs twisted in an abnormal angle while a pool of red painted the ground. I whipped around to Blake, who was staring at the ground with a pained expression on his face. "When the hell did this happen?" I growled angrily.

Selene erupted in another bout of tears, and I looked down ashamed. I whispered a silent apology to Dylan who was glaring at me and walked over to Blake, taking him away from Dylan and Serena. "What happened?"

"I don't know."

"What do you mean, 'I don't know?'" I growled angrily. "Why do you not know?"

Blake glared back at me. "I just woke up too, man. Stop placing the blame on people. Here, Serena left this on top of her bag, probably before she…"

I nervously took what seemed like a small piece of cloth off Blake's hand before inspecting it. The fabric itself was thin, and sandy colored just like the military uniforms. A small inscription was scribed on its frontal face.

"Sorry, but I can't do this anymore. Selene, Ethan, I'm sorry."

It was a short message, and a confusing one as well. I couldn't make heads or tails of it and couldn't possibly think of what Serena was apologizing to me and Selene for.

"Do you have any idea why she did it?" Blake asked.

His voice sounded accusing, and I growled. "What the hell are you trying to say?"

He held up his hands placatingly. "Dude chill out. I'm not trying to say anything. We're all trying to figure out of this mess."

I sighed, raking my hands through my hair tiredly. "Sorry."

"It's fine, don't worry about it."

For the first time since I woke up, I noticed how weary Blake looked. His brown eyes were dull, devoid of the sparkle that I was used to, and his shoulders were sagging in exhaustion. Sand and dirt-caked almost every inch of his body except for parts of his face while old tear tracts drew squiggly, uneven lines on his cheeks.

"Hey, are you doing okay?"

His breath was ragged when he talked, and he had large bags around his eyes. "Yeah, I'll be fine. Just a little tired, that's all."

"If you say so."

I scanned back around and saw Dylan, who was now supporting Selene as she stood up. The tears had stopped running from her eyes, and she had an almost empty look on her face that made my heart clench tightly.

Nearby, Alyssa was leaning her back against a flat rock while she looked toward Selene with a sad expression in her eyes. She wasn't shedding any tears though, which wasn't unsurprising. The two had never been close.

"Alyssa," Dylan called, making her perk up. "Let's go. We're leaving."

"Wait," I called.

Everyone paused, staring at me wearily. I tried saying something, anything, but the words caught in my mouth. They looked at me, waiting expectantly. My watch vibrated against my wrist, and an alarm rang out in a crystal-clear tone. Something clicked in my mind, and with one smooth movement, I unlatched the strap of my watch, and held the small boxed screen in my hands.

"This symbolizes our loyalty to the mission. If keeping this small box is worth more than the lives that have been lost up to now, keep it on. But I refuse to hold onto this symbol any longer," I cried, the words slipping out of my mouth seamlessly.

The other glanced at each other, nodded. Selene's face was

marred with tears, and exhaustion was prominent in every-one's faces, but they all took their watches off their wrists, holding out in their hands.

"For Serena," I whispered, and heaving my arm back, I chucked the watch into the deep recesses of the ravine.

"For Serena," everyone whispered, and four arms cocked back, four watches bouncing down into the ravine.

There was no big fight, no dramatic moment of breakdown. The realization that our group, which had started with nine people at the get-go, was now down to five only left a dull aching in my heart. With one final look toward the ravine, I walked past Dylan, and the five of us continued our death march.

# Chapter 18

*August 6, 2103*

· · · ● ● ● · · ·

A SMALL SPECK OF gray appeared on the horizon as we all continued marching forward. The group's atmosphere had yet to recover after yesterday's incident. Any positivity that had grown in the short period after coming out of the headquarters had been dashed. Instead, it was replaced by an oppressive aura of weariness and bitterness.

"Damn General Bergen, I'll kill him when I get out of here," Dylan whispered furiously as he continued walking. I shot him a look of concern. Ever since yesterday, he had been whispering similar things incessantly with a glint of furious insanity in his eyes.

My gaze drifted to Selene, who was walking with a tired expression. She no longer seemed saddened in the expressive sense, but the impression I got from our brief conversation yesterday was that she was still suffering on the inside.

*"Selene?"*

*She didn't even turn around as she continued to lay down the tarp on the ground, getting ready to sleep. After a long day of traveling, we had ended up setting in a rock formation that put a roof over our heads.*

*"Hey," I called again. "How are you feeling?"*

*She didn't respond. I sighed and was about to move away to my own corner of the cave when she softly whispered, "I'm not doing well, in all honesty. Thanks for caring about me though."*

*I hesitantly held out my hands toward her but froze. Her voice sounded so hollow and empty, and my heart clenched yet again when I heard her lifeless voice. "Hey, you know that I'm here for you if you need. Right?"*

*She turned around and smiled weakly. "Yeah, I know."*

Ever since then, we hadn't talked again. It was nearly 1800 hours, late into the evening, and we had been walking endlessly for hours. The trip was long and arduous. Our water supplies were starting to run low, and we had started abandoning the hope that we would survive in the desert. Looking at the small gray building in the distance, which was our destination, my hopes weren't getting any higher.

The building was just slightly larger than the off-branch facilities that we had visited, but its condition looked worse for wear. The walls had massive holes in some parts while the door was loosely hanging by its hinge. Occasionally, a strong gust of wind would pass by, making papers fly out of the small holes in the sides.

Upon approaching the facility, I could tell the severity of the building's condition. The walls were thin, almost as if it were made from the paper, and I got the impression that the building was more like a tent than and actual permanent residency. One look into the building showed that I wasn't too far off.

The building was furnished in a very similar way to the off-branch facilities. Several desks were sitting around the walls while papers were scattered on top of them. A hastily constructed computer set up on one of the desks, now with cobwebs spanning the monitor and keyboard.

"Should we search the place?" Blake hesitantly asked, and Dylan nodded.

"We don't know if something useful might pop up. Let's still give it a search," he said, but I could tell that he wasn't too confident in our chances of finding anything there.

Since the structure was small, Dylan asked just me and Blake to accompany him into the building, leaving the two girls outside to wait. As soon as we entered, I could tell that there wasn't much. There were a couple of filing cabinets to my right, and then the small desk with the computers. A large rug sat in the middle of the room with a torn piece of rubber sitting on it, which might at one point have been an inflatable mattress.

"This is disappointing," Blake muttered, looking around the building. He didn't even try to search through the filing cabinets or the desk. We both knew that this building was a lost cause. Dylan and I had made the wrong decision coming here. But Blake didn't gloat or say anything about it.

I watched as Dylan angrily kicked the base of the desk, shaking the metal table violently. The computer setup tumbled onto the ground while papers flew in every direction. Each kick left small dents in the metal. "Damn it. Just grab anything that you two can find that might be useful and let's get out of here. We need to move. Fast."

Blake and I nodded, and immediately, Blake went for the desks, if anything just to placate Dylan's growing rage while I went for the rug. It looked comfy. Somewhat. Starting with one end, I started rolling up the thick rug, cringing in disgust as a couple of ants scuttled out from underneath it. Just about when I reached halfway, I jumped in surprise as I saw a small divider on the floor.

"Dylan," I called hesitantly.

"What?" he growled while continuously digging through the filing cabinets. "If it isn't important-"

"This is important."

He turned around and stared at me in confusion. Squinting his eyes, he took a second look and a small grin appeared on his face when he saw what I was pointing to. Eagerly, he came over and started helping me roll the rug up fully. When the floor was fully uncovered, all three of us, including Blake who came over to see what we were doing, had small triumphant grins on our faces.

The floor underneath the rug was a fake, and a small panel, just like the one from the athletic training facility was embedded in the ground. It was slightly different than the flooring, a minute difference that could only be seen by a keen eye. The coloring was just slightly grayer than the other parts, and to the touch, it felt much cooler. The small slab was separated from the rest of the ground with a tiny handle that was attached near the top.

Dylan glanced down at the slab nervously before bending down and lifting the panel out of the ground. With tremendous effort on his part, the small tile on the floor came undone with a loud groan. Inwardly, I sighed as I felt an overwhelming sense of deja vu.

The small hole in the ground was like the entrance to a sewer, and a long ladder stretching downward was attached to the walls of the hole, leading downwards. However, this time there was no musty forest smell. Instead, it smelled like nothing.

"Are we going down there?" Blake hesitantly asked, and Dylan shook his head.

"Let's talk together before doing anything. I sure as hell won't be going down something like this again so soon," he wisely said.

Dylan herded us back out into the desert area outside of the building and gathered us in a small circle, fixing us all with a straight look. "Alright, we have to make a choice. We're either going to go down there together, or not at all. I couldn't see anything down there which means that it's a fairly long trip down. I say we take a vote. Raise your hands if you want to go and keep them down if you don't want to go."

Alyssa was the first to raise her hand, followed by Selene, mine, Blake and Dylan's. We had a unanimous decision. Dylan nodded, and recommended, "Keep your supplies rationed and make sure you're looking out for each other's backs. We don't know what's going to be down there."

They nodded, and with a heavy sigh, Dylan led us back into the small building. Cautiously, he stuck his foot out and bumped it against the ladder. To my surprise, the ladder didn't rattle of shudder at all but remained firmly mounted on the wall, not buckling under the physical force.

"At least it's stable…" he muttered under his breath.

Putting his right foot in first, he started climbing down the thin rungs of the ladder leading down to somewhere. Alyssa followed in after him, trailed by Blake, Selene, and finally, me. Before I hopped in, I grabbed the panel and slid it back into place, the stone dropping back in its slot with a satisfying thump.

As we continued moving downward, the first thing that I noticed was the extreme darkness in the place. There wasn't a single speck of light coming from below. I stumbled, barely even having time to register the fact that my feet were on solid ground as I came to the end of the ladder.

"Hello?" I whispered.

"Here, follow my voice," Dylan called, and I stumbled forward, hand brushing against someone's skin. A female voice yelped, and I recoiled back, muttering, "Sorry, whoever that was."

"It's fine," Alyssa's voice replied.

"Alright," Dylan said, from somewhere close. "Let's try to stick together and look around for lighting. Or, if someone has a flashlight in their pack, even better."

"I think I do," Selene's subdued voice responded, and I heard rustling as metallic clinks came from my left. Several metallic objects hit each other, making a crisp, clear sound. Selene exclaimed in joy, and suddenly, a long ray of light illuminated our surroundings.

We were in a holding area, elevated from the rest of the facility a little bit. In front of us, there was a small set of stairs that led down to a more expansive section of the room. There were multiple doors that were set in a semi-circular formation to the opposite side of where we stood.

"Alright, Selene, go with Ethan and try to find a light switch. We'll stay here. If you can't find anything after ten minutes, just come back."

Selene and I nodded, and with her at the lead, we walked down the staircase, our boots clacking against the concrete ground with every step. We started around the left base of the stairs, hoping to find something, but to no avail.

"Let's try to other side," I encouraged, and guided Selene over to the other side. To my glee, there was a large panel with tens of switches on it, and a label above the panel read, "Lighting." Reaching out, I flipped pretty much every switch I could find to an "on" position.

The vibrancy of the lights that illuminated the room had me wincing, blinking to get the spots out of my eyes. Selene clicked her flashlight off, and the sight that met our eyes had the group jumping in joy.

The entire room was decorated in a monotonous gray

and concrete was used to line the walls while metallic slabs formed different walkways and staircases. Though, it had been left in disrepair with deep cracks forming in the walls with slimy water oozing through the cracks. Along the far edges of the room, deep, dark tunnels stretched away from the center. Metal plates were embedded in the wall on top of the doorways, but their labeling was now faded.

A loud bang noise interrupted my evaluation of the room. Off to the far-left side of the room, Dylan was ramming his foot against a locked door, making loud echoing bangs resonate. When the loose door came undone from the strike plate, Selene and I moved over to peer into the room.

The sight made me feel relieved and joyful. Large, metal shelving units stocked sparsely with boxes lined corridors wide enough for machinery to pass through. This had clearly been some sort of storage room for supplies among other things. Though, there was some evidence of the room having been ransacked before.

Still, there were still several boxes and crates intact, and they held supplies such as water, first aid kits, food, and more. A closer look showed that many of the boxes were torn apart with jagged tears, shredding the box into several pieces.

"Let's look for whatever we can find here, then move on," Dylan commanded.

We broke away to dig through different sections of the storage room. The best thing that I found during the thirty minutes that we were scrounging around was a full thirty-six case of sixteen-ounce water bottles with some flavored mixes.

When I came back to regroup, I saw that the others looked a lot more elated than before. They were all holding boxes of different sizes and were pulling out various objects like medical kits, food, and other essentials. One of the boxes even had a massive tent.

"Let's pick out the most important things here. Preferably compact but filling foods and lots of water. We can't overload ourselves," suggested Dylan. He himself was holding tightly onto a box full of ration bars.

For the next couple of minutes, we took the time to fill our bags with various bottles and bars, noting with happiness that our bags were several pounds heavier than it had been before we stepped into the room.

"Let's keep moving," Dylan called once all our bags had been filled. "There are a lot of different rooms that we have to check."

Going around the main atrium-like area, we checked around the different rooms, but they were all useless compared to the storage room. One room was filled with papers and filing cabinets, another with vehicles but no keys, and another with large rifles and guns that we just couldn't carry around without being hampered. Although, we did take several old MP-9 pistols along with some holsters.

The last path that was left in the atrium was the long, dark tunnel that was in the center. All the lights above the long path were broken, so the tunnel was shrouded in darkness. Dylan hesitantly started taking several steps forward, before leading us into the dark space.

My heart lurched in fear every time I heard something in the darkness. Even just a cough or sneeze from the others made me jump in fear. It started softly, but Inthmus' screams of pain gradually grew louder inside my head, and my heart pounded wildly, shaking my entire body, making me experience fear. True fear.

Each minute felt like an eternity, and the darkness felt constricting. I frowned as the dark tunnel didn't seem to come to an end. A constant dripping sound was coming from beyond the roof of the narrow tunnel. The whispers of curiosity, which had been coming from the others, had subsided a long time ago as the novelty of walking in the darkness wore out.

Suddenly, I felt a gust of wind pass by me as something shifted. I couldn't see anything, as it was still dark, but I got the impression that we were no longer standing in a tight tunnel. Indeed, as my eyes slowly focused on the area, I found that the dark tunnel had ended abruptly, leading the way to a sight that we certainly weren't expecting.

If the storage room was large, this room was gargantuan. Relatively speaking of course. In total, the entire room was probably around ten acres in size. It was multiple stories tall, and long, zig-zagging catwalks spanned across the length of the room at many levels. But it wasn't the size that had caught us off guard.

What is that smell?" Blake asked with disgust in his voice. "It smells like rotten food, but like...worse."

"Look for light switches," Dylan said, pinching his nose tightly. "Then we'll decide where to go from there."

It didn't take long to find them. The large panel of lights was to our immediate left, and after flipping them all, several hundred lights from the ceiling illuminated the large room in a white glow, giving way to a sight that had us shocked and disgusted.

On the far side of the room, there were rows upon rows of cells that were embedded in the wall. The wall of cells went three stories high, long catwalks lining each floor. They were of various sizes. Some were large, big enough to fit about three to four people while there were also some that were small enough that it barely left a single person enough room to stand.

To the right, there was a pile of junk that was stacked up carelessly. It was just like a mound of different belongings that were meshed together into one gigantic heap.

In the center of the room, there were several steel shipping crates that were stacked upon each other unevenly, leaving gaps in between them in random places. It was almost as if the people in charge of handling them had gotten bored and started playing Jenga.

The extra lighting revealed all the coloration in the room, and it also revealed the identity behind the horrid stench that we had been smelling ever since we stepped into this room.

"I-Is that blood?" Selene stuttered, covering her mouth with her two hands in horror.

I nodded grimly, noting the dark stains that were splattered all along the walls and floor. Especially inside of the jail cells, it was severe, the walls painted in a thin coating of that blood as if it were a fresh batch of paint on the wall. Fortunately, or unfortunately, all of it was dried up, meaning that whatever had been the cause for it was long gone.

"Let's regroup and figure out what we have to do," Dylan called, a disgusted look on his face. He forcefully turned his gaze away from the walls and floor. "I don't want to stay here if possible. Let's figure out what we can get out of this place, then bounce as soon as possible. Also, make sure that you all are staying in groups. I don't want to risk splitting up in such a place. As soon as you see something off, you scream. Got it?"

We nodded. Dylan and Alyssa stuck together, checking out the mound of objects while Selene and I were looking through the warden offices that were at each end of the rows. Blake was staying near the middle of the room, searching the outskirts.

The first office that we entered wasn't all too exciting. In fact, it was quite plain. A desk sat in the far back corner with a couple of empty picture frames sitting along one half while a large computer occupied the other half. Nothing else in that office remained. Not even papers.

"Let's move onto the next one," I suggested. Selene followed me out and walked across the prison cells toward the next office space on the other end of the long row. While walking, I took a quick peek into the cells and cringed in disgust, covering my nose with the collar of my shirt to keep the stench away. Selene was doing the same, though she looked green.

We reached the office that was at the other end of the row, and this one was a little bit more exciting. A little bit. It was a basic office space like the other one with a desk and computer. There weren't any picture frames, though. Instead, the desk was slightly smaller, leaving room for the one large filing cabinet sitting next to the splinters of what might have been a wooden chair in the past.

"Do you want to do the honors?" I asked Selene, trying to lighten the mood a little bit, but she shook her head.

"You can do it."

I nodded, and went over to the large filing cabinets, popping open each one. Out of the four large cabinets, there was only one that was filled with files. It had large stacks of manila folders that had faded white sheets of paper sticking out of it.

I gently took out the stack, tossing aside any that were either too faded to read or had uninteresting information. Only one packet of information really caught my eye, its title reading, "Building code: 206718 Worker's Report." Confused, I quickly skimmed through the information, shocked the more I read.

"What is it?" Selene curiously asked.

"They're records," I replied, hands shaking. "It seems like a report of workers that were supposedly used for a massive project, but this doesn't make sense."

"What doesn't make sense?"

"These records are from seventy-five years ago," I whispered. Inwardly, I was in awe. This facility was seventy-five years old, and who knows how long this place had been in operation before that.

"Wow, that's cool and all, but that's not anything importan-" Selene started, but a loud male scream of surprise interrupted her. It came from outside, near the center of the large room.

I rushed outside, shouting, "What's wrong?!"

Blake's panicked voice shouted back, "There's something else here! I heard it shifting around near the garbage bags in the corner!"

My heart, which was throbbing in nervously and excitement at hearing someone scream, settled down into its normal rhythm. Rubbing my hands through my hair, I sighed. "Maybe it's a rat or something. If you want to check it out, go ahead, but we're going to continue looking through the offices."

"We'll do the same," Dylan and Alyssa said from the mound of objects. "If you want, you can check it out, but if not, you can come over here and search through this heap of junk with us."

Blake waved him off. "Never mind."

I shrugged and went back into the room.

"What happened?" Selene asked in concern.

"Just Blake. He said he heard something near the garbage bags," I told her. "Let's keep moving and search the second-floor offices. The first office near the far-right edge was less bland than the other ones. Beyond the traditional desk and chair routine, there was also a large safe that sat near the back corner of the wall, wedged in between the desk and the wall. The lock was facing away from the entrance so that it would only be accessible to the person sitting at the desk.

I walked over to it, and experimentally gave it a couple of tugs. It wouldn't budge at all. The rusted handle stuck firm to the metallic door of the safe and the safe stayed still, rooted as if it was fastened to the wall. Tightening my arms, I gave it a couple heftier pulls, grunting as it wouldn't move at all. The small keyhole on the handle staring back at me, mocking me for not being able to get it open.

"Do you want me to try?" Selene offered, but I waved her down.

"Let me try something before that."

She pouted but stayed back. From the small hidden sleeve pocket on my left arm, I pulled out the small swiss army knife that had remained forgotten for most of the trip. I sifted through the different tools, flipping open the half-saw and blade knife, screwdrivers, and others until I reached a little peculiar tool. It started as a thin screwdriver with a square, blocky body, but near the end, it thinned out and started moving in zigzag until the tip, which was pointed.

"Is that a lock picking rake?" Selene asked. "Have you had that the entire time?"

"Yes?" I replied, confused.

"You know you could've probably used that to open the doors in the other buildings rather than having Blake kick it down."

I rested my forehead in my palm, cursing myself for lack of insight. Selene was laughing quietly while my face burned in shame. Instead of dignifying Selene with a response, I started picking at the small handle lock with a bent-out-of-shape paper clip acting as my tension rod. The rake rattled inside the lock but didn't click very easily.

Blake's startled cry of panic came from the outside again, followed by the alarmed shouts of Dylan and Alyssa. I exhaled exasperatedly and turned to Selene. "Can you go check that out really quickly, please? Let them know that this joke isn't funny the second time."

"Alright."

I kept scratching the rake through the lock hole, grinning as a couple of the pins snapped into place. Suddenly, the office door swung open with a loud crash, and Selene barreled through, shouting in alarm, "Ethan! We need you outside. Now!"

I frowned at her hastiness and panic that was clear in her eyes. There were unshed tears that were lingering in them, an untold sadness that reflected on her face. I peered back at the lock, and pleaded, "Are you sure? I'm almost done with the-"

"*Now!*" she yelled, and I jumped up to my feet. Leaving the small swiss knife lodged in the lock, I rushed outside, partially on my own accord and partially because Selene was dragging me along by the arm. As I stood on the metal catwalk, it wasn't immediately clear what the issue was. Partially, it was because I couldn't see that far. I made out a couple of humanoid figures, but they were covered in the shadow of the crates that were in the middle of the room.

"What's going on?" I asked Selene, but she was already running down the stairs toward Dylan, who had his gun out, pointed toward the humanoid figure. Suddenly, the person in the shadows darted out and landed on top of the stack of crates in the center of the room.

As the light shined directly onto it, I realized that it was not really a question of who, but *what*. The figure resembled a human from the outside, but its fingernails were elongated, almost looking like claws, and the skin on its flesh almost seemed rough like the exoskeleton of an insect rather than the smooth skin of a person. Its eyes had a frenzied and feral look that didn't belong to a human's face. A crimson liquid was dripping down its right arm, marking dark stains on the faded gray crate.

"Who are you?!" Dylan, who was standing in front of the crate shouted. He was looking up toward the creature, and it stared down right back at it.

"Maybe the question is, what are you?" I said, still in shock and disgust at seeing the creature. "Blake, where the hell did you find this?"

"I don't know. One moment I was just looking around the room for something, then the next thing I know, this thing just darts in front of me!" he shouted in panic. He was holding out his MP-9 pistol at eye-level, training it on the creature.

Fumbling around with my own pistol in the holster, I pulled out my MP-9 pistol, loading it and training it toward the creature. From the second floor, I got a good angle, but the creature was still a far distance away.

If the creature recognized the danger that it was in, it certainly didn't show it. Its sharp teeth were still borne toward us while it was crouched down on all fours. Suddenly, it started taking slow, calculated steps forward as it leaped off the top crate and started making its way down toward the ground.

My grip on the pistol tightened, finger hovering over the trigger. The creature was now crouched low on the floor on all four limbs. Now that it got closer, I was able to see its features a lot better. Even though it looked and resembled a human, its body parts showed anything but. Its arms and legs were bent at awkward angles, and the skin on its feet and hands seemed hardened, like paws or some other modification.

"Who are you?" Dylan asked one more time. His voice was trembling, and he wasn't even trying to hide the fact that he was nervous just looking at this creature. His finger on the trigger was trembling.

I warned, "Dylan, don't do anything rash."

He nodded stiffly, keeping his eye trained on the creature.

We were at a chilling standstill as silence overcame the large room. The only sound we could hear was the dripping of water seeping through from the ceiling. The creature turned its head to the side, as if curiously amused about the whole situation. Its nose and eyes twitched every couple of seconds.

Suddenly, it pounced. It was *fast*. Almost like a cheetah, it ran on all four limbs and made a straight line toward Selene going from zero to sixty in almost the blink of an eye.

"Selene!" Dylan and Blake shouted in panic. A couple of loud bullet shots rang out, echoing off the walls, but none of them hit the creature. It was almost halfway to Selene, getting ready to pounce with its claws and teeth bared. Selene was rooted in her spot, trembling.

My hands moved naturally as if they had been doing so for years. They whipped around to the front, index finger already ready on the trigger. The barrel of the gun was pointed toward the creature midair, letting out two consecutive shots. One missed, skidding against the concrete floor while the other embedded itself in the calf of the creature, making it hiss in pain as it tumbled to the ground. Selene yelped and ran behind Dylan who had reloaded the gun and had it pointed toward the down creature.

Slowly, I made my way toward the end of the catwalk near the stairs, and slowly made my way down, keeping my pistol trained on the creature's head. It was still, not moving a single inch. Slowly, Blake, Dylan, and I moved to surround it from all three sides, our pistol trained on the thing.

"Is it dead?" Blake asked nervously. His gun was also shaking in his hands.

"I'm not sure," I replied uncertainly. The creature wasn't moving, not even breathing from the looks of it. But I wasn't so sure if it was dead or not. It had only taken a shot to the leg after all. Blake started slowly approaching it, gun held firm in his hands pointing toward the thing's head. He was almost standing right next to the creature now, his fingers tightened on the trigger. But the creature didn't move.

I sighed a breath of relief and loosened the grip I had on my pistol. Dylan and Blake were still looking at the creature wearily, but slowly, they also started putting their pistols down.

"I guess it's dead," Dylan muttered dully.

Dylan hesitantly kicked the beast, and when it didn't move, he laughed nervously. "What the hell man? That wasn't so hard."

Suddenly, the thing's feet twitched, and all three of us fumbled to raise our guns, firing just as it started lunging toward Dylan. Its claws were borne, shiny white teeth glinting underneath the white fluorescent lights. A couple of loud gunshots rang out in the spacious hall, and a couple of red patches appeared on its body as the bullets lodged themselves into the creature. The figure skittled to a stop with its right arm outstretched, its five fingers digging deep puncture wounds into Dylan's chest.

Slowly, the two crumpled onto the ground, like two falling logs.

# Chapter 19

*August 7, 2103*

· · · · ● · · · ·

W E WATCHED IN shock as Dylan crumpled to the ground almost in slow motion, groaning loudly. The creature was almost positively dead now, its eyes devoid of the ferocity that we had seen before.

"Dylan!"

Alyssa's hoarse voice tore through the air like a sharp knife as she kneeled beside him with tears running down her face. She buried her head in the crook of Dylan's neck as he tried to weakly smile. He started coughing violently, blood leaking out his mouth in uncontrolled shudders.

"Selene! Medical kit! Please!" Alyssa cried desperately. Selene moved quickly, bringing out a medical kit with saline solution, gauze pads, medical tape, and another solution capped inside of a bottle. She hurriedly handed it over to Alyssa who frantically started trying to apply pressure to the wound.

"Alyssa, stop," Dylan hoarsely cried, grabbing at Alyssa's hands. She shook her head, tears still dripping down her cheeks. She kept on pushing down against the wound with a large, white cloth even as blood leaked through her fingers and drenched her hands in a crimson layer.

"Alyssa…"

His voice was getting weaker by the second, and his grip on Alyssa's hand was loosening. I grimaced and looked away as I saw the life fading from his eyes. His gaze was becoming less and less focused until it was clouded over, his eyes unfocused.

Alyssa's sobs echoed in the large chamber as she cried over Dylan's limp body. At some point, Blake had moved the other creature's body, much to his disgust, into one of the cells that were still open. He backed away, giving Alyssa some space to grieve. Selene was alone as well, sitting on the floor with a look of shock on her face. Silent tears were rolling down her eyes while she had a faraway look. I imagined that being a second away death could not have been a pleasant experience.

"Are you okay?" I hesitantly asked.

She shook her head numbly, and grasped at my uniform sleeve, holding it tightly as if it were a lifeline. I sat beside her, gently taking her hand in my own and started rubbing small circles on the palm of her hand. Her sobs were becoming louder and louder. Off to the side, I saw Blake standing with an awkward expression on his face.

"You're okay now. Don't worry," I whispered into Selene's ears, but her sobs didn't decrease in volume at all. She just kept on weeping and weeping until she could no longer cry. After her tears dried, she leaned her head against my shoulders and rested there. Meanwhile, Blake started nervously walking over toward Alyssa and started talking to her in hushed whispers. I couldn't hear what they were saying.

Shortly after, Blake came over to me, and asked, "What do you want to do now?"

"I don't know."

"Well, you better figure it out soon."

His voice was weary and saddened but underlain by an unknown determination that I couldn't pinpoint the cause of. "Well?" he prompted.

I glanced at Selene, who was also staring up at Blake with tired eyes. She looked drained, but still resilient, ready to go at a moment's notice. "Let's figure out where we can go from here. We can decide whether we're moving forward or going back to where we were. Blake, can you go around the room and look for any other places that we could go?"

He looked nervous about going alone again but nodded with an audible gulp. "Alright, what do you want me to do when I find something?"

"Come back, and we'll regroup."

Blake briskly nodded and walked off, searching the room once again. I continued to rub small circles into Selene's hand as she kept trembling in fear and shock. Minutes later, I whispered. "I'm going to check on Alyssa, can you stay here for just a second?"

Selene nodded, giving me a look of understanding. "Make sure she's okay too."

Alyssa was still sitting next to Dylan's body, a blank look on her face. She was still whispering words in Dylan's ear, muttering, "Please come back, don't leave me."

My heart sank like a brick in water, and I suddenly felt ashamed for what had happened back at the headquarters, when I had decided that my own personal prejudices were more important than helping someone who was standing at the doors of death.

"Alyssa, I'm sorry," I whispered.

She shook her head. "He's not dead yet. He's just sleeping. He always jokes like this, did you know? Even when we were back in Sector 66, even when-"

A choked sob escaped her lips as a fresh wave of tears

started falling down her cheeks in waves. I stood there awkwardly, not really knowing what to do. Hesitantly, I sat down next to her and wrapped an arm around her shoulders as she continued to cry. I lost track of how long she cried in my arms, but Blake had come back at some point and was talking to Selene about something, to which she was nodding periodically.

"Alyssa," I called softly. "We need to go."

She shook her head, refusing to move from where she was sitting. "Not yet."

"Alyssa," I called again. "We need to keep moving. Dylan would've wanted us to keep going."

I reeled back in surprise as Alyssa violently snapped her arms out of my grasp and shouted angrily, "Don't talk like you know Dylan! You don't know anything about him! He's gone, so stop using his name like you know what he's like!"

Another wave of sobbing renewed, and she angrily slapped at the ground. Her face was flushed red with fury at the same time. Hesitantly, I stood and walked over to Selene and Blake.

"I found a door," Blake started. "It leads to some kind of garage area that has a long tunnel leading somewhere. I'm not exactly sure where it goes to, but it's probably our best chance."

I sighed inwardly. I was starting to get tired of dark tunnels that led to obscure places.

"Do you have any idea where it might feed into?" I asked.

"It leads north, toward Sector 247, but I don't know if it's a straight channel, or if it leads to some other place. That's to be determined."

That sounded much better than "a dark tunnel leading somewhere."

"Alright then, lead the way."

Blake nodded and pushed us toward a corner next to the far-left end of the prison cells. Selene gently whispered something in Alyssa's ears, but she kept on shaking her head, muttering.

"Ethan, Blake, I need a moment."

"Selen-"

She fixed me with a glare, and I closed my mouth with an audible click.

"Alright."

I watched silently as Selene walked over to the stack of items near the right side of the room and picked out a large, silky cloth. It was entirely black, with a large image embroidered near the middle as a design. Selene gently wrapped it around Dylan's body, and then turned to me.

"Can you help me move it over?" she asked, eyeing the gap underneath the crates.

"Yeah," I whispered morosely.

The two of us hefted Dylan's wrapped body over toward the stack of crates in the center of the room. With a thick marker, Selene wrote on the bridging crate on top, *Here lies Dylan, a leader, family, friend.*

Alyssa, who had tears running down her face in waves, walked up to Selene and hugged her tightly, bawling in her arms. The sound of her sorrow echoed in the spacious room for minutes on end, never abating. Guilt and sorrow picked at my heart. *If I had been faster, if I had been smart, if I had been more aware.*

The realizations and questions that I asked myself stung more than ever. I started realizing that nothing had changed. I was still here, asking the same questions that I'd been asking two months ago back in Sector 36. Part of me was still stuck there, standing in front of the building windows at the mercy of mini-me's judgement.

"Let's go," Blake whispered.

Finally, we said goodbye to Dylan, and Blake led us to the far-left corner of the room. There was a small swinging door with a faded label that read, *G--A-E*. Blake swung through the door, and we followed, not really knowing what to expect.

As we entered the room, Blake flicked a light switch to the right, basking the room in yellow light. It was a lot smaller than the other room had been, maybe about a fifth of the size. The far wall near the back was lined with cars while the long tunnel that Blake had been describing was to our left, directly in front of the entrance to the room.

"Do those cars have gas and keys?" I asked.

He shrugged. "I don't know. We can check, though."

All four of us trudged toward the cars and looked for keys and gas but found nothing. Disappointed, we came back as a group.

"No keys, no nothing. But the tunnel is still there, so we can just walk it if we need to," Blake suggested. The prospect of going through that tunnel, which didn't seem to have an end from what I could see, wasn't very appealing.

"Well, at least the good thing is that if there are cars, there must be an outlet to where they go, right?" Selene said optimistically. That was one positive thing.

"Then what are we waiting for?" Alyssa growled. "Let's hurry up and move. I don't want to be here any longer than I have to." Her words were chipped, the sorrowful tone now nowhere to be seen.

I peered into the tunnel, and it was dark, not a single bit of lighting being visible anywhere down the long tunnel. "Try to find a little bit of lighting first. We won't be able to see very well if we go in as it is now, and we might miss our exit or something."

Blake nodded, then started prodding with the light panel

near the entrance again. After several minutes of flickering lights, I heard a soft hum as multiple lights lit up in the dark tunnel. The lights glowed in a soft amber tone from where they were embedded in the wall.

Fortunately, the ground was paved with asphalt, making the walking slightly easier. I signaled back to the group, waving them through into the tunnel. With heavy feet, they started walking, going down the long tunnel while hugging the right wall. I silently hoped that someone would come down through the other end of the tunnel to help, but after thirty minutes of silent walking, that hope was dashed.

The long walk was getting monotonous, and the only form of entertainment that I initially found was counting the number of lights embedded in the wall. Eventually, that game became boring as well, so I twisted my bag around my body and pulled out the small file that I had stashed in there from my brief search in the headquarters. If there was ever a time to start reading something, it was now.

The document seemed quite old and the print was fading, but the words were legible just fine. It seemed like an abstract for an experiment. The paper read:

*The Second Advent Project Phase Three Abstract: This study models high-speed adaptation of the human body to extreme circumstances. Data analysis from decades of study reveal that it is possible for technology to genetically modify an entire species artificially. As a result, the study concludes that the application of such technology in widespread amounts is likely to bolster the capabilities of a person, bringing us as a race closer to the next step of the evolutionary process.*

*Methodology: Through live experimentation, the serum was tested to be highly effective. Slight variations in the formulation process exist, but there have been no significant side effects reported from this difference.*

*Future research must determine if this differentiation can be purposefully induced during the manufacturing process for the serum.*

*Findings: The experimentation process of the study reveal that the injection of this serum enhances a person's overall senses and physical attributes. Mental disparities between pre-injection and post-injection must be studies further for increased quantities of data.*

*Limitations: N/A.*

*Practical Implications: CLASSIFIED*

Was this what had created the creature from before? It was only mere speculation at this point, but it started to make me wonder what those buildings out in the desert were really made for. To think, that those buildings had been in place for seventy-five years. It also filled me with fury. *Why didn't the government do anything about these buildings?*

The thoughts continued to plague my mind, and for some reason, my thoughts drifted back to the old dream that I had while near the ravine. *You do not know your enemies,* I remembered the voice saying.

"What is that?" Blake asked curiously. He saw the sheets I had in my hands, and I cursed, berating myself for not being careful enough. But at this point, I didn't really care, so I told him truthfully, "These were the papers that I grabbed from the headquarters right before I left. Do you want to read through them?"

"Sure," Blake said, and I handed him the top paper that had the abstract on it.

Meanwhile, I started flipping through some of the other pages that were inside the large packet but couldn't make heads or tails of what I was reading. The papers were diagrams of bombs and nuclear missiles that didn't seem to belong in a paper about genetic modification. It had complicated designs and mathematical calculations that I couldn't even start making heads or tails of.

"Are you serious?!" Blake shouted. I figured that he must've been done reading the papers. "This sounds like something straight from science fiction…"

I nodded silently and continued walking along the path while Blake continuously muttered under his breath. He silently passed it around from Alyssa, then to Selene who read it dispassionately. Although, Alyssa had a new fire burning inside her eyes, and I hoped that she wouldn't do anything irrational because of it.

Another hour or so passed by, and my legs were getting tired. They were wobbly from exhaustion, and my muscles burned. It felt like I couldn't walk forward another step. But soon, we came across a large stone wall that sat in front of us.

"This must've been for the cars…"

The stone gates looked like they were supposed to open to the sides, splitting right down the middle, but at the moment they were closed.

"Is there any way that we can get it open?" Selene asked.

I looked around, and to the far-right side, there was a small keypad that looked like it might've been the code to unlock the large gates, but it was now dead, the screen completely blacked out.

"No."

"We can still go up through there," Alyssa noted, and we turned our heads. On the left side of the wall, there was a long ladder that led upwards, presumably toward the surface.

I sighed in relief, although an underlying sense of fear overcame me. Was this the end of our journey? Or would there be something else on the other side? I wasn't so sure. This felt all too much an anti-climactic ending to a journey that started so awfully.

Hesitantly, I followed as Blake, Alyssa, and Selene started climbing up the ladders, small pieces of metallic debris following down and hitting me in the face. The ladder didn't go up that high, and soon, Selene abruptly stopped, making me almost run into her.

"Hey? Why'd we stop?" I asked curiously. I heard several slams before something popped like a balloon. Light poured in through the now open space near the top. It wasn't bright, but it was still a welcome change to what I had gotten used to during the long time I spent underground. Clouds were looming over us threateningly.

Blake scrambled out of the small hole followed by Alyssa and Selene. Finally, I poked my head out and stood up on the solid ground, brushing the loose sand and dust off my pants and sleeves. When I looked up, I stared into the barrel of several rifles that were trained on me.

"Drug the spares," I heard, and with an excruciating jolt of pain, I lost consciousness.

# PART 3:
# Coming Home

# Chapter 20

*August 17, 2103*

· · · · • • • · · ·

B EEP...BEEP...
EVERY PART of my body felt numb, the nerves on the surface of my skin oblivious to everything that was happening around me. My mind felt blank as if all my thoughts had been stripped away from me.

*Beep...Beep...*

The soft, rhythmic beats which sounded in the distance began to overwhelm my senses as an uncomfortable heat started flaring up across my body. I felt every nerve in my body tingle as the sensations became hotter and hotter. The soft beating in the distance screamed louder until the pulsing beats sounded like they were coming from right next to me.

*Beep...Beep...*

A prickling pain jabbed at my eyes as a harsh light shined above me. It was like a miniature sun that was right above me, but instead of golden light, it casted an irritating white light into my eyes. My head was throbbing as if a bull had mauled into it. Even the slightest twitch of my body made me feel like I was on fire.

"Oh, you're finally awake."

Opening my eyes, which was slowly adjusting to the

bright lighting, I slowly took note of the room I was in. The walls were stained beige, the paint chipping in places, and paintings adorned the walls. To my left, monitors and machines were beeping away, many of them having tubes that were connected to my arms and legs. A breathing mask was attached to my face, the clear plastic rubbing against my nose. A tall woman with an emotionless expression stood to my left, holding an E-Board held tightly against her chest.

"Where am I?"

She replied, maintaining her flat expression, "You are in the medical wing of Sector 247's Genetic Research Facility. Currently, your location is Room C248, and the time is eight in the morning. Does this satisfy your inquiry?"

I must've still been hazy, because the first thing I blurted out was, "Why are you talking like that?"

I cringed inwardly as I realized how rude the question must've sounded, but the nurse just tilted her head to the side, and replied, "I do not understand your question."

Sighing, I instead asked, "Who brought me here? Where is everyon-"

I paused, wondering why the second question instinctively came out of my mouth. Who was I referring to? *Who are these 'others'?* I thought, and a sharp pain ran up my head. Some images flashed through my head, and I remembered the underground facility, Dylan dying, leaving me alone. There was also this lingering sensation on my shoulders that I couldn't place.

Her fingers rapped against her E-Board, and she read, "Unit 142 discovered your presence exactly ten days ago. You and your companions were relocated to this facility soon after. Your conditions were most severe. The conditions and locations of your companions are classified pieces of information that cannot be loaded from the database. The doctor will be here shortly."

My head stung in pain again. "What companions?"

But the nurse didn't answer. She stepped out of the room, and I was alone again. My head still felt extremely groggy, and everything still felt like a blur. Every time I tried to remember back to what had happened after we got out of the underground experiment facility, my head started throbbing, and I could barely recall anything.

A few minutes went by before a short, clean-shaven man walked in while tapping at his E-Board. "Ethan Holfstras?"

I tried to nod, but a sharp pain in my neck dissuaded me, so I responded with a weak, "Yes. That's me."

He scanned my body before continuing, "My name is Dr. Hayes. I'm sure you're confused since you were out for quite some time. Your brain scans show that you aren't doing too well, so let me try to keep this explanation brief. Our soldiers found you just a little way from our sector and brought you into intensive care. You got lucky since you were barely holding onto life when we found you. That was a week and a half ago, and luckily, you've come to rather quickly."

"What about my companions?" I questioned.

The doctor made a confused look. "What companions? You were the only one that we found out there in the desert."

"The nurse just said something about companions. Did she not?"

An annoyed look flitted across the doctor's features before he replied, "She must've misspoken, then. As far as I know, you were the only one that was found out there in the desert."

He tapped the E-Board several times before recommending, "You've got enough to process, Ethan. Let your mind rest for a day or so," he responded.

"That's what I thought," I whispered uncertainty. "Companions…me?"

The throbbing in my head returned thrice-fold, and I asked, "What is going to happen to me from here on out?"

He smiled at that at least. "There should be no permanent damage. I'm not sure what you went through, but your physical injuries were all superficial at best. With a little bit of rehab work in the next week, we should have you up and running to go."

That was good news. News that I wanted to hear. "Where will I go after this?"

He shrugged. "I'm afraid that I can't help you there. But we got a call from the General from Sector Nine, his name was Kyle Bergen, I think? He instructed us to call him when you woke up. So, I suppose that's what I'll be doing now."

Anger filled my veins when that man's name was mentioned. "I'd rather you not call him, doctor."

He shrugged. "Sorry, but I don't have much of a choice. Not listening to his words is almost equivalent to treason. Besides, he might be your only ticket to get back home since no one from this sector can give you a ride back to toward the inner sectors."

I frowned but stayed quiet. "What will I do while I'm here?"

"Whatever you want to. We can get you started on physical therapy as early as today after our first checkups. But for now, you should probably rest. We'll get you on some melatonin until the afternoon. After that, we'll see how you are doing. Does that sound good?" he asked.

I nodded my head wearily. "Yes, that should be fine."

He gently pushed me back into a comfortable position on my bed and checked the mask that was covering my mouth. Soon, I heard a soft hissing noise before drowsiness overcame my body, and my eyelids were closed against my will.

# Chapter 21

*August 18, 2103*

· · · · ● · · · ·

"**Y**OU'RE ALL READY to go," was the first thing I heard as I woke up once again. The light entering the window was less vibrant than the overhead light, and through squinted eyes, I saw Dr. Hayes sitting on a chair across from the foot of my bed. Everything was still the way it had been earlier except for the fact that I felt less nauseous.

Looking to my left, I noticed that the medical equipment that had been there was gone along with the mask that had been on my face. The room was stripped of any of its identifying features, and it seemed like a normal, rather plain bedroom.

"General Bergen called early in the morning and will be here in a little bit. He appears to have been at a nearby facility waiting for you," Dr. Hayes explained, almost as monotonously as the nurse had.

"You're just letting me go?" I questioned. "Didn't you say that I still had physical therapy and stuff I had left to do?"

"I have no choice. If it was my choice, you wouldn't be leaving quite yet, but he insisted, and he has superiority over me."

I was deciding whether I felt betrayed or nervous. "You didn't suggest anything to him?"

He glared at me. "Of course I didn't. Shouldn't you know better what happens when you question people of authority? Your mark should've given you plenty of reminders."

The brand at the base of my neck stung, and I fingered it with my hands, glaring right back at the doctor. "That was uncalled for."

He shrugged. "This is a give and take society. Let's get you up. We'll put some food in your body before we send you off with General Bergen again," he added.

I nodded. Gently, he guided me off the bed and onto my feet. My arms and legs felt a lot less inflamed than they did just yesterday, but it was still difficult to walk without help. Dr. Hayes led me down the hallway and stairs and into the dining hall. I could tell he wanted to strike up small talk, but he seemed to stray away from the thought. Instead, he directed me towards the breakfast buffet and explained, "You probably aren't all too hungry, but get something into your system."

The thought of eating made me a little bit nauseous, but nevertheless, I grabbed a plate and start piling up small amounts of food. It was a very welcome change from the ration bars that had kept me going for the past few weeks.

Dr. Hayes sat down across from me and asked, "Are you doing fine? I mean, I understand you haven't had much time to recover and that everything might've been a big shock, but I just want to make sure you're comfortable."

"I don't know how I feel," I muttered, poking at the scrambled eggs with my fork.

"Here," he responded, reaching into his pocket. He handed me a small card with his name and number. "I know you haven't had the time to get comfortable with me yet, but if you ever need somebody to talk to, I'm more than willing to listen. This part is rough, and I absolutely wouldn't blame you for being afraid."

Was I afraid? Really, I mostly felt queasy from forcing myself to eat. "Thanks, Doctor. I'll keep you in mind if anything goes south." I forced a small smile, receiving a nod of approval from him.

His eyes drifted over my shoulder and behind me, I saw a nurse, the same one that had woken me up yesterday, standing there. "Dr. Hayes, I've been informed that Mr. Ethan Holfstras should be getting ready rather soon. His General has entered the sector."

My General? If anything, he was really the last person I wanted to be associated with.

"Thank you, Lydia," he answered. "Let's go, Ethan, we can wait for him out front."

Thankfully, that meant that I didn't have to keep tossing food down my throat forcefully. But at the same time, my heart was pounding against my chest at the thought of seeing General Bergen again. It had been nearly three weeks since I had seen him last, and my opinion of him most certainly hadn't gotten better during that time.

"The entrance is just right outside at the end of the hall, Ethan. I'll let you take your own pace out there," Dr. Hayes told me. I slowly stood up from my seat and made my way out of the double doors of the dining hall. To the right was an open waiting room and another set of double doors, which I approached.

I was met with a blast of searing heat to my face and body, contrary to the cool air inside the facility. Dr. Hayes walked out right behind me, closing the doors as we stepped out onto the small raised platform. I quickly noticed how barren the road network was. The buildings all around us had boarded up windows and not a single car was in sight.

Though, soon enough, a black sedan pulled around the corner, stirring up a trail of dust behind it. It was eerily similar to the vehicle that took me from Sector 36 to Camp Daedalus. When it got closer, I saw the doctor stand up straight and give a salute before the car even pulled up in front of us. As it started slowing down, the passenger seat window opened. General Bergen was sitting there with a smug look on his face, his eyes hidden by tinted sunglasses.

"Good to know that at least one of you made it out of there alive," he said, no remorse in his voice. My blood boiled underneath my skin, my teeth vibrating in anger. I tightly grasped at my pant legs until my hands became white as paper.

"Yes, I survived. Something that everyone else didn't do. Why the hell would you send us out there if you knew that it was that dangerous?!"

He reached up to his face and plucked the glasses off, staring at me with a stony expression. "It wasn't supposed to be hard. You all *made* it hard. I gave you an easy path back to the base when I drove you out. Don't blame their incompetence on me."

"Incompetence?! They were strong and talented! Yet even then we were screwed because of you. You never intended on giving us a chance in the first place!" I huffed, heavily breathing.

Unexpectedly, he didn't shout back or deny my words. Instead, he pointed to the back of the car. "Get in," he muttered, before turning his gaze to the doctor beside me. "You did well Dr. Hayes. Thank you for contacting me as quick as you did."

"No," I growled. The two men turned their heads toward

me. "I won't be going where you are. You no longer have control over what I do from here on out."

The General sighed and waved Dr. Hayes back toward the research facility, to which he obliged. He pointed again to the back of the car. "Get in. You're not getting out of this sector if you don't, and I sure as hell won't be coming back here anytime soon."

As he finished, the back seat of the car popped open, and it irritated me to see how confident he was that I was going to get inside. At the same time, he did have a point. Gritting my teeth, I hesitantly stepped forward and got in the empty back seat. After I pulled my feet in, the door automatically closed, and the car engine started revving up.

"Good, now that you're done with your temper tantrum, we can talk about some real stuff. And before you get all angry, listen. This is actually important information. Your little burst of anger can wait," he added, fanning the fire.

"Fine," I growled.

"Good."

Shifting around in his seat, he reached back and handed me a large stack of paper that was pinched together by a large clip. "Give it a read. Let's just say it's a...reward, for finishing Camp Daedalus and completing the mission I gave you before you left."

Scowling, I swiped it off his hands and looked at the title. It was called, *"Operation Nabu Strike."*

"What is this?"

"Just read it."

Groaning, I flipped to the first page, which had a brief, overarching description.

> *Operation Nabu Strike*
> *Following the increased attempts to infiltrate our*

*nation, the United Republic Department of Military hereby authorizes the organization and execution of "Operation Nabu Strike." The Republic DOM recognizes the severity of the threats that are being posed to the capital's southern border and recommends implementing this project as a pre-emptive intel strike against the Blighted people of the East. Classification level Nine. The information outlined in this folder is as follows: member recommendations, recruitment background information, training outlines, and mission outlines with parameters.*

"My question still stands," I started. "What is this?"

He huffed, and answered, "It's exactly what it sounds like. You've heard of the increasing attacks on our southern border, haven't you? You even saw the threat indicator in the basement intel room back at the base."

I vaguely remembered the diagram of the Republic on the massive screens. "Yes, I remember," I replied curtly.

"Well, they've been getting worse while you've been milling around in the desert with your little ragtag group. Each of the Generals on the Board was asked to find a recommend a candidate for the operation."

It took me a second, but I finally realized what he was trying to say. "No way. No way I'm going to be part of some military pet project again. Come on! Even you must have some limits for what you ask of people!" I shouted, getting worked up.

"Calm yourself down, and listen, you little punk. This isn't about you, this isn't about me. It's about what's at stake, which is the whole goddamn country. Do you understand?" the Alpha General angrily responded, and I sat down, a boiling rage building up inside myself.

Much to my chagrin, he pulled a cigarette out from

somewhere and lit it inside of the car. Smoke started filling the car, and I coughed a couple of times from the fumes. "Sorry, sorry," he apologized, and he opened the car window, letting the smell filter out. For some reason, it felt so wrong hearing the word "sorry" coming out from his mouth.

"So? You decided that you'd let one person live from your camp and that would be who you took?" I accused, fixing him with a scathing glare.

"Not exactly, but something like that. I was genuinely serious when I said that all of you should've made it back. Your scrappy choices are what got you into this situation. But anyway, it's not like you have a choice about this issue anyhow."

What he said at the end incensed me while my stomach sank uncomfortably as I felt a foreboding feeling in the depth of my guts. "What do you mean I don't have a choice? Of course I have a choice, don't I?" I asked indignantly. He tossed something toward the back seat, which I recognized immediately.

"Isn't this my graduation pamphlet? Why do you have it?"

"Read the section for Hannah Kamiya. I've even highlighted it for you," the Alpha General muttered, not even bothering to look back.

I flipped through a couple of pages before landing on Hannah's. It had her picture, a face I hadn't seen for a long time. Tracing my fingers along the page, I thought of how good it would be to see her again after all this time. But then, my eyes came upon the highlighted part of the page. I began reading out loud, "-various different sectors. When she was thirteen, she worked closely with Dr. Francis Collers of Sector 48..."

That name hit me hard, as if someone had taken a mallet to my head. "Dr. Francis Collers... isn't he-"

"Yes, he's one of the head medical researchers for the military. And the conversation you heard at the military base-"

"Was about Hannah?"

"Unfortunately," he muttered. Silently, he pulled out another cigarette and lit it, enveloping the car in dark fumes again. "Here's the choice you are given. Either, don't be a part of Operation Nabu Strike, and I personally won't blame you, but your friend will lose everything she has right now. Imagine it, negative paparazzi, a ruined reputation, and no future. She's already treading on thin ice with the mistake she made with Dr. Collers' project, but I can grant her a blank slate since he technically works under me. The other option is-"

"To go, obviously," I finished, staring down at the pamphlet.

"Of course," he said smugly.

"How do I know that you're not tricking me?" I accused. "You've done it plenty of times before."

General Bergen scoffed. "Somehow, I knew you'd say that."

He fumbled around with something near the front seat again, and another manila folder came flying back, filled with several thin sheets of paper. When I opened the folder, my heart froze in place, and my breath hitched.

"Full immunity. Guaranteed."

There were two images on top of a stack of papers, one was an image of person, someone who I knew very well. In the picture, the person was dead, killed by a thin slit that was made across his neck. In the other picture, there was a crude scratched drawing of a wolf-like figure.

"Holton Bordias. I'm sure you're familiar with him. After all, you killed him, didn't you?" General Bergen mocked.

"H-H-How-"

"Now, here's the final deal. Either you join Operation Nabu Strike, and Hannah gets full immunity for her mistake and you get full immunity for the murder, or on the flip side, you both go to jail. Or for you, maybe the execution block. The people have gotten rowdy after this murder, you know. We're on the cusp of revolution."

The decision was simple. "I'll go."

"Good," he simply said, and became quiet again. "You've made the right decision. The others will have already been there for several weeks, so you're behind. Familiarize yourself with the schedule and what they expect of you."

Leaning back in my chair, I started sifting through the rest of the packet, questioning whether I was truly making the right decision. But soon, I realized that it didn't matter. Regardless of whether this was the *right* decision, this was the *better* decision. There *was* no other decision that could be made.

Something that General Bergen said didn't sit right with me. "You said that the others have already been there for several weeks? Where am I going right now anyways?'

"The program started up already, so you're behind. It's the consequence of taking so long to finish the final assessment."

The anger, which had stayed in the back of my mind, flared back up. But instead of shouting in anger, I grit my teeth, bottling those emotions and pushing them deep down. I growled, "What would you have done if more than one of us survived?"

He hummed amusedly as if he was thinking about something interesting. "Well, I would've thought of something. But it's never happened before, why would that change?"

That implication settled in my mind uncomfortably like a heavy rock. "This has happened before?"

He didn't respond.

"Also, you never answered my other question. Where are we going?"

He hummed lightly, before answering, "To the home of the Republic military. Sector Two."

I closed the packet of papers and slid it in the back pocket of the passenger's seat. Leaning sideways, I rested the crown of my head against the window, basking in the chilling sensation crawling down my neck and to the rest of the body. The dunes of sand and plains of cacti rolled by, and the turmoil in my head continued.

# Chapter 22

*August 19, 2103*

· · · · ● · · · ·

G ENERAL BERGEN REMAINED silent throughout the trip. I guess he really didn't have much to say, though I certainly wasn't going to complain about that. Although my immediate anger was satiated with my little outburst, I still felt underlying anger that was blistering underneath my skin. I wasn't sure if I'd be able to contain myself if he crossed the line with his comments one more time.

Instead, I watched the countryside pass by the window; the desert had faded into rolling hills a long while ago, and soon turned into forests as we traveled northeast toward Sector Two. Along with the landscape, the sectors transitioned to a much more high-class area with bigger homes and a much more liberal application of technology on the streets. The often stone and concrete buildings of the outer sectors were replaced by metal and glass superstructures in the inner sectors. Whereas the smaller, two-lane roads of the outer sectors were barely worn at all, the multi-lane highways that the inner sectors sported had constant repairs around the cascading river of cars.

Soon enough, the urban structures became more grandiose in design and size until we finally reached the ring roads surrounding the Inner Sectors. Core Ten. The Sectors for the Elite. The Corrupted Sectors. What people called these sectors differed based on their own opinion. But factually, these sectors were the group of sectors that were designated to serve special roles, therefore deserving of a special name.

As we pulled up to the ring roads, a man in a silver military uniform directed us to the side, leading the car toward a security draw gate. Multiple soldiers with guns were at the point, directing their wary gazes toward the vehicle. For the first time in a while, I heard General Bergen speaking as he muttered, "Stupid procedures wasting my time…"

I gazed out the window in both awe and trepidation. The security surrounding the Inner Sector borders was way overkill. All the entryways were surrounded by military vehicles, and extreme surveillance through cameras and the like were planted on top of the steel draw gates. Guards were all over the place, and it almost felt like I was entering a prison, rather than the center of government and economic activity.

"Identification?" a gruff voice asked.

"Here," General Bergen replied, handing him a small card.

The soldier didn't even take it. As he noticed the gold coloration of the identification card, his eyes darted toward the passenger seat. When he made eye contact with the General, his hand retracted as if he had been stung, a panicked look shadowing his face.

"G-General Bergen, it's good to see you again, sir!"

"Stand down and get your act together. Haven't you all been told to increase security?"

"Y-Yes, sir!" the soldier shouted. He retreated from the car, and moments later, the draw gate started swinging open. Slowly, the car passed through the barrier between the outer and inner sectors. I felt a shiver going up my arms as the car passed through. The last thing I saw as the car continued forward was a soldier yelling and pointing a gun at some family that was sitting inside their car with frightened expression on their faces. *'Some security...'* I thought.

Turning to the General, I asked, "Why is security being tightened?"

"The same reason that they're calling for Operation Nabu Strike. The DOM has ordered security to be tightened as a precaution. You'll find out once we get you up to speed, but the situation is much worse than what you probably are imagining," he informed me.

As we passed into Sector Ten, one of the border Inner Sectors surrounding the Capital, I couldn't help but notice all the soldiers that were moving around. Some were stationed outside of banks, entrances to railway stations, and other random buildings.

"Is it always like this?"

General Bergen snorted while looking outside the window. "Security is a little bit tighter, but yeah, this is what it's like. People are paranoid about attacks and safety. Cowards are what they are. Rich taxpayers basically hiring out the military. It's disgusting," he mumbled under his breath. I wasn't sure if he was responding to me or if he was just thinking to himself.

I took in the sights of people moving around, going about their daily lives. On the streets, I saw some teenagers around my age who were loitering around on the streets while two adults were arguing nearby. Near the corner of the block, two children in fancy-looking clothes were tossing rocks at a smaller child who distinctively had a brand near the base of his neck. Absentmindedly, my hands rose to my neck.

After a bit of driving through the ring roads and the local

streets of Sector Ten, the car took an exit off the main road. On the horizon, I could see the bustling airspace over the sector as well as the characteristic haze of the inner sectors. As we approached, the car again took an exit and began circling around the outer edge of Sector Two. Looking in, I could see the towering condominiums of the sector's edge. Overall, Sector Two had a much more modern feel than the outer sectors and even compared to Sector Ten, it had a more refined feel to it.

The car slowly approached a towering white building in the distance.

"Here we are, the military base of Sector Two," General Bergen announced with pleasure, and my mouth nearly dropped.

The expansive white building was nothing like the military base that hosted Camp Daedalus or what I imagined an above-ground base to be. Where I expected dull, gray concrete walls lined with barbed wire fencing, this base was the complete opposite. The parts of the building not covered in glass were decorated by a sparkly white stone that I could not recognize, and the design seemed almost futuristic, as if it were a technology hub rather than a military base.

The building was two stories high, and it took up a massive chunk of land, about thirty acres, on the ground. A tall metal and glass tower extended in the center above the rest of the building with skywalks jutting out from it leading to several floating "orbs." The building was pretty much just a cylinder with an oddly shaped tower in the hollow center.

In the distance, I could see drones coming in for a landing, going into the building through somewhere on the roof while thin blue wires inconspicuously wrapped around the perimeter, creating a nearly invisible fence.

"This is the main base that controls a lot of the central information for the entire country. There are smaller bases that dot the sector, but this is the main one," General Bergen explained.

"Why is the building designed this way?" I asked curiously. "Doesn't it stick out like a sore thumb?"

General Bergen laughed a little, as wrong as that sounded. "It's protected enough that the design isn't a problem."

That was a very mysterious response. One that I didn't really understand while looking at the base since the only form of protection I could see was the thin perimeter of fencing. General Bergen must've noticed my confused look because he elaborated, "You'll find out soon enough."

As we reached the front entrance of the base, the car stopped behind a translucent gate for a few moments before continuing forward. The gate didn't really open, though, so much as it kind of fell away. The technology of the base was already bending my mind, and I didn't know if I'd have the energy to take it all in.

A translucent barrier that covered an open portion of the building also faded away as the car got close. We continued moving forward until the car stopped on top of a white platform. As expected, the car began to rise in a sort of elevator, but instead of a dark chamber, natural light poured in through the glass windows that looked outwards. The floor even turned the car around so that we could see the amazing view of Sector Two. It was quite a breathtaking view, and I was almost lost in the moment. Sadly, as quickly as the show started, the car pulled back from the elevator shaft into a wide, open space.

The car slowly rolled to a stop in a large reception-like room. It was very similar to the foyer at Camp Daedalus except for the fact that there was no large statue and the Republic emblem on the ground was painted in white and gold outlines.

All four of the car doors clicked, signaling that the doors had been unlocked. General Bergen opened the car and swung himself out, and I hastily followed him as he walked up to the reception desk near the front of the large room.

"I've brought my candidate for Operation Nabu Strike. Is General Heitman here?"

The receptionist nodded with a smile before she glanced at me. Her eyes turned frosty before she picked up the phone next to her. Dialing a couple of numbers, she held the earpiece against the ear, and said, "General Heitman? Yes. Yes. Yes, he is here right now. Alright. You too, sir."

She hung up the phone and turned to General Bergen. "He will be right down. Please go to the central tower and meet him at the first-floor lobby there."

General Bergen nodded swiftly and motioned for me to follow him. I gave the receptionist another glance who shot me a frosty glare in response. Her eyes fluttered toward my neck, and I grit my teeth at the attention.

We walked down a winding spiral staircase before arriving at a crossroad of some sorts. The intersection had a long catwalk that led toward the central tower. Its sides were framed with glass, the catwalk itself crafted out of white metal.

"Why is everything so white?" I asked General Bergen, and he shrugged.

"The geezers must've liked white when they built this place."

The long catwalk led right into a larger atrium-like space that was extremely spacious. A large statue crafted out of some other white metal reflecting the sunlight stood at an impressive height in the middle of the room. Its nameplate also read, "Tyler B. Whitman." Above the statue, there was a chandelier made from various glittering stones of varying colors, sort of resembling the solar system.

"Stop gawking and let's keep moving," General Bergen chided. My gaze shifted back toward ground level, and I saw General Bergen swiftly walking toward a pair of people that were standing next to the massive statue. One, who looked very old, had an entirely white uniform with various medals and ribbons dangling off his chest and arms. His hair was white, and he had a full beard around his mouth.

"Kyle Bergen, General of Sector Nine," General Bergen formally introduced, stretching his hands out toward the man. He directed his gaze towards me, and announced, "This is Ethan Holfstras of Sector 36, the sole survivor of Camp Daedalus 274."

The other man took General Bergen's hand with a small smile. "Gregory Heitman, General of Sector Two. I also have here with me my assistant, Lieutenant James Dyer. It's a pleasure to meet you."

I noticed that General Heitman was purposefully glossing over me, even though I was standing right in front of him.

"Thank you for your recommendation, General Bergen. I'm sure that he will be an important part of the mission," General Heitman said, but I didn't hear any sincerity in his voice, even though his visage seemed friendly enough.

The Lieutenant turned toward me with a small scowl. "Welcome to Sector Two. This military base will be your *temporary* residence for the foreseeable future until Operation Nabu Strike commences. We will start out with a short meeting in a conference room, then you'll have a chance to catch up and meet the others."

I watched as the two Generals made their final farewells and parted. General Heitman started walking forward toward a different part of the building, again not sparing a single glance toward me. Lieutenant Dyer followed General Heitman, and I hobbled along, frowning at being ignored by the pair.

They led me toward a secluded area in the main tower section of the building, and my anxiety continued to rise as we headed down a spiral staircase. Neither of the two spoke a single word, nor did they explain what we were doing all the way down here in what I presumed was a basement.

I tried opening my mouth, but no words came out.

"Here we are," Lieutenant Dyer suddenly said, and he, along with the General, was looking toward a single sliding door that was embedded into a glass wall. The door led into a massive room that was filled from top to bottom with massive server towers with multicolored blinking lights.

General Heitman pressed his thumb against a small pad on the wall, and a small light scanned through his eyes. He also pulled out a small phone-like device from his pocket and put it into a slot inside of the wall.

The door opened with a hiss, and the Lieutenant motioned me to follow him in with a sneer. He led me all the way to a small pedestal in the center of the room. The base of the pedestal was connected to several of the server towers by thick rubber cables. Lieutenant Dyer messed around with some buttons before turning toward me. "Put your hand in the center."

He stepped to the side allowing me to stand up onto the glowing black plate that was embedded into the pure white pedestal. I hesitantly pressed down my hands on the plate, recoiling in shock as something bit at my hands. Cautiously, I looked but saw nothing there. My hand looked fine too.

"Well? What are you waiting for?" the Lieutenant's impatient voice urged.

Nervously, I held out my hand toward the plate once

again, pressing it down carefully. The shock came once again, but it felt less painful. Small green lines started filling the previously black panel until the entire board flashed green.

"You can take your hand off now."

With a heavy sigh of relief, I jerked my hand away from the pedestal, watching as General Heitman and Lieutenant Dyer walked out of the room. Their behavior was starting to grate on my nerves, and my head was throbbing in annoyance. But I recalled what was at stake, so I silently followed them without protest. I made a mental note about the existence of this room, however.

At the top of the staircase, General Heitman turned toward Lieutenant Dyer and commanded, "Show him to his room. After you're done, bring him over to the conference room halls and find me there. Make sure that you don't take too long."

"Yes, sir!" he responded as General Heitman walked through the connecting skybridge toward the main part of the building.

"Come with me," Lieutenant Dyer's sharp voice called, and he started leading me up a staircase that wrapped around the entirety of the tower. We walked up and up until we reached the second floor. The second floor was just a large glass ring around the inner circumference of the cylindrical tower that had different doorways leading to the glass "orbs" that I had seen earlier from the outside.

Lieutenant Dyer led me into one of those orbs labeled 2B, climbing up a slowly inclining sky bridge to do so. When we finally made it inside of the small "orb," I was met with a sight that I didn't expect. The entire structure was dedicated to dorm rooms, a short semi-circle of doors having been placed near the outer circumference. A somewhat cozy common space was in the middle of the circle of doors which couches and a TV set.

"These are the men's halls," began Lieutenant Dyer. "Across the facility is the women's halls. You'll check into your room every night and check out in the morning. All your other necessities will be here as well, including 24/7 dining, training, and many more areas. The layout is rather basic, and we've reserved a special area for your unit. I'll take you to your room, and your fingerprints against the doorknob will be enough to unlock the door. Just firmly grip the knob and you should hear a click."

He told me all this without looking directly at me once and with a very reluctant voice. In fact, Lieutenant Dyer looked as if he was entirely disconnected from the world. We swung around the small circular common space until we reached room 220, which was on the opposite side from the entrance. He motioned for me to open the door, and I reached out to grab the knob, jumping in shock as the locking mechanism inside automatically turned to let me in.

The room was less of a dorm or bedroom and more of a lavish one-room house. Just at a glance, I could see a comfortable seating area with a television and a Dashboard. Off to the back was a countertop and sink, and a few cupboards and drawers added to the small kitchen area. I stepped in and let the door close behind me.

My boots clicked against a tiled white floor, and the furniture inside was made in similar colors to the rest of the base: gold and white. To the left of the entrance was a personal bathroom and, although small, was much more welcoming than a shared showering hall. As I stepped further in, I noticed the rectangular lighting panels in the ceiling distrib-uting ample, warm light throughout the room.

The seating area I'd noticed before looked almost as comfortable as the bed that was leaned up against the large window in the far side of the room. It was inviting, calling me to lay down in it. The Dashboard was where it always seemed to be, across from the bed. The screen was mostly blank for now, merely showing a holographic display of the entire facility.

"Here are the two things you need while you are at this base."

I turned around as Lieutenant Dyer took out from his pocket a pristine white watch and a similar phone-like device to what General Heitman had. I held them in my hands experimentally, and asked, "What are these for?"

Lieutenant Dyer didn't answer me.

My wrist, which had felt empty ever since I got rid of the black watch from Camp Daedalus, once against felt complete as I strapped the new, sleek white watch on my wrist. Immediately, it lit up in a flash of white light, green lines darting across the screen. Just seconds later, it chimed, "Biometric scanning complete."

As I held the phone in my other hand, it did the same, chiming, "Biometric scanning complete," just seconds later.

"The watch functions like the Dashboard, as you should already know, and the phone, which we call an Egg, serves other purposes which you can figure out later. But importantly, it's a third security requirement for some high-profile locations around the building," Lieutenant Dyer explained.

I looked down at my watch. A flurry of text was already skittering across the screen reading, *Pre-Orientation Meeting: 1630 Hours.* The time read 16:15.

"You'll have an opportunity to look around a little bit later, but for now, you have a meeting with General Heitman. Let's go," he called, turning around to leave the room.

As we made our way again through the winding halls and staircases, Lieutenant Dyer went back to his old, dispassionate self and didn't say a single word to me during the entire trip. Once on the first floor, we left the tower toward the main cylindrical portion of the building. There, he led me up to the second floor to a wing of rooms that looked entirely dedicated to business conference rooms.

He prodded me into a room labeled "C-214."

The room was set up quite simply. A long mahogany desk sat in the middle of the room with multiple crimson cushioned office chairs surrounding it. The atmosphere felt chilly, the air conditioner running at full blast. General Heitman was already there, sitting on the opposite side of the long table while typing away at some laptop that was set on top of the desk.

"General Heitman, I brought him back."

He finally looked up and said, "Thank you. You may go back now."

Lieutenant Dyer saluted the general and swiftly left the room, but not before shooting me another heated glare. Nervously, I stood there, scratching at my arms, not really knowing what to do.

"Take a seat," General Heitman commanded, addressing me directly for the first time.

I hastily sat down in the chair opposite from his, noting that the chair was very comfortable and made my entire body sink into the cushion. It made me feel a lot calmer than I had been just a few seconds ago. General Heitman didn't speak a single word. Instead, he continued to look at me across the table with a piercing stare, making me fidget in my seat uncomfortably.

"I would advise you to watch where you step while you are here," he started, making me flinch. His gaze shifted toward the base of my neck, which I hastily covered with my right hand. "Hiding it doesn't do you any good. You either run away from it or confront it. But that's not why I've brought you here."

He rummaged through a large bag that was sitting next to him on the table and pulled out a large manila folder. He set it on top of the table and pressed a button to the side. To my surprise, the outer edge of the table started shifting, rotating as it brought the folder closer toward me. When it reached me, General Heitman pressed another button, and the shifting belt stopped.

"This is a brief mission detail for Operation Nabu Strike. Everyone else has already received this information many weeks prior, so you have a lot of catching up to do," he stated. There was no insult or pity behind his words. He simply spoke the facts bluntly.

"What exactly is the mission?" I asked curiously. "I was told that there would be a mission related to the Eastern Federation, but not exactly what it would be."

"It's nothing more than a simple recon mission to the East. They're attacking our border and infiltrating into our country, but we have no idea why. That's what this mission is about."

"And my status as a Bastard? Will that affect me while I'm here?" I asked nervously, being equally blunt as the general.

He snorted in response, to my immediate frustration. "Your status will affect you as much as you let it. If you want to hide the fact, then be my guest. If you want to tell them, then do so. Just know that all of the others that you will meet are from the Core Sectors."

My head was swimming from that information, and I thought back to the brief conversation that I had with Carter just days before he was expelled from Camp Daedalus. *"But you should see what they do to people like us in the Core Sectors. I heard they literally use us Bastards as slaves."*

I gulped as the General continued to look at me with interest. "Is that all for today?" I asked.

"Yes, it is. Read through the information thoroughly and make sure that you ring Lieutenant Dyer up when you are ready. You can do that with the Egg he handed you earlier."

I took that as a dismissal and stood up, leaving the room.

Tracing back my steps, I walked through the winding hallways until I was back where I started, back in my room. The soft mattress of the bed still called to me like a siren's song, tempting me to go and lay down, just for a moment. I shook my head. Instead, I pulled out the Egg that Lieutenant Dyer had given me right before he left. It really was just a phone.

When the screen lit up, the wallpaper was the Republic's emblem. I saw various options on the home screen. There were basic news apps among other things, but there were also specialized options such as "Room Maintenance" and "Dining Hall Services."

I clicked on the option labeled "Dining Hall Services," and a long list of food options came up. *That's why Lieutenant Dyer said that this room had everything that I would ever need,* I realized. I could practically just stay holed up in my room and get everything I needed right here if I wanted to.

I called for ten water bottles along with some small snacks that I could keep in my room. The phone let me know that it would be about ten minutes before the food would arrive. So, during that time, I decided to explore the room just a little bit more. First, I started with the closet, which had ten new, clean uniforms hung up for me. Again, they had gotten my size right. Each uniform was jet black, pockets running down the arms, chest, and legs. Oddly, mine was a little bit different than the others' based on what I'd seen so far. Mine had a slightly longer collar that stuck closer to my body, which I soon realized was meant to hide my brand.

Quickly, I changed out of my sand-colored uniform into this new one, which I found was much more comfortable than it looked. Then, a soft chime rang through the room as someone arrived at the door.

On the other side, I saw a very short, plain guy standing stock still with objects gathered in his arms. He was wearing a military uniform, but a downgraded version of it. It was just a single layered jumpsuit that clung to his skin, and there were no pockets on it. It looked eerily similar to prison jumpers.

"Ten bottles of water and nutrition bars?" he said. His voice sounded hoarse and lifeless. Hesitantly, I reached out my hand to grab the items out of his small hands as he saluted once. As I raised my hand to salute him back, the guy flinched back as if he had been slapped. He quickly bowed once, then ran off. Just before he left, I saw part of his uniform intentionally cut out near the collar. There was a black tattoo mark near the base of his neck, an image of a wolf preparing to bite into his neck.

# Chapter 23

*August 19, 2103*

. . . . **.** . . . .

I LAID DOWN ON the bed, staring up at the ceiling with a blank mind. For thirty minutes, my thoughts were continually occupied by the memory of that cursed brand. Carter's word again echoed hollowly in my mind. *"But you should see what they do to people like us in the Core Sectors. I heard they literally use us bastards as slaves."*

Shock still coursed through my veins, and I started wondering if there were more of them here in the base. If there were, where did they live?

My eyes drifted back to the ten water bottles which were now sitting on the ground next to the bathroom. The granola bars were scattered on the small cubby underneath the Dashboard, and the sight of them made me feel disgusted on the inside, as if I had been tainted by something foul.

Papers of all different sizes were scattered across my bed, all part of the gigantic manila folder that General Heitman had handed me about an hour ago. I wondered how long they were willing to give me before they got fed up with me not calling Lieutenant Dyer.

With a loud groan, I sat up in bed, holding some of the papers in my hands. Most of them were miniature replications of the map displayed in the underground Intel Division room at Camp Daedalus. Otherwise, the papers were general daily reports about activity on the border. The most recent one, which was from just two weeks ago, was the most intriguing.

> *August 5th, 2103,*
> *Location: Marais Des Cygnes River*
> *Current Situation: The Blighted have gained ground on Republic soil along the Marais Des Cygnes River, and have set up military camps within our borders. Short gunfire conflicts within the area resulted in the majority of casualties for the Republic.*
> *Casualty/Damages: The ratio of the casualties heavily favor their forces. Republic casualties: ~24,000. Federation casualties: ~1,000.*
> *Recommended Action: Retreat and move Republic lines back to Bull Creek.*

As a sifted through the papers for a couple of hours, I found that most of the other reports were in a similar vein, the tension culminating in this most recent report. I got the gist of why the military was eager to carry out Operation Nabu Strike so quickly. Every day, the Republic was being pushed back, somehow.

As time ticked on, I felt the need to contact Lieutenant Dyer sooner rather than later, so I set the folder aside and called him on my Egg. Instead of hearing his grating voice in return, however, the schedule on my Dashboard simply updated. *"Meeting. 1830 Hours. C-211"*

I leaped up from my bed and took a moment to gather the loose sheets of paper back into the folder. Walking out of the room with folder tucked under my arms, I drew my collar up nervously. Two other guys passed by, chatting animatedly about something, and they didn't even stop to give me a second glance. I sighed in relief.

Going back through the skybridge and into the main building, I was once again back in the large area dedicated to conference rooms. As I got closer to C-211, I heard subdued sounds of a male and female voice talking beyond the heavy door. I put my Egg up to the scanner and let myself in and saw General Heitman standing at the front talking to a girl around my age.

As soon as I entered, they both turned around, the girl watching me with a cold, expressionless stare. Her cold blue eyes were like chips of ice boring into my soul.

"Mr. Holfstras, this is Ms. Heliodoro, or Elisa," General Bergen introduced, and her familiar-sounding name sent a shiver up my spine. *Stop thinking like that,* I chided myself. Elisa's flowing blonde hair bobbed as she walked over to me. When she got closer, I stuck out my hand, but she never took it. I retracted it awkwardly.

I waited for her to say something, but she just stood there, watching me.

"Ms. Heliodoro will be the leader of Operation Nabu Strike," General Bergen continued. "She's aware of the activity on the border and has been working hard with the rest of your squad to prepare for the Operation. As I've said before, I expect you to catch up quickly, so get acquainted and follow the orders of Ms. Heliodoro."

I nodded in response. "Of course, General Heitman."

A slight smile rose on Elisa's face which disappeared as soon as it formed.

"I've added you to my contact list on my Egg. It's getting a bit late tonight, but I do expect you to try to contact me as often as possible to catch up on everything," Elisa explained, gesturing to her phone device. While her voice wasn't as emotionless as her facial expression, it was still a far cry from being friendly.

"I'd be failing myself if I didn't."

She nodded at my response and gestured for General Heitman to continue. "That's exactly what we want to hear, Mr. Holfstras. That's all for this meeting, I needed you to meet Elisa. Keep looking into those documents, and you can begin training tomorrow. Feel free to do whatever you wish during your off-time. You're dismissed."

I glanced between the two and began backing out of the conference room, walking back through the winding hallways. Elisa was already making me feel uncomfortable, and I felt confused. She had been unnecessarily unfriendly even though it was only the first meeting. My eyes widened, and I ran all the way back to the room in a panic, tossing the manila folder on the bed before darting into the bathroom. I stared at myself in the mirror. The brand on my neck was still hidden underneath the thin fabric guarding the neck, which meant the only reason she might've treated me like that would've been-

"Damn him..." I growled, slamming a frustrated fist onto the marble countertop. I continued to stare at my reflection, furious at General Heitman. He had given me a promise to not tell anyone yet had already blown it within the first couple of hours.

Frustrated, I stomped back into the room, looking around for something to let out my pent-up anger. Snatching the folder off my bed, I chucked it across the room, scattering pieces of paper everywhere. My head was still pounding in anger, and I saw the time, *19:00*. Picking two water bottles off the ground, I marched out of the room, heading toward the training facility.

As I went down the long sky bridge, I grabbed at my Egg and pulled up a map of the base. The athletic training facility was in the main cylindrical portion of the building on the first floor. It took me nearly twenty minutes to get there, but when I did, my mouth dropped in surprise.

If the training facility at Camp Daedalus had been advanced, this one was even more so. There were many people milling around using various pieces of equipment. Every single one of them had little eye visors on, but I couldn't fathom why. The room itself was somewhat like the other facility except for the fact it was colored white as far as I could see, and it was slightly more compact. Off to the side, there were multiple separated rooms that were empty while people were standing in them, moving around as if fighting an invisible foe.

"Is this your first time here?" someone asked.

I turned around. Right next to the entrance, there was a woman sitting at a reception desk with an emotionless smile on. "Yes, this is my first time."

"Then here," she said, pulling out a clear eye visor from underneath her desk. "This visor is called the C-Track. It will allow you to keep track of how long you've been in the facility, give you progress checks, and recommend training regimens based on your performances. Please sync it with your Egg. That C-Track will only be accessible to you."

"Thank you," I whispered in awe, running my finger along the edge of the visor. The receptionist turned away, looking forward again; out of the corner of my eye, I saw the coal-colored brand on the base of her neck. With a grimace, I walked into the athletic training facility, syncing the C-Track with my Egg. As soon as the syncing completed, the device hummed, and I put it over my eyes.

It was incredible. When I looked around the room, it was almost like playing a game. Short explanations of each device/training activity appeared on the screen, and recommendations for using that piece of equipment appeared.

I walked around, watching other people exercise while exploring the features of the C-Track. The people inside of the empty white rooms were apparently doing something called, "Virtual Walking," a form of mental training activity.

Eventually, I came upon a small space that was dedicated to a shooting range. It was separated from the rest of the facility by a thick, soundproof glass wall with a metal door. The range was long and used live bullets. Several semi-corporal vapor trail targets were lined up near the back end of the range which was about fifty meters away.

There was only one person in the room. His back was turned to me, so I couldn't tell his age, but his blond hair stuck out like a sore thumb, and it reminded me of Elisa, to my annoyance. I made to turn around and leave but stopped as the guy started shooting. He had a small MEG-9 pistol, a smaller than standard pistol that was mainly used for stealth operations, and was firing away at the targets. He never missed. Each bullet continued to pierce through the targets' heads as he went from the left to the right.

Hesitantly, I reached out and opened the door, entering. "That's impressive," I told him as he finished.

The guy turned around and smiled, "Oh, thanks. Are you here to give it a try as well?"

I shook my head nervously. "No, not today. Maybe some other time."

"Come on, why not? You came in here watching me, it'd be unfair if I didn't get to watch you too!" he protested, his blue eyes practically pleading.

"Um, I really shouldn't-"

He fixed me with a stare, and I sighed. "Fine."

The guy grinned and put the pistol back into a small holster on his hips. He motioned me over and showed me a rack of various pistols. I glazed over several Beretta pistols, which made me involuntarily shiver for some reason. In the end, I grabbed a standard SM9 Pistol off the rack and experimentally held it in my right hand. With my left, I filled up one magazine of bullets and slid it into the gun.

I walked up to the range, eyeing the ten targets that were spread out horizontally. Glancing back, I saw the guy smiling, watching me with a keen eye. Even I could tell that he wasn't just looking on for entertainment.

Turning back, I trained the pistol toward the targets, just as my visor lit up and read, *"Mid-Range Targeting Exercise."* My muscles guided me once again, moving on their own. From the left to right, I shot bullet after bullet methodically, hitting every single one in vital points. I grimaced as I missed the last one.

"That was great!" the other guy called. I fidgeted as the other guy stood there smiling. Now that I focused more on him, I could see his features more clearly. He was *young*, maybe only as old as I was. His face was stretched in a contagious grin as he held out his hand. "I'm Elisedd Heliodoro, by the way, spelled with 2 ds."

Hobbling over, I shook his hand, the last name making me perk up. "Any relation to Elisa Heliodoro?"

Elisedd raised his eyebrows. "You've met my sister already?"

I grimaced. "Yeah."

Instead of chiding me for my rude gesture, Elisedd bellowed in laughter, clutching at his stomach as the sounds of his broken bouts of laughter echoed off the walls. Confused, I waited for another minute before Elisedd settled down.

"What's so funny?" I asked.

"Y-Your face," he panted, getting over his last fit of laughs. "I bet you thought my sister was some cold-hearted girl who hates you for no reason, right?"

*Well, it's not for no reason,* I thought, holding my hand against my neck. "Y-Yeah, I guess so."

Elisedd exhaled loudly one last time before explaining, "Don't worry man, she's not always going to be like that. She just does that to new people before she really gets to know them. Just give her some time."

Somehow, I really doubted that Elisa would be warming up to me anytime soon, but I gave Elisedd the benefit of the doubt.

"So, why are you here? You look like a new face to me," Elisedd asked curiously.

"Operation Nabu Strike."

"Ah," Elisedd said. "You're on our squad then."

"Our squad?"

"Yeah. Our squad. Elisa is the leader, and I'm also on the team. There's also Rag and Alex, but I'm sure you'll meet the two of them at some point. You know what? Why don't you come here tomorrow morning, and I'll introduce you? How does that sound?"

I cringed at the prospect of having to wake up in the morning, but nonetheless asked, "What time?"

"Six in the morning."

I groaned.

# Chapter 24

*August 20, 2103*

. . . . ● ● . . . .

I YAWNED. THE DASHBOARD was still screeching as the alarm I set up for 05:45 was echoing off the walls. My eyes were groggy, and I wished for nothing more than to just go back to sleep. But the Dashboard reminded me, *"Elisedd: 0600 Hours."*

With a groan, I turned the Dashboard off and silently left the room. Elisedd was already waiting by the common space. Apparently, all the males from Operation Nabu Strike were living next to each other. Elisedd had another kid right next to him.

The other guy was short, maybe only just coming up to my chest. His face was dotted with small freckles, and he had nasty bedhead. His black eyes were bloodshot, and he was shooting filthy glares at Elisedd, who didn't even bother to acknowledge it.

"Hey! Are you ready to go?"

"Yeah…" I muttered, my gaze trailing over to the other kid.

Elisedd followed my gaze and exclaimed, "Let me introduce you to each other. This is Rag, short for Ragnvald.

He's from Sector Eight, a little way out, but he's a pretty cool dude."

Rag waved his hand at me somewhat tiredly. He didn't seem like a bad person at first glance, just someone that was too tired to be up this early in the morning. Rag turned to Elisedd and complained. "Why did you only drag me up this early in the morning? What about Alex? Why isn't he here with us?"

"You know he likes to sleep in."

"What about me?! I like to sleep in!" Rag protested, waiting for an answer.

Elisedd just shrugged and started walking toward the sky bridge. I laughed, heaving in mirth as Rag disbelievingly looked toward Elisedd's slowly retreating back. He sighed and ran after Elisedd while I followed close behind.

In silence, we walked down to the training facility, which was empty this early in the morning. The woman at the counter was gone, replaced by a short, scrawny boy that was probably no older than fourteen.

Elisedd led us past the shooting range and toward a makeshift fighting ring that was set up. "Most people don't use the actual boxing ring," Elisedd explained. "Most people would rather just go through the virtual version without pain. But I say no pain, no gain, so I like to dish it out in the real world."

I nodded. That made sense. It probably also helped muscle development since just the muscle memory wouldn't get you anywhere if someone was stronger.

"Rag, you want to go first?"

"Sure," he replied.

The two stood up on the ring, staring each other down. Elisedd was in a low, athletic stance with his hands out in front of him while Rag laid low, almost coming down to Elisedd's waist height. They circled around each other, looking for an opening that they could exploit.

Rag struck first, using his low stance to try to sweep out Elisedd's legs from underneath him. Elisedd leaped back, then threw a low side kick toward Rag's stomach. It made direct contact, and Rag stumbled back a bit before regaining his balance. He looked swift on his feet even though he was a bit on the scrawny side.

The fight continued for a long time. Although Elisedd most certainly had the upper edge in terms of strength, Rag's dexterity and swiftness allowed him to keep up. Finally, Rag made a mistake. He went in for another low sweep but went in too deep. Elisedd landed another hard kick to Rag's chest, making him tumble to the ground.

"I give," Rag groaned, holding his chest in pain.

Elisedd grinned and helped him up. "You've gotten a lot better than how you were doing when you first got here."

"Well, yeah. You've been beating me up every single day since we got here," Rag accused with a glare. Elisedd had the decency to look sheepish.

As Rag came down from the arena, Elisedd called, "Ethan, you want to give it a go?"

I hesitated, and started, "I-I don't think that's such a good-"

Rag pushed me, shouting, "If I get treated like a punching bag on the first day, then this kid gets to be treated like a punching bag on the first day too!"

He pushed me toward the arena and practically threw me up onto the platform where Elisedd was waiting in his athletic stance. Hesitantly, I got into the same stance I always did: my feet spread shoulder-width apart, my left palm was out at an angle, and my right hand stayed close to my body in a tightly closed fist.

I circled around him while Elisedd stood still, following my motions with his eyes and turning his body in place to keep me in front of him. Even though I really tried, I couldn't find any openings that I could exploit without getting pummeled back.

"Come on! Get him!" Rag called from the sidelines and I snorted. *Easy for you to say when you're just looking in.*

Elisedd taunted at me with a grin. "Come on, you heard him."

I growled and lunged at him with my right fist reared back, ready to punch forward. Elisedd was still standing motionless in his original position. But as my hand tore through the air toward his face, Elisedd ducked, and the fist went sailing past him. I felt the air get knocked out of my lungs when Elisedd plowed his knees into my gut.

Stumbling backward, I looked through narrowed eyes at Elisedd, who was now hopping lightly on his feet. He started moving forward in a sprint with his own fists reared back. Rag was still yelling from the sidelines, but his voice faded away as the edge of my vision faded to black. I could only see Elisedd in my sights.

As he came in close with his fists geared toward my face, I moved. I darted to the side, letting his fist pass by me harmlessly, and swept my legs in a high arc to try and hit his head. I grinned. Elisedd was off balance with no way to move, and I saw his eyes widen once he realized that. *I win,* I thought.

But suddenly, Elisedd disappeared from my sight, and I looked down in surprise. In a desperate move, Elisedd had crumpled in on himself, knees folding as he laid down on the floor in a last-minute attempt to dodge. I twirled around on my left foot in a full circle as my kick missed, and I felt a hard impact against my back that tossed me to the ground.

"Alright, stop, stop, I give," I groaned. My stomach was still hurting from the first time that Elisedd hit me, and now my back erupted in a new wave of pain. *That's going to leave a nasty bruise,* I thought.

"That was pretty impressive," a soft voice called from outside of the ring. I turned around in surprise to see Elisa striding toward the arena, sweat glistening on her forehead. Her blond hair was wrapped into a ponytail that lightly swayed behind her as she walked.

"Hey, sis," Elisedd called jovially.

"Elisedd, what did I say about doing your crazy exercises today?"

"To not do it?"

Elisa glared at him. "So why are you out here, at seven in the morning, doing *exactly* what I told you not to do?"

"Cause I'm older?" Elisedd replied cheekily with a grin. I saw Elisa's face twist into an annoyed scowl before her gaze shifted back toward me.

"Please don't let this idiot influence you. He's a bad person to be around if you're serious about making yourself better. He just wants an excuse to beat other people up."

"No, I don't."

Elisa glared at Elisedd one more time, before announcing, "Today, General Heitman has requested that we do group training. Since we only have about a week before deployment, he suggested that we work together more."

Elisedd's happy face immediately shifted into a more serious one. "Alright. I'll make sure that everyone is ready for the exercise. Is it team versus team again?"

"Yes."

Grins appeared on Elisedd and Rag's faces.

"Boys," Elisa muttered, shaking her head disparagingly

when she saw their grins. But a small smile appeared on her face as well, contrasting with her previous cold expression. "Just make sure that all of you are ready, and get Ethan up to par as well."

"Alright, will do," Elisedd responded. Elisa walked away from the arena and left the training facility. I turned around to see Elisedd and Rag still grinning with devious expressions.

"What was that all about?" I asked, confused. "Why are you two getting excited all of a sudden?"

"You'll see soon."

With that cryptic message, Elisedd grabbed Rag and ran out of the training facility, making me follow behind them. They went all the way back to the common space, and with a short goodbye, left to their own respective rooms to do something. I was still confused, but one look at my watch showed me an update that I hadn't put there myself. *"Simulated Team Battles: 1500 hours."*

I sighed, and retreated to my room, lying down on the soft bed while drifting off to sleep. Whatever this training thing was could wait. Sleep came first.

GENERAL HEITMAN AND Lieutenant Dyer led us to a much larger simulation room. Somewhere during the middle of the journey, the other squad, led by their captain Eugene Oanez, separated from ours, following General Heitman while we ourselves were stuck with Lieutenant Dyer. The room was like the forest at Camp Daedalus, though this one was a more arid, slightly urban area. We entered through large double doors which led toward a steep ramp. The dusty entryway was surrounded by tall stone walls, and just I could just make out a raised platform in the distance.

We stepped through into the dry heat, a dusty haze filling the air. When we reached the peak of the ramp, and I got a better view of the area. We were in a bit of an opening between buildings, a long pathway connecting our open area to the raised platform I'd seen earlier on the other side of the long straight. To the right was another narrower platform, and behind a half-wall to the left was a passageway. In the far corner, in front of the passageway, was a dumpster and a small gap behind it.

As we looked around the area, Lieutenant Dyer began explaining the rules of our next assessment. "These games are meant to test your teamwork and strategy, so focus on that, not the competitive aspect. The teams will be the two squads taking part in Operation Nabu Strike. One of you is on the defense, the other is on the offense. For this exercise, you will be supplied with simulated weapons and grenades.

"If someone is hit enough times, they are out for the round, and automatic sensors will disable your weapon and you'll have to exit through the nearest doorway, which you'll find scattered throughout the arena. You'll also have a top-down map on BigEgg tablets we'll provide for you, which will not only show you the layout of the arena, but also the positions of your teammates. It'll also display the number of times that you can get hit before you are 'out.'"

"One thing you will notice is red boxes on the map," he continued to explain as he handed out the BigEggs. "Those are the flag points. Attackers must reach those points and gain control for a set amount of time, or eliminate all defenders to win the round. Defenders will obviously defend these points and either eliminate all attackers, prevent attackers from gaining access, or regain control of the point before the attackers hold control of the area for a set amount of time.

"Attackers can gain control by copying a string of infor- mation that will be present inside of an unlocked safe at those locations. One person on the team will get a special golden BigEgg which is the only one that the code can be copied onto. The defenders will have a reset code that will scramble the message, which is when the attackers lose. Any attacker eliminated while carrying the golden BigEgg must drop it at their feet before leaving the arena. I'll give everyone five minutes to explore the arena and the starting zones, indicated by green points on the map, before I pick your sides. You're free to go."

With that, we dispersed across the arena. I walked across the long, straight asphalt-paved path that led to the raised platform in the distance about a hundred meters away. Near the seventy-five-yard mark, just as the path was feeding into an inclining ramp that went up to the platform, I came across a four-way intersection. To my right, there was a small square chunk that had been carved out of the wall, leaving enough space for about two people to fit in. To my left, there was another long passageway, which had an immediately declining ramp leading to another long straight pathway. It tunneled under another catwalk that ran perpendicular above the new path.

I moved past that intersection, going up the inclining ramp to the first flag point. It was set up in a very simple setup. The flag point was a small, boxed in space that had a lifted railing section around the edge. It came up to around waist height. A couple of small, metal crates surrounded a safe that was sitting in the middle.

"Hey, Ethan! Let's move together!" Elisedd called, and I looked back. In my excitement, I had forgotten about the rest of the group, who were now just catching up. Alex was missing, though.

"Sorry about that. I got a little bit excited," I apologized. While I was talking, Elisa and Rag had taken a scan of the first flag point and urged us to move on. Instead retracing our steps and going down the ramp, I continued forward. There was a winding catwalk that went straight for about twenty-five meters, perpendicular to the long path. It took a sharp left, leading to the portion that I had seen earlier on top of the burrowing tunnel path.

The path disappeared between two buildings after we crossed above the lower pathway. A staircase led downwards, and another sharp right turn directed us toward a very open, expansive area.

There were two "stories" to this middle area, which I could see on my BigEgg. The lower floor of the spacious area fed into the other side of the burrowing tunnel we saw before, while we were standing on the upper portion right now. A medium height ledge separated the two floors.

To my left, there was a long walkway that led to a choke-point in front of the attacker's starting point. From that chokepoint, there was also a large decline that led to a set of double doors which were to my right. When I looked straight, I saw a dimly lit tunnel that had a staircase leading upwards near the end. This was the centerstage of the arena.

I hopped over the short wall onto the long decline and walked through the double doors on my right. I arrived at some sort of T-intersection. To the left was a flag point behind a wall; another double door and a hole in the wall granting access from that side. On the right was the "burrowed" section underneath the catwalk that I had seen earlier, and I could see the shallow cubby just above the ramp.

I turned left towards the second flag point and through the ajar doors, saw how much more chaotic this point was. Boxes were everywhere, even a stack right next to the other end of the tunnel which I had seen before. The flag point itself only took up a small corner about a fifth the size of the space and was flanked on many sides by boxes. The back-right corner of the space was a platform raised about a foot above the rest of the area, which also had plenty of concealment.

Finally, the left of the space had a much deeper cubby space and a tunnel entrance, which would connect to the other tunnel through a staircase, according to the map. Also, according to the map, I only had a minute to finish exploring, so I began jogging through the rest of the arena.

Connecting the lower and upper tunnel was an enclosed room with a few pillars for cover, and an open doorway to my right led out into another open space, very reminiscent of the first flag point. A ramp was on the right with a raised platform on the left. Dashing up the ramp, I made a left turn towards a long, open walkway. About halfway, I saw the large open centerstage through a gap between two buildings. I was now standing in the starter's position for the attacker team.

Finally, on the far end of the open area was a small enclosed space with two sets of doors that led back to the entry area that we had first come through.

As we grouped back up with Alex, who probably had been exploring the area by himself, or sleeping, Eugene's group also came around to meet up with us along with General Heitman. Lieutenant Dyer came back, and told us, "Elisa's squad will start on the offense, and Eugene's will start on the defense. I'll show each of you to your start positions, and I'll also hand out your weapons and grenades. Once your watches go off, the offense has fifteen minutes to gain control, and defense has five minutes to regain control. It's one round, and the point is team play and strategy, not necessarily on the outcome of the round. Got it?" We all responded with a firm nod.

He took Eugene's squad down the long pathway towards the raised flag point and turned left towards the dark room under the catwalk. According to the map, that room was the defense's starting area. As they disappeared around the corner, Elisa began talking.

"If this is a strategy assessment, then we need a strategy. As we go, we can create different names for all the areas just for consistency. I will be leading the group, as designated by my role as leader, but I'll have Alex helping me with the strategy."

Everyone nodded in agreement, although Alex seemed a little bit reluctant in doing so.

"If I may," I interrupted, getting flashbacks to the survival exercise during Camp Daedalus. "I don't think splitting up would be the best idea. Working together and taking one chokepoint would probably work best especially if their defense is going to be split up. Right? Let's make sure to communicate really well, just passing on information and such, and we can work together to figure out what needs to happen throughout the exercise."

The others nodded in agreement.

Lieutenant Dyer called, "Follow me."

I turned and watched him walk past us, continuing through the two double doors and signaling for us to follow. We lightly jogged to catch up with him as he made his way past the open space outside of the doors and up to the back area of the arena.

He stopped back in the gap between the two buildings I had seen earlier. "This is the offensive starting area. Stay in this area, and once your watches go off, you have your fifteen minutes. Work well together and keep an eye out for exit doorways. Once you're out, you're out for the round. I'll step out, and I'll set you guys off in a moment. Oh, and here is your golden BigEgg," he told us, handing Rag a large golden tablet before stepping out at an exit point.

Just a few seconds later, rhythmic beeps began emitting

from our watches. I glanced down at mine to see a timer, now at three seconds, counting down. As it reached zero, it buzzed loudly, and we were free to go. A timer now sat above the map image and counted down from fifteen minutes.

I watched as Elisa and Alex butted heads together and started formulating a plan in low whispers. Soon, they came out of their small meeting and came over to the rest of us near the fourteen-minute mark.

"Alright, here's what we're doing. Alex is going into the tunnels to the left. His job is to hold position and prevent the defenders from getting curious, while also keeping a presence and preventing them from feeling safe. Ethan and Rag, you should gain access to forward positions in the middle of the arena, preventing them from coming through the double doors or from Flag Point One, as we'll call it. Go, now. Elisedd and I will press through the door room and hold a position in the deep trench area. Are there any complaints?" Elisa inquired. There were none.

"Then move to your positions," Elisa called, grabbing Elisedd and dragging him over toward the closed double doors. As Elisa and Elisedd disappeared behind into the small room, Rag and I were approaching the large open area in the middle, opposite of the double doors. Holding out a signal to stop moving, I listened, trying to hear something, anything that would indicate where the other team was hiding. It was silent, except for the occasional shuffling noises that Rag would make with his feet.

Cautiously, I poked my head out from behind the wall, peering down toward the middle area. Behind me, I felt Rag pushing against my back as he poked his head out as well. I didn't see anything at first, but in a fury of motion, three of them stomped out across the double doors, coming up the inclined middle toward us.

"They're pouring through the middle doors, three of them!" I cried through the mic piece.

"Get into cover and don't take too much damage, we can poke out together and take them out one by one!" Elisa shouted through the earpiece, a couple of staggered footsteps coming through.

"There's three of them? Do you think I should try to get into Flag Point Two?" asked Alex.

"Go for it. We can overwhelm them ourselves toward the other chokepoint. Alex, you push through to Flag Point Two. Ethan, Rag, try to distract them as much as you can. The more you can take down the better. Just keep them occupied. Elisedd and I will try to get onto Flag Point One," Elisa commanded.

The connection in the earpieces fizzled out, and I motioned for Rag to push out from where we were hiding. Gunfire started almost immediately as I held my rifle out and started shooting at them. Rag was shooting wildly from behind me as well.

A loud screech filled my ears as my vision was blinded by something. The gunfire subsided for a moment. Once I got my bearings back in order, I took stock of what had happened. Despite the continued gunfire, no one had "died" yet. We were all still standing. Rag retreated behind the wall while the other team appeared to have the same idea and retreated further away from the middle area, standing near the double doors.

Rag's voice filled the communication channel in the next moment. "One's pushed through the walkway in the chaos. As of now, I think we have four of them in the middle. Flank them quicker, we're trying to exchange gunfire but I'm almost completely down. I can only take two more shots."

Elisedd swiftly replied in the affirmative, before cutting

out. I waited behind the wall with bated breath, only sighing in relief when I couldn't hear any footsteps or gunfire. But I didn't dare peek out from where I was standing. They probably had their guns trained on us. Rag, who was catching his breath from all the excitement was leaning against the wall as well, while still alert.

"Alright," I started, looking at him. "We're going to stay low for a little while. If they decide to push up and come to us, we'll be ready, and we'll have the advantage, but we're not going to instigate a fight. That could be deadly."

Rag nodded and worked with me to take up positions, holding out our guns toward the middle area, hoping that someone would push through. But we were awarded a dull silence.

"Flag Point Two is clear, though I think I just heard some gunshots from outside the double doors. One could be flanking somewhere," interjected Alex.

I looked at my map, hoping to find Elisa and Elisedd pushed in far enough toward the long pathway toward Flag Point One, but was disappointed to find that they were only as far as the blue dumpster and watching around the corner. In my deep thinking of the situation, I missed the gun barrel that peeked out from the corner and the short burst of fire that came through. I swore as I saw my points going down, leaving me dangerously close to elimination. Unfortunately, Rag was completely out, his face sporting a defeated look as he dropped the BigEgg where he stood a few feet away. He'd stumbled out into the open in the brief chaos.

"Rag's out! The golden BigEgg is down! We have people pushing up the middle area!" I fervently shouted into the earpiece.

I felt a surge of adrenaline enter my body. I froze and was overwhelmed with energy and confidence. As I saw two people turn around the corner, their guns trained at me, a string of bullets came out from my gun, catching them in the shoulder. However, they didn't go down. They had to be precariously close, nearly "dying," but at that moment, my bullets ran out, and swiftly I headed behind the wall again where I could hear the clatters and clicks of guns firing.

"One down outside of the middle doors, we're still missing one of them somewhere. We know where three of them are, though," called Alex.

"I'm going to try and swing back around the middle area from Flag Point One. Ethan, keep your presence there quiet as much as possible and make sure that they don't push up toward you. Elisa, follow me," Elisedd called, before cutting out.

I felt the rush of adrenaline coursing through my body, pushing it to go forward and reign hell down on them, but following orders, my mind went against my body, shutting those urges down. Squatted, I stayed hidden behind the wall in wait for support.

"Elisedd and I got one down in flag point one, but we still need to eliminate the people in the middle area in order to get to the flag point," Elisa called, making me feel relieved.

"Alright, I'll try to head through the doors that you went to and get to Flag Point One. I-"

"No, don't," Elisa interrupted.

"Why not? Isn't that area clear of the other team?"

"Yes, but there's a seriously long gap that you would have to cross, and I'm not risking having to lose the tablet in that gap where they are free to shoot us. We'll clear the middle and go through there. I-"

The voice cut out suddenly, and to my shock, the dot representing Elisa disappeared from the small map on the tablet that I was holding onto.

"Elisedd? What happened?"

"They got her from the middle area. One was staked out on the catwalk, and we didn't notice. Don't worry, I got him down. We've still got three people against their three. We're still in the clear, although Elisa certainly doesn't seem happy," Elisedd reported, chuckling toward the end.

I sighed in relief. The odds were still even. "Alright Alex and Elisedd," I called. "Try to break through and get rid of the people near the double doors but be careful. They probably have at least two rifles trained on you," I continued to command.

"I'm surrounded, I'll just try to keep them distracted. Make sure to keep your eyes out for the third person, wherever he mig-" Elisedd's microphone suddenly cut off as another dot disappeared from the small radar on the tablet. We were down another one.

"Dammit," I muttered under my breath. "Alex, we're going to need you to pull off an incredible feat here. Do you know if they are aware that you're camped up near flag point two?"

"I'm not sure," came the reply. "I don't think that they know. Would you like me to try and take out the people that are in the middle area? I can go through the tunnels and probably get behind them."

I grit my teeth and started gnawing at my fingernails. Then, I came to a decision. "Yes, try it. That's the best bet we have."

Alex muttered, "This is such a drag…"

The communication cut out, and just seconds later, I heard a single gunshot followed by a burst of others. I waited excitedly for positive results but was disappointed when Alex's radar blip disappeared without any negative response from the other team. Cautiously, I peeked out quickly, just to get an idea of what had happened, and to my disappointment, both enemies toward the middle were still alive with the last one MIA.

The golden BigEgg was just out of reach, and I had at least two enemies holding positions against me. I had to make a quick move, so I reached into my belt and grabbed a smoke grenade. Tossing it next to the wall and waiting for it to go off, I heard a flurry of gunfire ripping up from the doors. I was forced to crawl on all fours, under the gunfire, to grab the golden BigEgg.

Immediately, I darted up the incline and towards our starting point, hoping to wrap around to where Alex had been by Flag Point Two. Hearing the gunfire die down in the middle, I became aware that the enemies could move to anywhere. I wasn't safe from behind anymore.

As I approached the entrance to the tunnel, I slowed down to avoid making too much noise. I held my rifle up, ready for any enemy presence. I waited for a moment and checked my BigEgg, which was counting down quickly from 43 seconds. I had to move quickly. To the right of the tunnel, where a staircase led towards the middle door area, an enemy head popped out. I quickly reacted and fired off a small burst before dashing out into Flag Point Two, throwing subtlety out the window.

While I thought I was safe in my approach, I suddenly heard a gun firing from behind a set of boxes. I dove down and gave myself a moment to react before inching my way across to a different position. My rifle was directed towards the source of gunfire in case of the enemy suddenly rushing me down. The bulky weapon just didn't respond smoothly like a pistol. So instead, I grabbed the pistol from its holster, holding it out in front of me.

I finally felt safe enough to poke my head out and fire off a few shots onto the defender, quickly knocking him out of the fight. A small feeling of satisfaction entered my body, but ignoring it temporarily, I took the golden BigEgg toward the safe, seeing that I only had ten seconds left. Prying the safe open, I scribbled down the small message that was there on a sheet of paper. *This is the message for this exam.* How anti-climactic.

I peered back toward the BigEgg that I originally held and sighed in relief as it was no longer counting down the seconds, but was lit green, counting down from five minutes instead. My muscles relaxed a little bit, and my tunneled view of the world collapsed as my eyes became my own again.

My focus was dedicated toward the tunnel, with my eyes darting toward the doorway to my left periodically. In just a few seconds, I was rewarded with my prey. The final enemy just came through the tunnel area, his eyes widening as he saw my position near the back wall. He must've not expected that. I raised my pistol, firing toward him, the bullets already careening on their way to him, but instead of having a panicked look, I saw him intentionally collapsing his legs as he went down onto the floor right as I started pulling the trigger. He grinned, and with a small pistol held in his hand, he fired twice at me. I peered down and saw with disbelief as two little red dots emerged on my stomach. The counter for how many bullets I could still take went down to zero.

They had won.

# Chapter 25

*August 20, 2103*

· · · · ● · · · ·

AS I WALKED through the tunnels beyond the doorway, I heard a subdued cheer ring out in the distance. I followed several arrows on the ground that led me to an open room where the rest of the squad and the others were standing. My squad had disappointed looks on their faces while the other group was cheering and congregating around the last kid who had won the game for them.

"Nice try Ethan," Elisedd said solemnly, a downtrodden expression on his face. All four of them, minus Alex, had an extremely disappointed look on their faces, but no anger. They didn't seem to be blaming me, which I was grateful for.

"Attention!" General Heitman called. He was standing on a small podium at the front of the room with Lieutenant Dyer by his side. "Congratulations to Oanez's unit for winning this game. For the next week, you will be doing similar exercises on different landscapes in order to get used to working as a team and making sure that you all are ready for the mission. In one week, you will be deployed to the border."

General Heitman's announcement brought everyone back down to Earth, and Eugene's group stopped celebrating. They stood at attention, listening to every word that was coming out of General Heitman's mouth.

"In one week, Eugene's group will be shipped toward the west near Sector 27. From there, you will enter in. Elisa's group will be deployed directly en route from the Capital toward the border. From there, it is up to you to complete the mission that is given to you."

We all nodded in response and saluted General Heitman as he walked out of the room. Eugene herded his group out of the room as well, and we were the last people standing around in the small room.

"Hey, sorry-"

"Don't," Elisedd warned. "It wasn't your fault. We all made our own mistakes, which led us to our downfall. We'll work on it throughout this week. Right Elisa?"

"Yes," she growled, clenching her teeth. Her fists were balled tightly, grasping at her pant legs. "It's only around four right now, so go grab something to eat. Be back in the large simulator room by five."

Elisedd nodded and left the room. Hesitantly, I followed him out toward the dining hall while Alex and Rag went back to their own rooms. We stood in line, and I passingly thought back to the exercise and how many different decisions I could've made to win us the game.

"Stop," Elisedd warned again. "Stop thinking about that match. If you keep thinking about it, you'll make mistakes in the next match, then we'll lose those ones too. Then Elisa will *really* get angry."

"Wasn't she already angry?"

"Trust me. You've haven't seen her get *really* angry yet, and I hope that you never will have to."

Silently, I went through the line and grabbed a hamburger and some veggies off the belt. We sat down next to a large window that overlooked the entire downtown area of the

Sector. The view was great, and below, I could see people milling about, going on with their daily lives.

"So, you want to tell me about yourself or something?" Elisedd asked friendly. He was munching on a cheese-burger with an inquisitive look. Hesitantly, I bit into my own hamburger, eyes widening at the taste. It was really good. In fact, it was a lot better than almost everything I'd had in my lifetime. This food was like five-star gourmet food compared to that of Camp Daedalus.

"I know," Elisedd said with a teasing look. "It's terrible, right?"

I looked at him as if he was crazy but didn't answer the question. Silently, I kept on eating the burger until it was entirely gone. I then answered his first question. "What do you want to know?"

"I don't know, things you like, what you think about this operation, anything."

I hummed. "I don't know. This operation in my mind seems all a little bit out there to me. I'm still trying to figure out what I'm doing being a part of this operation to be honest."

"I hear you, I hear you. Just another question."

"Ask away," I muttered, chowing on a piece of boiled broccoli. Even the vegetables tasted good.

"Do you prefer men?"

I choked on the piece of broccoli I was chewing, coughing loudly as Elisedd slid me a cup of water. After gulping the entire thing down, I glared at Elisedd who was laughing.

"What the hell man?" I asked with a slight glare. "Where did that come from?"

"It was just a question, no need to get all flustered. I mean, I don't mind if you do, but I was just curious. You just always seem kind of aloof and bored if you know what I mean. It was a valid question."

*No, it wasn't!* I wanted to shout but kept silent.

"A lot of the girls here are hot if that's what you're worried about," Elisedd joked, wiggling his eyebrows. My face burned in embarrassment, and I silently wished that I had gone back to the room rather than coming here with Elisedd.

"Let's just go," I begged, and Elisedd let out another loud laugh before leading me out of the dining hall and back toward the large simulation rooms. There were still around ten minutes before five, but Elisa was already there, reading something on her Egg.

"Elisa! Ethan doesn't prefer men!" was the first thing Elisedd shouted, and my face burned up once again. I could probably cook an egg on my face.

Elisa sighed loudly then looked to me with an "I told you so" look. "What did I say about hanging out with Elisedd? I told you that you wouldn't like it, but you didn't listen, did you?" she chided with a small smile.

"It's not my fault," I weakly responded, and Elisa snorted, going back to scrolling through her Egg. We stood there awkwardly for a couple of minutes before Alex and Rag arrived, bringing the whole squad back together.

"Alright, now that we're here, we'll try to get a little bit of training in before we have more matches against Eugene's squad. Hopefully, we won't get swept this whole week before the mission. We-"

"I brought the bottles and monitors you requested," a meek voice stated. I turned around, and there was another girl with the downgraded military uniform on, which I realized was more a servant's uniform than anything else. Her brand was exposed to the world and several scar marks marred her arms and legs.

Elisa walked over and plucked several water bottles and a case full of little computer chips out of the girl's hands.

"Thank you, I appreciate it," she told the girl with a smile who jumped as if startled. She gave a short salute and ran off to wherever she came from.

Elisa turned toward us and held the case of chips out in front of us. "These are chips that will record what happens inside of the simulations. It'll help us decide how we can better improve our strategy, how we can improve at the personal level, and hopefully, help us win."

The case went around the group, and each person plucked one out of the case. It was only about as big as the pad of my index finger; I looked around, wondering where to put this. The others were screwing the top off their watches, revealing complex circuitry with several spaces where additional chips could fit in. I copied their motions and slid the small chip inside one of the slits.

"Did everyone get their chips fitted in?" Elisa asked, and we nodded.

"Great, let's go in then."

Elisa took us into the simulation room, where the entire landscape had changed. We were still in some type of arena, this one much more temperate than the last one, but this one felt like a dockyard of sorts. I could almost smell the sea in the air.

"Listen up, guys," Elisa announced. "This exercise is designed to help us develop our group into a unit. Essentially, we have to gain access to that building," she explained, pointing to a gray, boxy building.

"There'll be numerous guards patrolling the building, all of which are just moving targets. Though, cameras and IR sensors will be able to see you, so keep low. Also, they're able to fire back. Our goal isn't to kill everybody, it's to get into a vault in the center.

"Oh, and each time we reset, the interior layout changes,

so there are no suicidal attempts to learn positions. We *must* use our assets to succeed. I set the course to medium, so their shots and positions should be rather easy to handle. And remember, only shoot at them if you feel like you need to. We could theoretically make it through without shooting our weapons at all, especially on medium, but let's just try to pass it first. The countdown starts now," she concluded.

"This is the perfect exercise for me," I heard Rag mumble through my earpiece. "I could probably do this alone."

"Remember Rag don't get cocky. Nobody can do this alone. The security here is meant to be top-notch and just one person would be too easy to track. Spreading our footprint wide is what we need to do," Elisa reminded him.

He nodded before formulating a plan. "Let's spread out and take note of all the possible entrances. Make sure to keep an eye out for any guards or cameras that might be situated around. Then we can decide to send in people or create a new plan."

We nodded, agreeing with that plan. Slowly creeping towards the building, we took note of the different windows and doorways. The windows looked inaccessible, but they would probably be more lightly guarded than the doors. If anything, our best bet might've been on the-

"What do you think the roof looks like?" Elisedd asked.

Rag looked towards him and back at his BigEgg, skimming across the map. "There might be an entrance, but we don't have any rope or climbing gear. I don't expect everybody to be able to get up there."

He continued, "I'll assume they're guarding the more exposed windows. If these are sensibly set up, I imagine we can get through some of the windows in more secluded areas of the building."

As he said that, he glanced up and down between his

tablet and the building. After just a moment, he extended his arm and pointed towards a section of the building, leading us toward it. "I'm going to need two of you to place your hands together to make two small platforms and lift me up. I want to get a glimpse into this room," Rag commanded.

Alex and Elisedd made their way under the window, crouching down and holding their hands in a way to let Rag stand on them. Rag inched the window open slightly and tossed a small device inside. Jumping down, he explained, "It's a small, autonomous drone. It'll make its way to the security center and I can use it to temporarily freeze different security cameras, along with getting a full view of everything they can see."

"In the meantime," added Elisa, "Let's get moving. We're not timed, but we also don't have forever."

Rag nodded as he brought us towards the window. "As far as I saw, that room was fairly clear. Let's get two people in there, holding steady while we get access to the rest of the building."

Alex and Elisedd opted to go in, both muscling up the wall onto the windowsill and sliding into the ajar window. A thumb stuck out, indicating that we were good to go. With a nod, Rag continued around the building, leading us towards some small windows at one of the corners.

"I'll go in alone from here," Elisa said. She lifted herself up the wall and slid the window open, forcing herself into the building.

"We're going to make a diversion, Ethan. A big one. I'm going to try to cause some unrest near the front to draw attention so everyone else can make their way upstairs," Rag explained as he continued around the perimeter of the building. "Then we'll be able to get the objective done with a little bit of flare."

I sighed at his antics, discovering a new side of Rag. Whereas before, he seemed meek and supportive in everything the squad did, now it was clear that he probably had just been waiting for the right moment to be assertive and lead. I silently follow Rag as he made his way around the building, ending up at the front entrance. He pointed above the door, and I noticed a discreet security camera pointing forwards.

"My drone is in the security room," Rag whispered. "If we hug that wall, we can avoid the camera. Everybody inside, I don't see any hidden cameras. Go ahead and begin clearing the halls."

He and I both continued along the front side of the building. Stopping in front of a wide window, he began explaining, "This is one of the main front rooms. If we can get inside without being noticed, we can probably shuffle behind random furniture and get out unnoticed. I just need you to keep an eye on how you're moving."

I simply nodded in agreement, and Rag turned back towards the window. He reached his hands up and pulled his eyes towards the bottom of the window, peering inside. He seemed to be reassuring himself before pushing his fingers under the window, forcing it open. I pulled myself up as well once he entered the window.

The guards weren't facing the window, but instead, two watched towards the door. I quietly slipped onto the floor and crouched down, following Rag along the edge of the room. He continued closer to one of the guards, raising his rifle and gesturing for me to point mine at the other guard. We pulled our triggers and put a simulated bullet in each of the target's skulls.

I stepped forward to twist the doorknob when an alarm went off. "Who tripped the alarm?!" Rag shouted. Silence ensued in the following moments, and Elisedd lightly whispered, "What were we supposed to do? Clear the halls and then what, just stand there?"

More silence.

"Meet me outside of the front entrance," Elisa said coldly. Rag and I made our way into the hall and out the front door, waiting for the rest of the group to convene together. Elisa wasn't very happy, and we were all a little stressed. She began making her way towards our original starting area once the others arrived.

"We're going again," she commanded, making all of us groan. With the touch of a button, the simulated environment eliminated all the faux bullet holes in the walls and the "damage." Once again, the timer ran down, and we dashed off to our positions.

"Again," Elisa urged, making us groan. This was already the third time, and we were getting tired. But we pushed ourselves up without protest.

"Again."

My legs were feeling limp as if they were made of jelly.

"Again."

Everyone was practically dead by now.

"AGAIN."

ELISA HAD MADE us go through seven rounds of the simulation until she was satisfied. It was more like she was accepting the results for what they were. While they were certainly better than the last couple of times that we had done them, we still weren't able to complete the full objective. By the end, we had managed to take out five of the enemy team before Elisedd was taken out in a one versus one situation. I couldn't blame him, though, since he had been the one doing all the work during that round of simulation. He was one tough guy.

"We still weren't able to complete the objective," Elisa noted monotonously. I flinched and hung my head ashamed. The others did so as well, disappointed looks fluttering across their faces.

"Do you all know why?" she asked, and I racked my brain around for the answers, but still couldn't find one. No one else could speak either. They all silently racked their brains without giving an actual answer.

"Anyone?"

No one spoke up, and Elisa sighed loudly. "We're failing because we're not supporting each other," she tiredly said, the time spent in the simulation showing on her face as well.

"What?" Rag asked in disbelief.

"You heard what I said," Elisa replied. "Every time we go into the exercise, we're doing our own thing, trying to do things for ourselves rather than helping each other out. It shows in the way you move, the way that you attack, and the lack of communication. This is our problem, and I intend to rectify this issue. Go to your rooms for today, and we'll continue this tomorrow. We're going to make sure that we can clear the expert difficulty before we are deployed."

We took that as a dismissal and began filing out. I was at the back of the line, waiting for everyone to file out, and just before I left the door, I peeked back. Elisa was still standing there, staring at the ground with a pensive look on her face while her arms were crossed across her chest.

"Aren't you leaving?" I asked, making her turn toward me.

"I'll leave in a while. I need to go over what we did today and how we can improve for tomorrow," she muttered, still in her monotonous tone.

"Oh, okay."

I silently closed to door behind me and went off to my dorm room to sleep.

# Chapter 26

*August 24, 2103*

· · · **•** · · ·

THE NEXT FEW days went by at a turtle's pace, the looping schedule becoming boring quickly. Every day, we woke up and ate breakfast before spending at least three hours going through the simulation exercise. With the amount of times we went through the exercise, I practically had the simulation's landscape generation tendencies memorized. The buildings were always next to a long corridor, the stairs always curved to their right, and the area was always the same size. At least, that was until we stepped beyond "medium." After that, it was a completely different ballgame. That was when weird twists and unpredictability came into play, and my previous knowledge no longer helped.

"Elisa! Let's go out to the city!"

It was Elisedd who protested, much to Elisa's chagrin. "What?"

"Let's go out into the city!"

Elisa scoffed, turning away with a look of disbelief. "You've actually lost your mind this time. Deployment is in four days, and you want to go out to the city? We need to go through the simulation more times."

"Why not? We don't know how long we're going to be away, so why not get a breath of fresh air before we leave?" Elisedd begged with his hands pressed against each other. "You *know* we need it."

Elisa hesitated, but shook her head vehemently. "No, we can't afford to lose any more time. Haven't you forgotten that we've already lost to Eugene's group twice?"

"Yeah," Elisedd whined. "But we also beat them once as well. Elisa, stop making excuses, you know you want to go as well."

Elisa bit her lip, twirling a long strand of hair in her fingers as she stood deep in thought. Eventually, she sighed. "Fine. Let's go out. We're not staying away for too long, though."

Elisedd cheered jubilantly along with Rag and Alex. I couldn't really muster up any excitement since I didn't know what it was like in the city, but cheered along with them, nevertheless. "We're going to get changed, meet us in the lobby in fifteen minutes!" Elisedd shouted excitedly, then ran back toward the dorm rooms.

"Is he always like that?" I asked Elisa, and she sighed loudly. "Unfortunately."

"How do you deal with him?

"I don't."

I chuckled awkwardly as Elisa walked off toward the female dorms. "I'm going to get ready as well. I'll see you later."

"Yeah."

When I got to my room, I started digging around the closet for clothes. To my dismay, all the clothes that were in there were for military purposes, meaning that they were pitch black with thick fabric. It would stick out in the city like a sore thumb. The only thing remotely normal was a long-sleeved undershirt that had a tall neck. But it was summer. It was hot.

Elisedd started knocking on the door, shouting, "Ethan! Let's go!"

"Just a minute!" I shouted back, frantically tossing clothes left and right. I still couldn't find anything remotely normal that I could wear in public. Hastily, I opened the door. Elisedd stood there, wearing a casual blue t-shirt with tan-colored shorts on. His eyes raked up and down my body curiously.

"Aren't you going to get changed?"

My face flushed in embarrassment. "I didn't really bring anything so…"

"Oh," Elisedd remarked. "Just wait a second."

Before I could stop him, Elisedd ran back into his own dorm room and just a few seconds later, came out with a pair of white shorts and another light blue shirt that was very similar to the one he was wearing. "Here, try these on. They should fit your size."

I took them hesitantly and closed the door. Changing out of my military uniform, I put on the short-sleeved shirt and shorts, but grimaced once I looked in the mirror. Although the shirt and pants fit well, it was a crewneck, meaning that it left my brand completely exposed. I tried shifting around the collar, but it wouldn't cover up the brand without the shirt folding at ridiculous angles.

I gazed back into the closet and saw the long-sleeved shirt staring back at me innocently. *Screw you.* Grabbing the shirt, I tossed it on underneath the light blue shirt and rolled up the sleeves until it cut off at my elbows. It looked a little bit awkward, but it was better than having my brand exposed.

"Ethan! Are you ready?" Elisedd impatiently called from outside.

Opening the door, I chided, "Be a little more patient, would you?"

Elisedd, Rag, and Alex were all waiting in the common space with bored expressions on their faces. Rag shifted around impatiently with a shady glint in his eyes while Alex, well, he sported his trademark dull expression.

"Why are you wearing that underneath?" Elisedd asked curiously, motioned toward my long sleeve. "It's going to be hot outside. You probably don't want to be wearing that."

"I'm not used to wearing short sleeves."

"Okay."

He bought my reason with little skepticism, and together, we walked through the central tower and down toward the main lobby. As we passed by the reception desk, the woman there shot me another heated glare before returning to her work. Fortunately, no one else noticed it.

Elisa was already waiting for us near the front entrance, dressed in a black blouse with jeans. Her gaze was fixated on her Egg while her feet tapped against the ground incessantly. When she noticed us, she demanded, "What took you so long?"

"Don't blame me," Elisedd called, holding his hands up in surrender. He pointed at me. "He was the one that was taking a long time to change."

Her gaze briefly shifted over to me before she sighed. "Whatever. Let's just get moving quickly. We're losing daylight."

The process for leaving was a bit arduous, requiring the guards to check our bodies with a detector to make sure that we weren't taking anything important outside of the base. Fortunately, all we had on us were our Eggs, watches, and for some, money. A commodity that I didn't have at the moment.

"This feels so nice," Elisedd sighed, and I chuckled as I

watched Elisa roll her eyes. But she also let out a small smile. The air outside of the base felt liberating, and the road leading out from the base fed directly into the heart of the city where the shopping and corporate districts were.

"So, where do you all want to go first?" Elisa asked, prodding us forward with a neutral expression on her face. "There's got to be something that you had in mind since you wanted to go outside."

But a quick look at her face showed that she was far from disinterested. In fact, Elisa looked the most excited to be out here in the city. Her usual scowl and stiff body movements were replaced by something lax, and I saw her eyes darting between the stores that were at ground level, eyeing them almost hungrily.

"Why don't you choose, Elisa?" Alex suggested lazily. He looked the most out of his element in the city. Every time a car honked, or someone shouted furiously, Alex jumped, startled by the sudden noise. He looked nervous merely by the presence of other people around him.

"Are you sure?" Elisa asked skeptically, but underneath, I saw glee hidden underneath the mask.

"Yeah, why not?" Alex continued. Underneath his breath, he muttered, "Anything to get out of the outdoors." Elisa didn't hear him, though.

Turns out, letting Elisa choose was one of the worst decisions that we made together during our short time together as a squad. It started normally, and Elisa excitedly chose a clothing store. But soon, we realized our mistake when she dragged us around clothing stores right up until the sun started setting over the horizon. Elisa dragged us around as if we were slaves. My arms became hangers for all different kinds of clothing, and even my neck became a temporary rack for a shopping bag.

In the end, it was Elisedd that suffered the most. In each hand, he was holding four different bags of different colors while a ninth was hung around his neck. Rag and Alex continually teased him about it as Elisa seemingly went through the entire shopping district of Sector Two before stopping. It made me wonder where she was getting all this money from.

But in the end, time caught up to us and the sun started to set, basking the cityscape with an orange glow. As the city infrastructure started transitioning into "night-mode," the lamps by the streets lit up and the windows of the buildings started pulsing various hues of light.

"That was a good day," Elisa cried with a small smile on her face. Elisedd looked like he was feeling the exact opposite. Whereas he started the day with his mouth spread out in a large grin, now he looked exhausted, his legs dragging on the ground as we walked along the street pavement.

"That was *not* a good day," Elisedd groaned.

Elisa mocking gasped, "Elisedd, you look tired!"

"You think?"

"Alright, you big baby," Elisa joked, turning around to face the rest of us. "I'll take him back to the base to drop everything off. You three can wander around a little bit before coming back, or just give me a call with your Egg, and we can come back out too."

"Sounds good," Rag said with a grin. As soon as Elisa and Elisedd were out of sight, Rag turned to me and chattered excitedly, "Do you want to do something fun? Every city has a place where we can do 'it.'"

I worriedly looked at him, wondering if he was suggesting what I thought he was suggesting. "You're not thinking of…" I trailed, watching as realization dawned on his face and he waved his hands frantically in front of him.

"That's not what I'm talking about! It's something else, just trust me."

I disliked the mischievous look that he had in his eyes but couldn't find any malice or ill-intention in his words, so I shrugged. "Lead the way." Out of the corner of my eyes, I saw Alex's eyebrows rise, but didn't think much of it.

Rag led us toward the outskirts of the sector where the buildings were transitioning into residential apartments. I noticed that more people in casual clothing were milling about, although that term was relative. Even the "poor" people were wearing the most luxurious and outlandish clothes that I had ever seen. After walking a little more, Rag stopped and grinned. "This looks like the slums of this Sector. I knew I'd find it if I walked around long enough."

Slums?

The area we entered was similar, if not higher class than what an average middle-class family owned back in Sector 36! It was most certainly better than many of the buildings that I had seen during my travel down to Camp Daedalus, and this was the slums?

Along the road, the number of people walking by was sparse since the sun was about to go down. People were now starting the retreat inside their homes. A lone biker cycled down toward us from the other side of the hill we were walking up.

Suddenly, Rag threw himself into the path of the bike, and my eyes widened as they collided, throwing the two onto the ground. I rushed over to them, checking their conditions. The biker was heavily injured, blood leaking off the scrapes on his arms. On his chest, a sticker name tag read, "Charles." Rag was laying a short distance away with a small grimace on his face.

"Rag! Are you okay?"

"I should've just tripped the guy..." Rag groaned as he stood up.

The other kid on the ground was still lying in a fetal position, cradling his arms. When Rag stood up, he walked over to the other kid and held out his hand. When Charles shakily stretched his arms to grasp Rag's hand, Rag swiftly retracted the hand with an amused grin on his face. Rearing back his leg, he punted Charles in the stomach, making him cry out in pain.

"Hey! Stand up!"

My body froze in shock as I watched Charles shakily get up from the ground and bow down to Rag. "I'm sorry," he whispered with a trembling voice, and now that he wasn't lying on the floor, I could see the small branding on his neck. My blood chilled as I saw Rag's face twisting into a malicious smirk.

"Sorry doesn't cut it. You ran into me with your bike, and whose fault was that?"

Charles looked like he wanted to protest but stayed silent. Rag's smirk twisted into a look of fury, and he whipped his leg up and kicked Charles in the face, sending him crashing back onto the hard pavement. I stepped forward, opening my mouth to rebuke Rag, but Alex gripped onto my arms tightly.

"Don't."

"Why?!" I shouted angrily, staring as Rag continued to kick at Charles' head. Blood was spewing out of his mouth, and I could see a couple of teeth dislodged from where they used to be. He was curled up into a ball on the street and tears were leaking out of his eyes.

"Look."

I looked up, and my eyes widened, body trembling in fury. Nearly all the windows of the large apartment complexes nearby were open, and people were staring out the windows watching Rag injure Charles. A very select few were watching in concern, but most were actively watching with amusement, alcoholic drinks held in their hands. Some even had the audacity to jeer at Charles and encourage Rag, who seemed to be basking in the encouragement.

"Get him!"

"Kick him in the stomach!"

"Break his legs!"

"Piss on him!"

The shouts in the neighborhood were thundering, and I was standing in the middle of the road, watching it all happen.

"You want to give it a go?" Rag asked me, kicking Charles one last time. "He's not dead yet."

I didn't even hear his question. Blood was still pounding inside of my head, and my body was trembling, shaking furiously at the sight of these people approving this abuse and impending homicide. I couldn't even hear sirens in the distance. All the sounds in the neighborhood were singularly coming from the taunts and jeers of the citizens.

"Rag, we're leaving," I said in a cold voice. Glancing back toward Charles one last time in pity, I started walking away back toward the corporate and shopping district of the Sector.

"What?!" Rag protested in confused anger. "I haven't had my fix yet!"

Curdling anger rose from the depth of my gut, and the edge of my vision was fading to black, a hazy red covering my eyes. I stomped toward Rag and grabbed him harshly by the collar, bringing him up to eye level. He was struggling against my grip as I practically choked him with his own shirt. "We. Are. Leaving. Do you understand?"

"W-Why?" Rag choked, glaring at me. "Are you one of those Bastard sympathizers?"

"Bastard sympathizer or not, you're tainting the name of those involved in Operation Nabu Strike. So, screw your head back on. We're leaving."

Dropping him back onto the ground, I briskly walked back toward the brightly illuminated downtown, not even once responding to the boos and jeers that suddenly shifted focus toward me. It was only when the tall buildings started emerging again did I get out of hearing range of the boos and jeers. I saw Alex walking behind me solemnly, shooting me curious glances. Rag also had caught up at some point and was fixing me with a harsh glare.

The city was alive in full swing. The electronic panels on the walls were alit in advertisements and propaganda posters against the East while people laughed and conversed amongst themselves in hushed tones. Near the entrance of one of the alleyways, a small group of boys forcefully immobilized a small girl as they harassed her.

They held the defenseless little girl by the arms, digging a sharp rock into her collarbone. As they carved at the distinct wolf-shaped tattoo, I heard her terrified cries ring out through the city, and the image of hundreds of people chanting for Charles' murder flashed through my mind. *'You should see what they do to people like us in the Core Sectors. I heard they literally use us Bastards as slaves,'* a distant voice echoed, and I finally saw the world for what it was.

This twisted world allowed people to kill others on a whim.

When I looked up at one of the large screens hanging from the towering buildings, it was scrolling through a political advertisement. *"No Bastards means fewer taxes, economic prosperity, and freedom for all. Eliminate the root of society's problems!"*

The lay of the land became all too clear to me, and as I remembered all the downtrodden, beaten, and defeated people with that small wolf-mark on their necks, a new goal started forming in my head.

Vengeance.

# Chapter 27

*August 28, 2103*

· · · · ● ● · · ·

"ELISA, EUGENE, YOU two will be briefing with me before rejoining your squads. Meanwhile, the rest can go get fit with equipment in the garage. Look for someone named Gringie. At 2300 hours, we'll be shipping you all to the border and from there, you know what to do," General Heitman reminded us with a sweeping gaze.

The past four days had not been kind. After coming back from our excursion in the city, I made a concerted effort to avoid everyone, staying holed up inside my room except for the official exercises that were scheduled sporadically. Every time I saw Rag, who still acted as if nothing had happened, my blood boiled with red hot lava pouring through my veins. A red haze clouded my vision, and I wanted nothing more than an opportunity to beat him up, maybe even kill him.

It didn't go unnoticed. As soon as they noticed that something was wrong, Elisedd and Elisa immediately started their interrogation, questioning me about my "abnormal" and "destructive" behavior. I didn't dignify their questions with an answer. Even Rag had seemed nice in the beginning, and if he could become a monster on a whim, there was no one I could trust. Carter had been right.

"All of you except Elisa," General Heitman commented,

interrupting me from my thoughts. I noticed that Eugene's squad had disappeared at some point. "Go to the garage and get stocked for the mission. Also, get familiar with the people who will escort you to the border."

I returned a half-hearted salute before following the others into a large garage filled with military vehicles. The room was enormous. One wall was lined with black and white vans and Humvees while another corner held larger vehicles like tanks and the occasional jet and helicopter. Military personnel were milling about, doing maintenance and checking over the vehicles. As we walked in staring at the vehicles in awe, a short man wearing a military uniform hobbled up to us. "You four are here for Operation Nabu Strike, correct?"

"Yes."

"Great! I'm here to take you to the loading area for this mission. Once you all are stocked and ready to go, Pierre, Colton, Mike, and I will be escorting you in our Humvees until you cross the border," he explained as he led us zig-zagging through the lines of vehicles.

We neared the corner of the garage where there were several jet-black Humvees that looked new. They seemed freshly painted, the outer coating sleek and shiny. The man that was leading us at the front patted the hood of one of the vehicles. "This is my boogie, I guess. It's one of the newer models that the R&D department came up with. The motors are near dead silent and the acceleration is nice. All we need for this mission."

"Was it made specifically for this mission?" Elisedd asked, staring at the vehicle in awe. "It must've taken a lot of resources to approve and carry out such a project."

The man laughed. "No, this was an ongoing project. It was completed a couple of months ago. It just happened to serve the purposes of this mission the best."

"Oh."

I noticed that several other guys in uniform were also around the vehicles, tending to the cars with either cans of liquid or tools that they got out of nowhere. When they heard the commotion, they finally clambered over. "Hey, Gringie, we're just doing the final maintenance checks. Are they the kids?"

"Yeah, they are."

The man that just stepped out from inside one of the cars took off his stained gloves and held out his hands toward us. "My name is Mike; I'll be one of the drivers taking you to the border. Nice to meet you."

He seemed nonchalant enough. Going around, we all shook his hand and introduced ourselves briefly. The man had a bright personality, easy to get along with.

"Don't worry about the vehicles for now," the short man, Gringie, said. "We'll go to the supply room and get you the weapons and gear that you'll need for the trip first, then figure out something if we have time left over. Don't worry, I think we'll be spending plenty of time inside the storage room."

Gringie led us back further into the garage and through another door. It led into a smaller storage room, and when I stepped through the doorway, my eyes widened, surprised by the sheer volume of weapons on the racks. There were various models of rifles, some that were familiar like the standard MR20s, then there were some others that were less familiar and seemingly more advanced. Along another wall was a rack of handguns of various sizes. Grenades and other accessory gears were along another wall.

"Ben! Ben! Are you in here you lazy slacker?" Gringie called.

A low groan came from the back of the room and a guy stumbled out from behind the racks of weapons. His hair was disheveled as if he had just woken up from a long nap, and his glasses were crooked across the bridge of his nose. He had a coffee stain on his chest. "Why are you waking me up this early?!" the man spat.

"It's 1900 hours."

"So?"

"So, get your lazy ass out of bed!" Gringie shouted irritably. He groaned, tiredly rubbing his hand against his face. "Anyways, these are the kids that are going on Operation Nabu Strike. Get them suited up for the mission. I swear you're going to get yourself dismissed by General Heitman one of these days."

"Wouldn't that be the day," the man snorted. He turned his gaze toward us. "Come toward the back. General Heitman had me get a basic kit ready for each of you, though you are free to customize and take whatever you wish. Of course, I'm instructed not to give you anything beyond the compacts in terms of weaponry."

He showed us to the back room, where there were five bags along with vests that were lying flat on a long table. The vests were packed with frag grenades, stun grenades, and smoke grenades. The small flaps for ammo clips were empty, though.

"You'll fill those up depending on what you decide to take as your weapons. As I said, nothing larger than a compact rifle and even then, more than two in your squad might be too much," Ben advised.

I looked back at the storage room which was filled to the brim with weapons. Looking at all the choices, I felt like a kid in a candy store, except, these candies could kill.

<hr />

HOURS LATER, RAG, Alex, Elisedd, and I finalized our gear. Elisedd settled with a small KTECH 739 Bullpup rifle. It was powerful, but still small enough that it wouldn't be a large hassle. Alex also decided to pick up a larger weapon than a pistol. He grabbed a P90-SSMG.

My pack was mostly filled with ration bars, water, and extra supplies. On my hips, an N90 Semi-automatic pistol rested in its holster, extra rounds stocked in my vest pockets. Ben insisted that I also take a combat knife as well. As he handed me a fifteen-inch single edged knife, the image of Holton's dead body flashed through my mind. But Ben kept prodding the handle of the knife against my shaking hands, and I took it, sticking it in a small sheathe attached to my left arm.

The promised time was near, the clock nearly winding down to 2300 hours. Elisa had joined the group about thirty minutes prior and was getting her gear fastened onto her body. She seemed optimistic, humming a soft tune as she organized the gear on her vest. Eventually, all of us were set, ready to head out. Our minimal supplies were on our body and backpack, and we were lined up in front of Alpha General Heitman again, hopefully for the last time.

"Remember, you will be in unfamiliar territory. After you cross that border, communication channels will be cut, and there will be no instructions from us or anyone else. You all know what you're supposed to do. Figure out why the Federation has decided to invade our borders and report back. Is that clear?"

"Yes, sir," we responded.

"Remember, this is a strict reconnaissance mission. You're equipped for a fight, but that is not in the mission parameters. Good luck and I hope to see you all back here safe and sound by the end of the week."

His farewell speech was anything but melodramatic. It

was like any other speech, straight and to the point. As the General turned back toward the other soldiers, the five of us were split up into different Humvees. Elisa, Elisedd, and I went into one while Alex and Rag got in another. Mike, who was sitting in the driver's seat, turned the key making the engine roar to life.

"Are you ready?" he asked, and I nodded my head. Sweat started gathering in my palms, and my heart sank in anxiousness. My shoulders were already starting to get tired of holding the somewhat large satchel behind my back, but I quelled my complaints. Instead, I gazed through the heavily tinted windows at the General who was giving out orders to the others. After his mouth stopped moving, he nodded and gave one last look toward us before leaving the garage.

The van lurched, and with one last rev of the engine, started moving forward along with the two vehicles flanking our front and back. The mood shifted with the lighting as the artificial glow from the base faded away into the distance behind us. The natural darkness of the night overtook our visual senses.

"*Fortuna audaces iuvat*" Elisa whispered, rubbing her hands together.

"What does that mean?" I asked.

She smiled softly. "I'm not sure, but it always makes me feel calmer and more focused."

Elisa turned her gaze back to the front, pokerfaced. She closed her eyes, seemingly deep in concentration. I sighed and turned my gaze out of the window, watching the dark landscape roll past us. I wasn't sure why, but my heart started pounding against my chest, and instead of fear, I was excited to see what waited for us at the border. I licked my dry lips several times and whispered, "*Fortuna audaces iuvat.*"

It calmed me down.

# Chapter 28

*August 29, 2103*

· · · · ● · · · ·

THE HUMVEE RACED along the dark pavement for hours, finally stopping long after my legs had fallen asleep.

"Get out," Gringie ordered.

It was almost completely dark outside, and the place we'd been dropped at was an uncomfortably familiar setting. Dense forestry surrounded us from every direction, and an ominous wind blew through the clearing. The towering walls that I'd been expecting to see were nowhere in sight.

"Gringie? How far away from the border are we?" Rag asked scathingly. "Are you going to make us walk all the way over there?"

"No, this is it. The border between the Republic and the Federation. It's physically unmarked, and practically defenseless except for the patrols that run here every fifteen minutes. For the longest time, the two countries had a non-aggression and non-migration pact going, which meant that the government didn't have to spend money on a wall. The United States couldn't scrounge up the money to fund it either."

"Don't you mean the Republic?"

"No, I mean the States."

Rag closed his mouth with an audible click after that clarification.

"Why set up the large border wall near the capital, then?" I asked curiously, taking another sweeping look of the area. "Also, doesn't this make it possible for people to infiltrate into our country undetected?"

"To your first question, because it gives a feeling of safety," Gringie answered, swinging his rifle around from his back. "The real security is the ring system around the Core Sectors. On the second issue, well, we're not here to play twenty questions, alright? You-"

A glint of metal reflected off the moonlight and just seconds later, my ears rang as the thunderous cry of exploding gunpowder and wind impacted my ears. Repetitive metallic clangs glanced off the vehicle next to me, and several more rattling sounds of gunfire rang through the clearing. My head was roughly shoved down low as Gringie pushed me over to the other side of the Humvee.

I clumsily drew my pistol from its holster, ready to fire at a moment's notice.

"Stupid Federation soldiers can't even let a single thing go right," Gringie mumbled. Leaning over the top of the hood, he immediately shot several bullets back with his M16, but only hit wood. Laughter arose from all around us, deep in the forest.

"Identify yourselves!" Gringie yelled.

The gunfire abated, leaving the clearing in a tense Zen, the calm before the storm.

"Did you hear that? The Republican traitors want us to 'identify ourselves," a deep voice mocked, a chorus of laughter following soon after. I could only distinguish around ten people sitting back deep in the woods, which was good news for us.

"Gringie," I whispered nervously, gulping loudly. "We can k-kill them. Our squad can continue with the mission after we take care of this."

"No."

"What do you mean, 'no'?"

Gringie silently waited deep in thought, biting at his lips while frequently shifting his gaze toward the woods. "What I mean is, as soon as we begin firing to kill, they'll alert others, we'll be swarmed, and you might not even have a chance to get over the border. You'll be dead on the spot. Splat."

A thin sheen of sweat gathered on my forehead as I watched Gringie rest against the cold metal door, exhausted with a defeated look on his face. Suddenly, a few seconds later, his head snapped up. "Elisa, Elisa, do you hear me?"

"Y-Yes, I do," she nervously responded, crouched behind the Humvee. She flinched and ducked as another rain of bullets scattered the other side of the vehicles.

"On my command, you're going to go behind enemy lines, and make it through the border and into the east, do you understand?" Gringie hissed as Elisa listened with eyes wide. "I doubt that they have an accurate grasp of our numbers, so as long as you remain silent, they won't be able to tell. Do you understand?"

"Yes, but-"

"No buts. You just do as I say. Do you understand?"

"Y-Yes."

Gringie had a grim expression on his face as he started pulling out all the grenades out of his vest and reloaded his M16. The clearing was still dead silent, only interrupted by the natural sounds emanating from the forest and the gunshots resonating in the distance. Another haphazard spray of fire came from their end, and this time, Gringie returned fire, his M16 scattering bullets back toward the grove. A couple of strangled cries came from within the forest, but Gringie also let out a pained curse as a bullet tore into his left shoulder.

"Gringie!" I cried, moving over toward him in concern.

"Just wait for the signal!" he growled, holding out a hand to stop me from getting closer.

His face was contorted in pain, but with his uninjured arm, he shakily plucked a smoke grenade off the ground and pulled the pin out with his teeth. With a flick of his wrist, he tossed it in a high arc above the cars, landing it somewhere in front of the clearing of trees.

"On my mark, Elisa!"

He hastily picked up a stun grade off the ground, pulling the pin with his teeth. The long stick was firmly grasped in his hands, and in one smooth motion, Gringie lobbed the grenade over the car. "Go, go, go!"

A screeching bang was accompanied by a bright flash, and by the time the smoke was fading from the clearing, the five of us were running through the forest as stray bullets sent splinters flying off the trees behind us. Another loud explosion followed by several screams ringing out across the clearing, but we continued rushing forward, our eyes glued on the path ahead of us. Elisa was leading the group from the front, the rest of us in frantic pursuit.

Our legs continued to carry us deep into the safety of the forest. Even once the sounds of fighting and gunfire began to dissipate, we still ran. When the grove of trees opened to a straight, paved road, we didn't pause to wonder where the road led. We scampered right past it, diving back into the forest where we felt safe in the cover of the thick, oaken trunks of wood. Even when a wide, meandering river with thick, murky water impeded us, we didn't stop. We waded right through, reaching the other side at the expense of our dry clothing. To be honest, I wasn't sure how long we ran. Our minds went blank, our bodies propelled forward by fear, a raw fear that forced our leg muscles beyond their limits until the distant gunfire became mere pings in the distance. Only then, once our adrenaline wore out, did we finally begin to slow down.

Elisa plopped down to the ground, her head hung low. In fact, all five of us had our heads bowed in exhaustion as we sat down on the soft mud and fallen logs.

"That was…" Elisedd started, his whole body shaking. His head was cradled in his hands.

"Frightening? Crazy?" I supplied.

"Yeah…"

"Well, this is what it feels like, I guess," I muttered in a trembling voice. Pulling the small water canteen out of my bag, I took a long sip of the water, sighing in satisfaction as the water quenched my dry throat. A loud explosion— almost like a cannon sound—roared in the distance, making us jump in fright.

"Let's keep moving," I suggested.

Elisa tiredly nodded, a haunted look still prevalent in her eyes. Rag, Alex, and Elisedd stood up stiffly, their eyes darting left and right frantically. We were only about a few miles into Federation territory, so there was no time to relax. There was no such thing as "security" until we reached deep beyond their borders. With heavy steps, Elisa led us southward, and after twenty minutes of trudging through moss and mud, the forest cleared out to the grasslands, an entire field of chest-high plants dotting the land as far as I could see. Elisa hesitated in front of the invisible boundary between the forest and grasslands. She looked back almost longingly at the forest as if begging the trees to follow her and provide her cover.

"Elisa?" I prodded, gritting my teeth when I saw her hesitation. "We have to go."

She numbly nodded, shaking her head. With shaking steps, she continued forward. With each step, our boots sank into the ground, the wet soil swallowing up our feet. Travelling through an open field felt like walking in public naked, and the feeling consumed me like a tidal wave. With every step I took forward, my skin tingled, the abnormally frosty air brushing against my face and body uncomfortably.

Suddenly, something to my right shifted and instinctively, my hands were on my pistol. The gun was outstretched in front of me, the shaking barrel pointing into the expansive wall of plants, ready to fire.

"Ethan?" Elisa tentatively called, shooting me a sideways glance. She also had her pistol out in front of her, ready to shoot at anything.

"Drop your weapons!"

The shout came so suddenly from all around us. I kept my hands firm, shakily holding the gun out in front of me. My legs were quivering, and a sweeping chill dusted over my heart. My stomach sank, and only fell lower when multiple figures appeared from the bushes. Out in the open, the moonlight shone brightly, and I could see the figures clearly. They were all human, but their gear was markedly different from ours. Their rifles were bleached in white while their uniforms were painted a unique green color. What distinguished them from us, however, was the golden eagle emblem proudly blazoned on their chests.

"Drop your weapons!" the gruff voice shouted again.

With twenty or so people around us, I looked toward Elisa for guidance. But she wasn't faring any better. Her hands were quivering, the pistol in her shaky grip trembling in tow. Slowly, it slid out of her hands, plopping onto the ground. I tsked when I saw this, but reluctantly dropped my gun, holding my hands up in surrender. One by one, our weapons were discarded onto the ground, forming a pile of metal.

They started rounding us into a small circle, facing inwards. When I looked at the others, they were shaking with unbridled fear etched onto their faces. The cold barrel of a rifle poked my shoulder. It just lightly prodded me, nothing else. From above, a bright ray of light suddenly illuminated the area, making me squint. The low flapping sounds of helicopter wings finally became audible, and despite the situation, I took a moment to marvel how silent the rotary sounded. It was almost as if it wasn't even there.

"Commander Johnson! We found them!"

"Good," a sharp female voice replied. The owner of the voice was behind the squadron of men and women who had their guns shoved into our bodies. As she stepped into the light, I glared at her with all the hatred I could muster.

"That's cute," she sarcastically said. The woman was around Elisa's height, brunette hair poking out from underneath the military cap that she wore. Her face was hidden by the shadow cast by her cap, but I could tell that she was young, probably only about two or three years older than we were. A sophisticated pin with detailed etching was attached to the collar of her military uniform. Slowly, her gaze raked across the five of us, and she grinned maliciously.

My eyelids pressed against each other, heart pounding wildly in my chest as the barrel of the rifle dug into my shoulder blades. I waited for the explosive sound of gunfire and the shredding pain of a bullet tearing into my shoulder, but it never came.

"Knock them out and bring them back. We'll get some

information out of them in the Central holding cells," the commander ordered.

I felt something abruptly bash against the back of my skull repeatedly, and my vision swam. The others were getting similar treatment, their heads lolling limply as they were held by the collar of their necks.

"Welcome to the Federation."

# Acknowledgements

This project was a journey that lasted a long four years. It was something that started when two eighth graders decided that they wanted to write a book and to be honest, we regularly questioned if we would ever get to publish this story. Constantly, we wondered if our four a.m. sprees of writing and loss of sleep would ever amount to anything. In fact, I distinctly remember calculating that we had spent more time writing this book than sleeping during the summer after our junior year in high school. Yet, through those sleepless hours of work, five monstrous drafts, and an endless four-year fight with schoolwork, here we are.

Joseph: *"My first thanks goes out to God, who gave me a chance at living and a chance to write this book. Second, to my parents and little brother Joshua, who always kept me going with a healthy mix of constructive criticism and positive encouragement. Third, to Christopher. He probably would've had a healthier sleeping schedule had he not agreed to write this book with me; he was and still is a faithful friend who motivated me when I was down and stuck with me for all these years while undertaking this crazy journey. Fourth, to the anonymous person online who kindly asked for an "early birthday present chapter" when this story was a scrap of ideas online. Without that piece of encouragement, perhaps this story would've never taken flight and made it to this point."*

Christopher: *"I'd first like to thank my parents, whose continued support through the thick and thin of the past four years has kept me motivated to wake up daily and put my work into life and this book. Despite the long process of writing, which may have made it seem like we gave up, my parents constantly reminded me of the work that went in and what Joseph and I were capable of. Another thanks go to Joseph, and I can't put into words how thankful I am for him. His motivation and often annoying strictness kept me honest with myself. Without his work ethic, this book would've never been more than a twenty-page idea on a word document. My final thanks go to my seventh-grade teacher, Ben Schekirke, who never doubted the idea of a book, even when it was just a floating idea way back in 2014. He was happy and willing to help me edit and revise my book long before I was working with Joseph. While that original story idea is long gone, it helped spark the fire that led to this collaboration, and I don't know where I'd be without it."*

Additionally, this book would never have come together without the amazing individuals who helped bring everything together. Cheriefox.com, our amazing cover page artist, created a stunning design for us unartistic souls. Her artwork and eye for details are unparalleled, and her friendly, supportive attitude made it an absolute joy to work with her. Sarco Press, who helped us format the interior design, was always helpful and made sure that we were getting top quality work.

To be honest, this still feels surreal. We still imagine ourselves as eighth graders, starting this book without knowing the first thing about creating a plot. Perhaps we're still lacking in this department, but for us, *Mark of Ascension* is a memento of our four years of work, a lasting memory of our friendship. More importantly, we hope that this story can be an inspiration to you, the reader, and anyone who is plagued in life by the question, "Can I do this?" If two eighth graders who barely knew the difference between the present and past tense can write a book, you can probably do just about anything. Never stop doing what you love because of criticism. Criticism is never a stop sign. It is a jump pad that lets you ascend to new heights.

# About the Authors

**Joseph Y. Kim** finds his greatest inspirations in life from books, scrolling through the news, and from his own imagination. After discovering his love for creating a new world from scratch in his middle-school years, he has his time and effort to bring his ideas to reality. When not writing, his interests and passions include social entrepreneurship, playing the piano, and making new friends. He is constantly working on improving his craft and finds the greatest joy in helping others flourish in their own respective niche.

**Christopher Boom** is a long-time reading and writing teenager. Having a deeply vested interest in the dystopian genre, he's stepped up to the plate to write his own dystopian novels. Throughout school, he has participated in numerous creative writing courses and contests, further driving his passion for writing. Other passions of his include competitive esports, construction, and programming. While his hobbies are diverse, Christopher has worked diligently on his writing to put his best work onto paper and hopes to take his writing further in the coming years.